THE
TRAITOR'S
BARGAIN

THE
TRAITOR'S
BARGAIN

RAJAT ROY

Copyright © 2025 Rajat Roy

All rights reserved. No part of this publication may be reproduced, stored in a retrieval system, or transmitted in any form or by any means —electronic, mechanical, photocopying, recording, or otherwise —without the prior written permission of the publisher, except for brief quotations used in reviews or scholarly works.

Published by Emberline Books

EMBERLINE
BOOKS

ISBN: 978-1-7641299-0-9

CONTENTS

Prologue — vii

Chapter 1 The Twilight of Glory — 1

Chapter 2 The Gathering Storm — 61

Chapter 3 The Unmaking of Bengal — 99

Chapter 4 The Chains of Conquest — 147

Chapter 5 The Ashes of a Nation — 189

Epilogue — 237

Author's Historical Note — 239

About the Author — 241

PROLOGUE

In Delhi, the Peacock Throne still gleamed, but the empire it once commanded had faded into myth. By the mid-18th century, the Mughal dynasty had dwindled to a shadow of its former might. After the death of Emperor Aurangzeb in 1707, imperial authority fractured, leaving provincial rulers to govern in near-sovereignty. Among them, the Nawabs of Bengal held court over the wealthiest province in India.

Bengal - comprising present-day West Bengal, Bihar, Odisha, and Bangladesh - was a land of breathtaking riches. Its famed Dacca muslin was so fine it was called "woven air" - cloth so sheer it could pass through a ring. Its saltpetre, a key ingredient in gunpowder, fuelled the armies of Europe. Its silk, opium, and rice fed global markets. European merchants, dazzled by its abundance, called it *Paradise on Earth*.

Initially granted trading rights by the Mughals, companies like the British East India Company and the French Compagnie des Indes soon transformed their outposts into fortified enclaves. These "factories" – commercial hubs that doubled as garrisons and diplomatic posts – became centres of intrigue, ambition, and military might.

By 1756, when this story begins, the British had entrenched

themselves at Fort William in Calcutta, the French at Chandannagar not far away. Their war in the south - the bloody Carnatic conflicts - had taught both powers that in India, trade was won by the sword. In Bengal, they jostled for advantage: manipulating court factions, negotiating with the Nawabs, and laying the groundwork - perhaps unknowingly - for something far greater than commerce.

For the Nawabs, the European presence brought both wealth and anxiety. The silver that filled Bengal's coffers came at a cost: defiance, militarisation, and the slow erosion of authority. The fragile balance between the crown and the Company was beginning to tilt.

And soon, the tilt would become a fall. A clash was coming - one that would not only seal Bengal's fate, but reshape the subcontinent, and in time, the world.

This story blends historical and fictional characters. The following are real historical figures, listed in alphabetical order:

Admiral Charles Watson	Miran
Alivardi Khan	Omichand
George Pigot	Rai Durlabh
Ghaseti Begum	Raja Manikchand
Henry Vansittart	Robert Clive
Khwaja Aratoon	Roger Drake
Lutf-un-Nissa	Siraj ud-Daulah
Major Caillaud	Sumru
Major Eyre Coote	Swaroop Chand
Major Francis Kilpatrick	Warren Hastings
Mehtab Rai (Jagat Seth)	William Ellis
Mir Jafar	William Watts
Mir Madan	Yar Lutuf Khan
Mir Qasim	

All other characters, including the pivotal figure of Javed Hussain, are fictional.

THE TWILIGHT OF GLORY

A warm amber glow suffused the lively city of Murshidabad as the winter sun dipped lower in the sky, stretching shadows along the curves of narrow alleys and open squares. From the lofty minarets of the Katara Masjid rose the deep, melodic call to prayer, winding its way through crowded bazaars and the still courtyards of stately homes. Merchants halted mid-haggle, artisans set their tools aside, and the faithful turned instinctively toward the mosque, drawn together by the rhythm of devotion.

The Katara Masjid, a masterpiece of Mughal architecture, stood proudly with its intricately carved stone walls and graceful domes. On this chilly Friday afternoon in the winter of 1756, the mosque exuded an aura of sanctity and quiet anticipation. The spacious courtyard was already filling with devotees - some dressed in fine muslins and silks, others in more modest attire, yet all united in purpose.

The rhythmic shuffle of feet merged with murmured greetings of As-salamu alaykum - as the worshippers streamed in, forming rows with flawless precision. Inside, the smooth stone floors carried a cool, soothing touch beneath bare feet. The scent of attar lingered faintly in the air, mingling with the earthy aroma of the day's heat.

As the muezzin began the iqamah, signalling the start of the congregational prayer, a hush fell over the crowd. The Imam, an awe-inspiring figure with a flowing white beard, stepped forward. As he began reciting the opening verses of the Quran, his steady, resonant voice echoed through the vast hall and open courtyard, enveloping the worshippers in a profound sense of devotion.

Heads bowed in unison, foreheads touching the prayer mats or the stone floor itself, the sea of worshippers moved as one - bending, standing, prostrating. The only sounds were the faint rustle of garments and the Imam's recitation, punctuated by a chorus of heartfelt Ameen.

Beyond the mosque, the city of Murshidabad seemed to pause. In the markets, even those who did not join the prayer remained still, their gazes often drifting toward the towering minarets. The mosque, capable of holding two thousand faithful at a time, had become the heart of the city for this sacred and timeless moment.

As the prayer concluded with the salaam, voices rose in quiet supplication. Men exchanged smiles and adaabs, some embracing warmly as they shared the communal joy of another Jummah prayer completed. The mosque's steps and courtyard buzzed with renewed energy as friends and neighbours lingered, exchanging warm greetings, shared laughter, and the latest gossip.

Amidst the noblemen's section of the throng, two figures stepped forward - Javed Hussain and Mozammel Khan. Their presence commanded quiet respect, evident not only in the richly embroidered shawls draped with effortless elegance over their shoulders, but also in the measured grace of their stride and the unspoken authority in their watchful eyes. Both middle-aged men, they were high officials in the court of Alivardi Khan, the Nawab of Bengal, and had known each other since their youth.

The Bengal they knew was a shimmering jewel - its wealth drawn from rice fields and jute plantations, its artistry woven into muslin and silk, and its prosperity carried by trade routes stretching to the farthest shores. And the capital of Bengal was here in Murshidabad. Cradled by the meandering Bhagirathi River – a distributary of the Ganges - Murshidabad stood as a living testament to Bengal's magnificence. Its grand mansions gleamed under the winter sun, its markets hummed with trade, and its lush gardens whispered of an era steeped in Mughal refinement.

But as the noblemen trudged along the bustling thoroughfare, both wore expressions of quiet sorrow. For the much admired and loved Alivardi clearly didn't have long to live.

Finally, Javed broke the silence, his voice tinged with both reverence and despair. "Nawab Alivardi has been a fortress for Bengal, Mozammel. A shield against the Maratha storms that threatened to consume us. Few could stand where he did, holding firm with his bravery and cunning." His footsteps slowed as if weighed down by his words.

Mozammel nodded, his fingers tightening on the embroidered edge of his shawl. "Indeed, Javed," he murmured, his voice faltering for a moment. "Few could have held the Marathas at bay like he did - not just with his sword, but with his mind. Those alliances, those brilliant stratagems - we've been fortunate to see them firsthand."

Javed's face softened, a smile creeping through his grief. "And yet, we have seen that he was not just a general. Ah, the evenings in his court!" Javed's gaze drifted upward as if picturing those evenings. "Poets reciting verses, painters unveiling their masterpieces, musicians playing melodies that seemed to make time itself pause. And the Nawab, at the heart of it all, with his sharp wit and kind words. He understood the arts in a way few rulers ever could."

"His appreciation was genuine," Mozammel said, his voice soft as though addressing the memory itself. He paused, his brow furrowing. "Not the shallow indulgence of a ruler seeking to impress, but the respect of a man who truly understood their worth. Do you remember how he rewarded those who excelled?" He glanced at Javed with a faint smile. "The poets, the painters - he brought the best from Shahjahanabad to Murshidabad, creating a haven of culture, even as the Mughal power crumbled around us."

Javed's throat tightened, the weight of loss already crushing him as he clung to each word spoken of the Nawab, as though speaking his name could delay the inevitable. "For all his love of art and refinement, he never forgot the farmers, the merchants, the common folk. He used to say no one should feel less safe in his reign than they do in their mother's arms. How many rulers can claim such benevolence?"

Mozammel sighed deeply, his gaze wandering at the waning sun.

"And how well he grasped the delicate play of power! His words about the Europeans - how they are like bees whose honey could be harvested if their hive was not disturbed. It was wisdom like that which has preserved our prosperity."

Javed chuckled softly, though the undertone was tinged with sadness. "And yet, he never hesitated to speak his mind, particularly to his generals. Poor Mir Jafar! I still remember the time the Nawab chastised him for his dithering."

The two men fell silent, the weight of their memories and the impending loss pressing down upon them. Mozammel halted mid-step, his gaze fixed on the horizon. "Bengal will never see another like him, Javed," he said quietly. "A soldier, a statesman, a patron of peace - the finest of companions. His golden reign fades away, taking with it an era." After a pause, he added gingerly. "Though I wish he hadn't let his affection for his grandson cloud his better judgment.".

Javed shot his friend a sharp look, his posture stiffening. They were in a public thoroughfare, and even the walls of Murshidabad had ears. For the grandson that Mozammel was referring to was the unpredictable and increasingly feared Siraj ud-Daulah, the 24-year-old heir apparent of Alivardi.

• • •

The noblemen continued their walk in silence, immersed in their foreboding at this wisp of a dark cloud that had appeared over the horizon of Bengal. Javed Hussain's mind drifted back to an evening two years ago, when Alivardi Khan had summoned his senior ministers to his private chamber.

The chamber was bathed in a warm amber glow, the flicker of oil lamps weaving restless shadows across the intricately carved walls. The faint scent of sandalwood hung in the still air, mingling with the muted rustle of silks as the ministers settled into their seats. Alivardi Khan sat at the head of a polished teak table. His frail frame, cloaked in fine muslin, bore the unmistakable marks of advanced age. The reverence that the octogenarian Nawab's presence commanded was, however, tinged with unease that night.

The ministers, seasoned men who had served Bengal loyally over the years, exchanged uncertain glances as they waited for the Nawab to speak. Alivardi's piercing eyes swept the room, and though his body had grown frail, the quiet authority in his gaze reminded all present why he remained the throne's enduring anchor.

"My trusted advisors," he began, his voice steady but tinged with the weight of years. "I have summoned you here to share a matter close to my heart and vital to the future of Bengal. My time is drawing to an end, and it is my duty to ensure the stability of the realm and the well-being of its people."."

The ministers leaned forward, their expressions a mix of curiosity and trepidation. Alivardi continued, "I have decided after careful consideration that Siraj ud-Daulah, my grandson, will succeed me as Nawab."

The silence that followed was deafening, broken only by the faint crackle of the lamps. The ministers were visibly shaken. Some swallowed hard, others lowered their gazes, while a few shifted in their seats, their eyes darting toward one another, searching for the courage to speak. They had long feared this day would come, yet hearing the words from Alivardi himself felt like a crushing blow, shattering the fragile hope they had dared to entertain.

Finally, one of them, Syed Imdad Ali, spoke with carefully measured deference. "Nawab Sahib, your wisdom is unparalleled, and we have always trusted your judgment. But... may we humbly express our views?"

Alivardi gestured for him to proceed. "Speak freely," he said. "I value your counsel."

Imdad bowed his head slightly before continuing. "Nawab Sahib," he began, choosing his words with the utmost care, "Siraj's youth is both his strength and his weakness. His passion can inspire, but... his impulsiveness has, at times, sown unease among your subjects."

Javed Hussain added, "Nawab Sahib, you have always prioritised the welfare of Bengal above all. Siraj's actions in the past... such as the rebellion in Patna,[1] ... have left many wary. Forgive me, but he appears to be more feared than admired."

Alivardi's expression softened, but his resolve remained steadfast. "I understand your apprehensions. Yes, Siraj erred in Patna. But he was young, misguided. I chose to forgive him not only because he is blood of my blood, my only grandson, but because Bengal cannot afford the turmoil of a disputed succession." His voice faltered momentarily before regaining its strength. "With no sons of my own, Siraj represents the future of this dynasty. My daughters have blessed me with only one male heir, and the weight of our lineage rests upon his shoulders."

The ministers exchanged uneasy glances once more. It was a truth they could not contest. Alivardi's three daughters had given him no other grandson who had survived so far, and Siraj, despite his flaws, was the sole male heir to the throne.

"Nawab Sahib," another minister ventured cautiously, "may we propose an alternative? Nawazish Khan, your son-in-law, is a man of wisdom and generosity. He is admired throughout Bengal and has already proven his loyalty and capability. Perhaps he could serve as a stabilising figure in these uncertain times."

Alivardi nodded thoughtfully, his eyes glistening with a mix of affection and sadness. "Nawazish is indeed a fine man," he admitted. "His union with my eldest daughter, Ghaseti Begum, has brought great joy to our family. But the throne is not his by right. It belongs to Siraj."

The ministers fell silent, realising that no argument would sway the Nawab's decision. Alivardi leaned forward, his gaze intense. "I ask

---

[1] In 1750, while deputy governor of Patna, Siraj ud-Daulah attempted to assert his independence. The revolt was crushed, but Alivardi Khan chose to pardon him.

only this of you: when my time comes, stand by Siraj. Guide him. Teach him. He will need your wisdom and patience, just as I have."

The room grew solemn as the weight of Alivardi's words sank in. The ministers, though dismayed, bowed their heads in deference. They could not defy their Nawab, even if his decision left them deeply uneasy.

. . .

The narrow alleys of the bazaar hummed with life - a symphony of clinking tools, the sharp calls of merchants hawking their wares and the steady creak of wooden carts laden with goods. Artisans worked under makeshift awnings, weaving stories into fabric, carving life into wood, and shaping grace from clay. The stalls overflowed with goods: vibrant silks from the hinterlands of Murshidabad, spices from the Malabar coast, and pearls brought by riverboats along the Ganges. Merchants haggled over ivory carvings and brassware, while traders from faraway lands marvelled at the abundance on display. Nearby the river teemed with boats laden with rice, jute, and indigo.

A weaver guided threads through his loom, creating muslin so fine it shimmered like gossamer in the sunlight, a fabric coveted by noble courts across Europe and the Ottoman Empire. Nearby, a potter spun his wheel, adroitly shaping delicate forms from damp clay, while a dyer stirred a vat of indigo, his arms stained blue as the rich scent of crushed leaves and earthen pots filled the air.

"Have you heard about the Dutch merchant who arrived yesterday on the sleek two-masted schooner?" the dyer, Ramu, asked the weaver beside him. "They say he paid nearly twice the usual price for muslin in Dhaka. Word is around that he seeks only the finest for a noble patron in Amsterdam."

The weaver, Gopal, smiled, his aged hands deftly guiding the shuttle across the threads. "Not surprising. These foreigners know our craft is unmatched. They pay well because no other land can produce such muslin - light as air and strong as silk."

Jahangir, the potter, joined the conversation with a chuckle. "And why wouldn't they? Have you seen what they make? Rough, clumsy cloth that tears before it's worn. It's no wonder they seek us."

Their laughter mingled with the lively hum of the bazaar. Though their words carried jest, there was a quiet pride in their tones. They knew that Bengal's artisans were not just makers of goods but custodians of an unparalleled legacy. Every woven thread, dyed cloth, and sculpted pot carried a story of mastery and tradition - a heritage so rich that even kings and emperors sought it from the ends of the earth.

Their banter was cut short by the sound of boots against the cobblestones. Two European traders wove their way into the bazaar, their crisp linen suits and powdered wigs setting them apart amid the flowing dhotis and embroidered angarkhas – long, loose fitting tunics - of the locals. Yet, theirs was not an unfamiliar presence. Like the Dutch and Armenians before them, they were another strand in the ever-expanding weave of commerce drawn to Bengal. Eyes lingered on them with the quiet curiosity reserved for those who called some distant lands as home, yet found their way back to these markets time and again.

Pierre Dubois, a Frenchman with an inquisitive gaze, paused near a loom, his fingers brushing the edge of the muslin. "Exquisite," he murmured in French, eyes widening. "Like holding a whisper in my hands."

His English companion, Richard Wickham, studied the scene with a calculating eye. "Indeed. But one wonders… how long does such perfection take? The slower the craft, the higher the price."

Dubois knelt near the potter's wheel, gesturing politely for Jahangir to continue. "This artistry… it is unlike anything I have seen. Tell me, friend, how long does it take to master such skill?"

Jahangir, rolling out the clay with practiced ease, arched an eyebrow. "Sahib, do you ask a river how long it takes to learn its course?

Or a tree how long before it knows to bloom?"

Dubois smiled, impressed. "A life's devotion, then."

Jahangir nodded. "More than that. It is not just my life, but my father's before me, and his father's before him. This clay," he lifted a half-formed pot, "carries their hands as well as mine."

Dubois exhaled slowly, as if weighing the depth of those words. Wickham, meanwhile, tapped his fingers against a crate of muslin, his mind more on profit than philosophy.

After their business in the bazaar was completed, the traders moved on and seated themselves beneath a banyan tree nearby. Sipping tamarind water from a clay cup, Dubois' gaze drifted toward the bazaar's bustle. "Bengal," he said, his voice tinged with a mixture of awe and calculation. "Every time I come here, I feel as though I've stepped into a fable. The wealth of this land… it is endless, non?"

Across from him, Wickham leaned against a wooden crate of muslin. A slow smile played on his lips, not of wonder but of consideration. "Indeed, Pierre. I've travelled to the Americas and seen the riches of the Caribbean plantations, but this - this is something else entirely. The muslins, the silks, the spices… there is no corner of the world that does not covet what Bengal produces." He ran a hand over the crate beside him, fingers pressing into the fabric. "Feel this, man. You'd swear it was spun from air itself."

Dubois leaned forward, brushing the cloth with care. "Ah, so fine! I've seen noblewomen in Versailles weep for such a treasure. They would pay fortunes to have gowns made of this."

Wickham exhaled lightly, as though considering an equation. "Fortunes they'll pay indeed. And fortunes we'll make - provided we know how to turn the tide in our favour." He glanced toward the bazaar, where merchants haggled, and silver changed hands with a nonchalant ease. "This trade is a river of wealth, Pierre, but one must know where to place the sluice gates. A deal struck in the right moment, a contract written just so… well, a man could do very well for himself."

Dubois nodded, his agreement instinctive though he did not grasp the full weight of Wickham's words. "The fields here, Wickham, they are the Gods' own work. Rice that feeds nations, jute that binds the world, and indigo that dyes even the courts of Europe in its majesty. How is it, do you think, that one land can hold so much bounty?"

Wickham's expression was unreadable. "It isn't just the land, Pierre. It's the hands that work it. Generations have perfected these crafts, refined these trades, yet they hold so little power over what they create." He tilted his cup, watching the tamarind water swirl. "A curious imbalance, wouldn't you say?"

Dubois frowned slightly, sensing something beneath Wickham's words. "And what would you do with such an imbalance?"

Wickham smiled, but his gaze was already elsewhere. "Only what any prudent merchant would do - find ways to make it work to my advantage." He took a measured sip, then set the cup down. "Tell me, Pierre, do you ever feel that we spend too much time merely transporting wealth rather than shaping it?"

Dubois hesitated. "I prefer honest trade, Richard."

Wickham chuckled, but did not press the point. "As do we all, my friend." He reached for another sip, his gaze lingering on the bustling marketplace. "As do we all."

The two merchants sat in silence, their gazes tracing the currents of commerce. Dubois saw a land of marvels; Wickham, meanwhile, studied the patterns of trade with a calculating eye, weighing the levers he could pull to bend the system to his advantage.

• • •

The humid air of Calcutta clung to his skin as the visitor made his way toward the looming silhouette of Fort William. It was a familiar sight yet one that never failed to stir awe. The fort, perched resolutely by the banks of the Hooghly River, seemed almost defiant against the chaos of the sprawling city around it. Its bastions rose sharply against the sky, cannons peering out like silent sentinels. Yet now, subtle signs of additional fortification work caught his eye - heaps of freshly hewn stone near the walls and scaffolding stretching like skeletal fingers against the sky, hinting at preparations to bolster its defences further.

Though he had visited many times before, the wiry man in his thirties found himself pausing as he approached the massive gates, where guards stood rigid, their red coats vivid against the sun-bleached walls. In a region where the French vied for influence and the Mughal grip weakened, Fort William stood as both a stronghold and a statement of British ambition

Beyond lay the inner sanctum - a realm of crisp order, where barracks stood in disciplined rows along cobbled paths, and the Governor's residence rose with understated authority. Even in its familiarity, Fort William, the East India Company's principal settlement in Bengal, exuded a sense of both impenetrability and ambition.

The visitor was William Watts, the chief of the British factory at Cossimbazar, a settlement near Murshidabad. His position granted him intimate access to the Nawab's court and its key officials, making him the high command's vigilant eyes and ears in Bengal's shifting political landscape.

Watts adjusted his coat as he entered the chambers of Roger Drake, the Governor of Fort William, his face set with resolute purpose. The air inside was heavy with the scent of ink and old parchment. Governor Drake, seated behind a broad mahogany desk strewn with dispatches and maps, looked up sharply from a half-written letter, his expression expectant yet weary.

"You have news, Mr. Watts?" Drake asked, dispensing with any pretence of formality.

Watts inclined his head, choosing his words carefully. "Your Excellency, my latest observations confirm what I feared," he began, his tone measured but laced with disapproval. "Siraj-ud-Daulah, the heir apparent to the throne of Bengal, is a man whose reputation precedes him - and not in any commendable fashion, I am afraid. He is widely feared and despised, and known far and wide for his depravity and cruelty. His character is a volatile blend of ignorance, arrogance, and malice, which, if allowed to ascend unchallenged, is certain to jeopardise both Bengal and the Company's interests."

Watts had long harboured doubts about Siraj's suitability to rule, but as he recounted his misdeeds, he could not deny a twinge of satisfaction. He was sure that a prince so despised by his people would only serve to galvanise the Company's cause.

Drake frowned. "These are serious accusations, Watts. Are they firsthand accounts, or mere exaggerations by the Nawab's rivals? Bengal's court is rife with intrigue."

Watts met his gaze. "My sources are close to the court and consistent in their reports - even Alivardi Khan himself acknowledges his grandson's excesses."

Drake's expression darkened as Watts pressed on. "His debauchery is unchecked. Even women, particularly Hindu pilgrims bathing in the Ganges, are not spared his henchmen. They are abducted straight from the river, their sanctity and traditions violated at his whim."

Watts let the words sink in before continuing. "His cruelty is no less appalling. During the monsoon, he takes perverse pleasure in deliberately ramming overcrowded ferry boats with his own vessel, watching with twisted glee as men, women, and children drown in the merciless currents."

Drake's fingers drummed a measured rhythm on the table, his eyes narrowing.

"This is the man set to inherit Bengal," Watts pressed. "The court is crumbling - not from external threats, but from his reckless rule. The senior commanders who once upheld Alivardi Khan's reign now seethe in silent resentment, humiliated and ignored. The very pillars of Bengal's military might now offer no counsel, only contempt. His erratic and despotic nature has alienated nearly everyone in his orbit."

Drake's tone sharpened. "And the French? You said he has their favour. What influence do they wield?"

"They have been shrewd, Your Excellency," Watts replied. "Their flattery has secured a tentative alliance, and they stand to gain much under his rule. Meanwhile, he detests us - perhaps because we refuse to indulge his whims."

Drake exhaled slowly. "A dangerous man."

Watts nodded. "More than dangerous - disastrous. His reign will be a blight on Bengal, marked by chaos, cruelty, and tyranny. If he ascends unchallenged, the Company will not only face an inept ruler but one bent on vengeance. We risk losing Bengal - not just to Siraj's wrath, but to French ambition."

Drake's voice was measured. "You paint a dark picture, Watts. If he truly poses such a threat, then the Council must deliberate with caution. Stirring the tiger may bring wounds we are not prepared to bear."

Watts's jaw tightened, but he bowed slightly, masking his frustration. "Of course, Your Excellency. I leave the matter in your capable hands."

Drake nodded, though doubt flickered in his gaze. "Keep me informed. We must remain vigilant."

As Watts left the chamber, his jaw clenched. He had delivered his warning, but Drake's lack of conviction loomed ominously. The storm was coming, and the Company's leadership seemed too paralysed by fear to face it.

• • •

Nawab Alivardi Khan breathed his last at dawn on April 9, 1756. The city of Murshidabad seemed to mourn in unison as news of his passing swept through its alleys. By mid-morning, the sound of muffled sobs and hysterical wails mingled with the rhythmic toll of the mosque's bell, a dirge that echoed through the city's winding streets.

Inside the palace, the air was thick with grief. Servants moved in hushed reverence, their faces streaked with tears. In the harem, the women's wails rose like a keening wind. In the grand audience hall, where a single oil lamp flickered unsteadily, Alivardi's closest relatives and advisors stood in solemn silence, their eyes fixed with melancholy on the lifeless form of the ruler who had guided Bengal through years of strife.

Siraj-ud-Daulah, his features pale but his jaw set, remained by his grandfather's side, his hand gripping the old man's still-warm fingers. The stillness of death hung heavily over the chamber, broken only by the quiet shuffling of feet and the occasional choked sob of an attendant who had served Alivardi his entire life.

Only when the call for the funeral prayers echoed through the palace did the mourners begin to gather, preparing to accompany the bier on its final journey.

The funeral procession moved slowly through the city. At its centre was the Nawab's bier, draped in white muslin, carried on the shoulders of his closest retainers. A single sprig of jasmine lay atop the shroud, its fragrance faded in the still, heavy air. The scent of sandalwood and burning incense curled upwards. Behind the bier, courtiers, ministers, and soldiers walked barefoot, their heads bowed in respect, their faces etched with grief. The steady hum of Qur'anic verses chanted by the ulema wove through the air like an unbroken lament.

The common people lined the streets, their eyes filled with sorrow. Men, women, and children stood shoulder to shoulder, many clasping their hands in silent prayer, others weeping openly. A fruit seller dropped to his knees as the bier passed, his shoulders shaking with sobs. A widow, her veil damp with tears, whispered a quiet dua, her trembling hands reaching out as if to touch the departing soul of the Nawab. Alivardi Khan had been more than a ruler to them; he was a father, a protector who had shielded Bengal from countless storms of war and strife.

As the procession crossed the bustling bazaars he had nurtured into prosperity, traders and artisans stepped forward, leaving their wares behind. Spools of silk, fragrant spices, and delicate filigree ornaments lay forgotten upon the road, the merchants too stricken with grief to care for their earthly possessions.

When the procession neared Khoshbag, the final resting place of the departed Nawab, the wails grew louder. The tranquil beauty of the garden cemetery, with its lush greenery and serene pathways, seemed to offer a solemn farewell to the departed Nawab. The scent of wet earth and blooming jasmine filled the air. Beneath the shade of an ancient banyan tree, a freshly dug grave awaited its honoured occupant. Yet beyond sorrow, there was a quiet solace - for Alivardi would forever rest beside his beloved mother, his journey in this world ending where hers had before him.

As the Nawab's body was lowered into the earth, the ulema's voices faltered momentarily, overcome with emotion. The first handful of soil was cast by Alivardi's grieving kin, followed by his loyal attendants. The soil was damp and cool, crumbling between their fingers as it met the white muslin of the shroud. The crowd, restrained by the guards, wept as one, their voices rising in a collective dirge. With each handful of earth, the weight of a lifetime spent in power, war, and vigilance faded away. No longer burdened by the trials of kingship, no longer weighed down by the battles and betrayals of his reign, Alivardi Khan would find peace in the embrace of eternity. And neither would his blissful slumber be ever disturbed by his flawed legacy - a legacy that would cause the magnificent edifice he had spent his life building and strengthening to come crashing down barely a year later. As the final prayers were said and the grave sealed, the people lingered, unwilling to leave. Many kissed the earth, vowing to honour the memory of a ruler who had lived and died in service to Bengal.

A warm breeze stirred the grass around the grave, carrying with it the scent of rain and the distant murmur of the Ganges. Above, the evening sky deepened into a sombre grey, as though nature itself mourned the loss of a great soul.

• • •

With the death of Alivardi Khan, the throne of Bengal immediately passed on to his anointed successor, Siraj ud-Daulah. It was a throne he was unwilling to delay securing for even a moment. At the same time as Alivardi's remains were being laid to rest, with the swiftness of a cobra striking its prey, he struck. His destination was Motijheel Palace, the residence of Ghaseti Begum, the eldest daughter of Alivardi Khan and the mistress of immense wealth – as well as influence in the Nawab's court.

Ghaseti Begum had openly backed Siraj's cousin, Shaukat Jung, as a rival for the throne, making her out as a grave threat. Murshidabad simmered with intrigue, and Siraj knew hesitation could cost him his rule before it had even begun. He had therefore meticulously planned to neutralise her power as soon as Alivardi drew his final breath.

Riding at the head of his troops, Siraj's eyes burned with vengeance, but beneath his resolve lay the weight of the imperative to secure the throne he had inherited. Though often called impulsive, he knew hesitation would be seen as weakness. Yet as he advanced, doubt whispered in his mind. Did they see a rightful Nawab or merely a boy clinging to power? He pushed the thoughts away, but they lingered, a shadow he could not shake.

As the expedition reached the gates of the palace, Siraj raised his arm, and with a single motion, unleashed the fury of his forces. The heavy palace gates didn't take long to buckle under the heavy blows. As the doors crashed inward, the palace, resplendent in its opulence - gleaming marble, gold-threaded tapestries, and chandeliers dripping with crystal, casting a fractured glow - seemed to welcome the intruders with open arms, beckoning them to plunder.

The first wave of soldiers surged through, their advance pounding the floor with a heavy, unyielding rhythm that sent a chill through the palace halls. The fiercely loyal palace guards, though hopelessly outnumbered, didn't yield without a fight. The sharp clang of steel against steel rang through the corridors, punctuated by the cries of the guards. But their resistance crumbled soon under the heavy assault. Blood smeared the polished floors, mingling with torn silks and broken ornaments.

Panic swept through the palace. Servants scattered, some fleeing down hidden corridors, others paralysed by terror. A few dropped to their knees, pleading for mercies. Chandeliers swayed dangerously as soldiers crashed into furniture, toppling tables, and shattering porcelain.

By the time the fighting subsided, Ghaseti Begum's defenders lay in bloodied heaps, their weapons scattered. Those who survived knelt in trembling submission, their heads bowed under the cold, unyielding glare of their conquerors. The air, thick with the acrid tang of blood, bore a stark and chilling testament to the new Nawab's ruthless resolve to extinguish even the faintest ember of defiance.

Siraj himself stormed into the inner chambers, his sword gleaming under the golden lamplight. Chests of gold and jewels were flung open, their riches spilling onto the polished floors. Rubies the size of walnuts and strings of pearls longer than a man's arm were swept aside as Siraj barked orders to seize every last treasure.

When he reached Ghaseti's private quarters, she stood waiting, her hands trembling but her eyes defiantly locked onto his. Her ornate silk robes and diamond-studded ornaments served as a glaring reminder of her immense wealth - and the threat she posed. Fear coiled in her stomach, but she refused to let it show. To bow before Siraj would be to admit defeat, and Ghaseti had never bowed to anyone - not even her father.

Siraj took a step closer, his lips curling into a mocking smile. "What a grand fortress of betrayal you have built, Begum. Did you truly think these riches would shield you from justice?"

Ghaseti straightened, a spark of steel glinting in her voice. "Justice? You desecrate your grandfather's memory by launching this attack before the earth over his grave has even settled, and you dare speak of justice? Is this the legacy Alivardi Khan left behind - his own blood turning against family before his body is even at rest? But know this Siraj - the throne you cling to is but quicksand."

Siraj's eyes narrowed, the mocking edge replaced with cold fury. But behind his fury was something deeper - an unspoken fear that she might be right. The foundations of his rule were far from firm, and every move he made was being scrutinised. The voices of his enemies whispered in his mind: 'A boy playing at power. A child unfit for a throne.'

"Enough of your games, Begum," Siraj snapped. "The time for mourning has passed. Bengal has a new Nawab, and he will not let the dead dictate the fate of the living. Your wealth, your schemes, and your scheming alliances have come to naught. Tonight, I am the Nawab, and you are nothing."

Ghaseti's defiance did not waver, even as his guards seized her arms. "You may strip me of my jewels, Siraj," she said, her voice steady despite the tension in the air, "but your reckless rule will never buy you loyalty."

By the time the night surrendered to dawn, Motijheel Palace stood stripped of its grandeur, its opulence reduced to a stark warning to any who dared to challenge the Nawab's authority. Siraj-ud-Daulah had not merely seized Ghaseti Begum's wealth; he had solidified his grip on a world steeped in intrigue and betrayal.

Ghaseti Begum was led away from her palace by the soldiers - to be transported to Jinjira Palace, a grim fortress where Siraj intended her to remain imprisoned for the rest of her days. Stripped of her wealth but not her defiance, she turned for one last look at Motijheel Palace, its grandeur now a bitter reminder of all she had lost. Yet in her eyes, there was no surrender - only the quiet fury of a queen who had been dethroned but not broken.

• • •

The balmy afternoon sun filtered through the carved latticed screens of the zamindar's[2] expansive drawing room, casting intricate patterns of light and shadow across the cool stone floor. Zamindar Rajendra Dutta, a man of considerable girth and an equally considerable fortune, reclined on an ornate divan. His robe, a fine weave of golden brocade, shimmered faintly as he sipped spiced sherbet from a silver goblet. From a nearby veranda, the distant murmur of boatmen along the river mixed with the occasional trill of a koel.

Before him stood Richard Wickham, private English trader, whose polished manners and disarming smile had already won over many of Bengal's unsuspecting nobles.

"Rajamashai" Wickham began, his voice smooth, with a deferential lilt as he bowed slightly, letting his pale blue eyes linger on the zamindar for a moment before continuing. "Your lands produce the finest silk I have ever laid my eyes upon. The lords of England would pay handsomely for such finery. I dare say, they would even compete to drape themselves in the splendour of your produce."

Rajendra Dutta stroked his chin, visibly pleased. "Our silk is indeed unparalleled, Mister Wickham. The skills of my weavers are unmatched. But tell me, he leaned forward, the weight of his curiosity clear, "what price do your lords offer for such fine goods?"

Wickham clasped his hands behind his back, feigning a thoughtful pause. "Ah, Rajamashai, that is precisely why I am here today. My

---

[2] A zamindar was a hereditary landholder who collected revenue for the ruling power and exercised local administrative authority.

buyers are desperate for such quality and are willing to pay handsomely - three gold mohurs per yard."."

The zamindar, his rotund frame draped in lustrous silk, raised an eyebrow. "Three mohurs per yard, you say? That is far higher than what the French or the Dutch pay. Are your buyers truly prepared to offer this?"

Wickham's eyes gleamed as he nodded. "I assure you, Rajamashai, this is no idle claim" he said, his voice dropping to a near whisper as if confiding a great secret. "My merchants in London... they are clamouring for more goods. Only yesterday, I received a letter -" he tapped his pocket for emphasis, though he produced nothing - "from a prominent merchant begging for sole rights to your silk trade." He leaned forward slightly, his voice laden with urgency. "Your silk, Rajamashai, is not merely sought after. It is longed for."

The zamindar's eyes gleamed. "And how much do you wish to purchase?"

Wickham's smile widened. "I propose a trial consignment of five hundred yards to begin with. Once this reaches London and earns its rightful praise, the orders will multiply."

Rajendra Dutta's broad face broke into a satisfied grin. "Five hundred yards it shall be. I will have my overseers begin preparations at once."

"Excellent, Rajamashai" Wickham said, bowing slightly. "But, as you are a man of great wisdom, I must confess one small matter."

Rajendra Dutta frowned. "What matter?"

"The buyers in England," Wickham said, his tone suddenly grave, "demand strict assurances. Silk of such extraordinary quality, as you know, cannot simply be bundled and sent like common goods." He let his words hang in the air, then spread his hands in a gesture of regret. "It requires secure warehouses, specialised containers, customs clearances at every port. All this requires an upfront investment. - but certainly, one worthy of such a treasure." He softened his voice, as if appealing to reason. "And to your reputation."

The zamindar's brows knit together as he shifted in his seat. "Investment? What do you mean?"

"Ah, Rajamashai, do not mistake me," Wickham said quickly, his tone conciliatory. "The buyers will reimburse every penny. But as per export norms of such high quality goods, the supplier must cover initial logistics costs. It is standard practice in European trade."

Rajendra Dutta's frown deepened. "How much are we speaking of?"

"Merely five hundred gold mohurs," Wickham said smoothly "A trifling sum," he added, with a reassuring wave of his hand, "compared to the riches this shipment will bring you - and the fortune you will reap from future orders." He inclined his head slightly, as though granting the zamindar time to absorb the offer, then added softly, "Consider it not a cost, but as the gateway to your future prosperity."

The zamindar leaned forward, suspicion flickering in his eyes. "And what assurance do I have that this 'investment' will be returned?"

Wickham's face softened into a winning smile. "Rajamashai, my own funds are tied up in this trade. To demonstrate my goodwill, I will personally contribute fifty gold mohurs toward the logistics costs. We are partners in this endeavour." He placed a leather pouch on the table with a satisfying clink, its contents shining through the loosened drawstrings.

The zamindar's scepticism wavered. "Very well. I will prepare the goods and arrange for the payment. But I trust you will honour your end of the deal, Mister Wickham."

Wickham rose and bowed deeply. "You have my word, Rajamashai. This partnership will bring riches beyond your imagination." He placed a hand over his chest, his expression solemn. "To me, honour is everything. A man is only as good as his word, and I stake mine on this venture."

Three weeks later, Rajendra Dutta stormed into the same room, his face twisted with disbelief and fury. He paced the room like a caged tiger. The overseers had meticulously prepared the silk and sent it to Wickham's designated warehouse near the Hooghly river. But when his men arrived days later to verify the shipment, they found the warehouse empty. Wickham and his clerks had vanished without a trace, leaving behind only scattered pieces of crumpled ledgers and the putrid stench of deceit.

"Scoundrel! Cheat!" the zamindar roared, slamming his fist on the armrest of his divan. "That slimy serpent has slithered away with my gold and my finest silk! I will see him dragged back in chains, or my name is not Rajendra Duta!"

His dewan[3], a gaunt man with hollow cheeks, shuffled nervously. "Sarkar, did I not warn you… this was a deal too good to be true"

Rajendra Dutta shot him a murderous glare. "How dare you speak to me of warnings now? Find him! Hunt him down!" He turned toward the guards stationed by the doorway. "Search the riverbanks! Question every boatman and merchant from here to Calcutta. Bring me news of that devil, or don't bother returning!".

But even as the zamindar bellowed his orders, Richard Wickham was already far downstream, aboard a small schooner bound for a secret anchorage. In the hold of the ship lay bales of silk, while in his cabin, a locked chest guarded five hundred gold mohurs. Leaning against the railing, Wickham let out a hearty guffaw.

"Greed makes fools of them all," he muttered, watching the riverbanks of Bengal slip away. "They count their gold, prattle about their wisdom - yet hand both to the first man who spins a clever tale."

With that, he raised a tankard of rum, toasting the glistening waters. "To Bengal," he said mockingly, "and its endless fools."

• • •

Two months had passed since Siraj ud-Daulah ascended the throne of Bengal, and any lingering hope that power might mellow the ruthless

---

[3] The dewan was the zamindar's right-hand man, overseeing land and revenue administration.

and impulsive prince had been thoroughly dashed.

At that moment, the young potentate was holding court in Kila Nizamat, the Nawab's fort and palace complex in Murshidabad. The expansive, high-ceilinged chamber was truly a hub of opulence, adorned with Mughal-style architecture, with intricately carved arches, gilded furnishings, and vibrant tapestries, as befitting the immense wealth and cultural refinement of Bengal. As on any other day, the chamber buzzed with a lively gathering of noblemen, high-ranking military officers, and wealthy merchants, joined by seasoned administrators and advisors who oversaw the kingdom's affairs. Among them were diplomats, traders, and emissaries from foreign powers, each manoeuvring for influence and favour in Bengal's ever-shifting political landscape.

Among those in attendance was Mehtab Rai, the current holder of the esteemed title of Jagat Seth. The Jagat Seths were a family of Marwari financiers who were awarded this title – which means *Bankers of the World* - by the Nawab of Bengal more than fifty years ago, as a recognition of their unparalleled financial clout. From their sprawling palace in Murshidabad, they controlled the minting, collection, and transfer of revenue in Bengal, wielding power second only to the Nawab himself. Their immense wealth and influence gave them the ability to act as kingmakers, shaping the politics of Bengal with a reach and reputation likened to the Rothschilds of 19th-century Europe. The Seths' machinations had secured Alivardi's rise to power – the military coup which secured the throne of Bengal for him was financed and masterminded by them - and anyone wishing to thrive in the region would find it prudent to cultivate their goodwill.

Today, however, the Seths' influence was about to face its most humiliating test. Siraj ud-Daulah, seated on his ornate throne, set his sights on Mehtab Rai, with eyes brimming with unrestrained arrogance. The Nawab's military ambitions had now turned to the district of Purnea, and for this expedition, he needed three million rupees - a sum he deemed the Seths were more than capable of providing.

THE TRAITOR'S BARGAIN

The room fell into a tense silence as Siraj fixed his gaze on Mehtab Rai. "You, Seth Mehtab Rai," he declared, his voice slicing through the air, "will provide the funds for my expedition against our treacherous foes. You have one week."

Mehtab Rai, dressed in his finest silks, felt the weight of every eye in the chamber upon him. His hands trembled as he anxiously twisted the hem of his shawl, beads of sweat gathering on his brow. He lowered his gaze, his voice quivering as he spoke. "Janab Nawab," he began carefully, "your servant has always remained loyal to the throne. But three million rupees…" He shook his head faintly. "Such a sum cannot be arranged, especially on such short notice. Even if every coffer under my stewardship were emptied, even if every merchant from Dhaka to Patna were to lend at ruinous interest, I would still fall short."

Siraj's eyes narrowed. "You expect me to believe that the house of Jagat Seth - who has bankrolled wars and decided the fate of kings - cannot produce this paltry sum?"

Mehtab Rai inhaled sharply, his throat dry. "I swear upon my ancestors, Janab Nawab, I do not deceive you," he said, his voice barely above a whisper. "Even the wealthiest of financiers have their limits. Giving away such a huge sum all at once would throw the entire flow of money and trade in Bengal into disarray." He raised his hands in supplication. "This is not defiance Janab Nawab, but the truth."

Siraj's lips curled into a sneer. "The truth?" he repeated mockingly. His fingers tightened around the hilt of the small ceremonial dagger at his waist. "No, Seth. The truth is that you fancy yourself with enough power and influence to refuse me."

A heavy silence followed, thick with tense anticipation. Then, without warning, the tempestuous Nawab sprang from his throne, covering the distance in a heartbeat, swift and predatory. In a flash, his hand struck the respected banker's face with a resounding crack. The force sent Mehtab stumbling backward, his shawl slipping to the ground.

"Circumcision might teach you loyalty," Siraj spat, his voice venomous. The words dripped with disdain, designed to humiliate. For a Hindu, the very suggestion was sacrilegious - a violation of faith and identity, an unthinkable disgrace.

Gasps rippled through the assembly; courtiers shrank into their seats, some shuddering at the sheer audacity of the insult, others averting their eyes from the hideous spectacle unfolding before them. Yet beyond shock and fear, a deeper horror gripped the room - an instinctive revulsion at the raw degradation of a fellow human being. This was not merely punishment or rebuke but the deliberate unmaking of a man, his dignity stripped away before their eyes. And he was no ordinary subject but a pillar of Bengal's mercantile power, now reduced to a figure of helpless disgrace.

Mehtab Rai, clutching his burning cheek, fell to his knees. His dignity in tatters, but his heart was gripped with a deeper, more primal fear. Siraj's reputation for cruelty and vindictiveness was no secret, and he knew that the Nawab's fury could extend beyond humiliation - to his very life. His lips quivered, but he dared not raise his head.

As Mehtab looked up, his heart palpitating. He saw Siraj's eyes burning with fury. 'Defiance will not be tolerated in my court!' the Nawab thundered, his voice crashing through the chamber like a thunderclap. His glare bore into Mehtab. 'You will deliver the funds, Seth, or you will suffer the consequences - ones you cannot afford to imagine.'"

The chamber descended into a suffocating stillness, the weight of Siraj's ruthlessness pressing down on all present. Even those well-versed in the ruthlessness of court intrigue felt a chill run down their spines. Here was a man who wielded power with no restraint, a ruler who demanded absolute deference, and in that moment, the nobility of Murshidabad understood one thing with absolute clarity – so long as he was on the throne, Siraj ud-Daulah's will was law, one to be questioned by none and carried out without the slightest demur.

Among those watching in stunned silence was Javed Hussain,

beads of perspiration growing on his brow. He had served the house of Alivardi Khan for years, had sworn fealty to Siraj ud-Daulah, but in that moment, all he felt was revulsion. It was one thing for a ruler to wield authority; it was another to revel in such naked display of absolutism. A ruler who saw his subjects as nothing more than pawns to be broken was dangerous, unpredictable. The thought came unbidden, like a whisper in the recesses of his mind: if Siraj could so easily strip away the dignity of among the most powerful of men in Bengal, what hope did the rest of the populace have?

• • •

David Pratt, barely nineteen and far from the rugged coastline of Cornwall, had come to India with dreams as grand as the opportunities promised by the East India Company. He had imagined daring campaigns, valiant charges, and a steady rise through the ranks, earning his commission through sheer ability and bravery. One day, perhaps, he might even command a fortress of his own.

Reality, however, had been far less glorious.

Each morning, the fort stirred to life with the rhythmic clang of the armoury being unlocked, the sharp calls of officers drilling fresh recruits, and the distant hum of the native quarter beyond its walls. The air was thick with the scent of gunpowder, sweat, and the ever-present dampness of the river. Pratt's duties were predictable - patrol the bastions, check the powder stores, stand watch over the wide Hooghly. Pratt had quickly moved past his initial disappointment with the monotony of his duties and had thrown himself into the work with a determination to prove his worth. But lately, the routine had felt heavier, the weight of foreboding pressing down on the garrison like the humid air before a storm.

Something had changed.

The fort's usual orderliness now carried an edge of unease. Officers spoke in hushed tones, their faces drawn with concern. Even the seasoned sepoys muttered among themselves about the tension with the Nawab. Governor Drake had ordered fortifications - walls reinforced, gun emplacements expanded - moves that had not gone unnoticed by Murshidabad. The whispers among the men varied: some insisted the Nawab would never risk war against the Company, while others swore that Siraj ud-Daulah was young, impulsive, and eager to prove himself.

In the mess hall, the air buzzed with speculation, though few dared to voice their thoughts too openly.

"You mark my words," one of the older privates muttered over his half-eaten meal, voice low but insistent. "The Nawab's not blind. He knows what we're building here. He won't sit idle forever."

A younger man scoffed. "What's he going to do? March down to Calcutta with his peasant army and throw himself against these walls?"

The private gave a dry chuckle. "You weren't here when he took Cossimbazar. Surrounded it overnight. We surrendered before dawn."

"Different place. Different times," the younger soldier insisted. "We've got cannons. Muskets. He's got matchlocks and spears."

Pratt listened, his pulse quickening. He had overheard an ensign joke, half in jest and half in warning, that they might soon be firing their muskets in anger. The remark had sent a thrill through him. A proper battle - an opportunity to prove his mettle. That was how men earned rank. That was how reputations were built.

"You'd best keep your head down, Pratt," a grizzled sergeant had muttered when he caught the younger man listening too intently. "Men who rush for glory usually end up in a shallow grave."

Still, as Pratt patrolled the ramparts that evening, he imagined the day when his name would be known far and wide. He could already see it - his orders ringing across the bastions, his command respected by men who had once looked down on him as just another lad fresh off the ship.

Beyond the fort walls, the Hooghly stretched dark and endless. The river had seen the rise and fall of empires, the passing of rulers, the ebb and flow of fortunes. In the fading light, the city beyond seemed distant, unknowable.

But Pratt cared little for politics or trade disputes. When war came, he would be ready.

If only he had known how soon it would arrive.

• • •

Siraj ud-Daulah did not proceed with the planned military expedition to Purnea, for which he had demanded finance from Jagat Seth. A graver matter demanded his attention. During Alivardi Khan's final days, troubling reports had reached Murshidabad: the British were reinforcing Fort William in Calcutta. These unauthorised fortifications were an affront to the Nawab's sovereignty. Ever the pragmatist, Alivardi had dispatched an agent to Calcutta, hoping to resolve the matter through reason and negotiation.

The agent had returned and brought with news that Governor Drake had not only refused an audience but had the agent forcibly seized and expelled from the city, treating the Nawab's emissary with open contempt.

When Siraj received the agent's report, his rage flared like oil thrown onto fire. The audacity of these English - no, their outright defiance! His temper, already infamous, now seethed with a fury that demanded reckoning. He summoned his ministers to the durbar hall. But this was no call for deliberation; it was a summons to war. To Siraj, the court existed to execute his will.

"Have we grown so feeble," Siraj began, his voice a thunderclap that resonated through the chamber, "that a handful of foreign merchants dare mock the authority of the Nawab of Bengal? Is this the land of Alivardi Khan or the dominion of those perfidious British? Shall we sit idle while they defy our authority? No - action must be taken."

He paused, his gaze sweeping the room like a blade. No one dared to meet his eyes. But an elderly minister, clearing his throat cautiously, ventured, "Nawab Sahib, Alivardi Khan himself sought negotiation before action. Perhaps if we assess their intent more thoroughly, we can -"

Siraj interrupted, his voice sharp as steel. "Negotiation? Haven't we had enough of that? Governor Drake," he spat the name like poison, "not only ignored my grandfather's reasoned overture but insulted us by seizing and expelling our emissary as if he were some common thief. This is not mere arrogance - it is a challenge, a declaration that they believe themselves beyond our reach, above our rule."

Siraj's tone grew sharper, slicing through the dense air. "And what do they do while mocking us? They strengthen their fort, prepare their cannons, and stockpile arms. They harbour traitors and fugitives under the shadow of those walls, daring us to act. Tell me, my ministers, shall we allow these traders to build their fortresses, defy our sovereignty, and quietly take our land piece by piece?"

Another minister ventured, his voice measured but firm, "Nawab Sahib, I think we should acknowledge that these British merchants, despite their arrogance, are not merely traders but representatives of a growing power. Their military prowess is not to be dismissed lightly. They have cannons, and their fort is well-stocked. Have we not heard of how their forces, though outnumbered, stood firm against the French and native armies in the Carnatic?" Pausing for a moment, he continued. "Perhaps we should explore the course of diplomacy a bit longer before engaging in confrontation?"

"Diplomacy?" Siraj thundered, slamming his fist on the armrest of his throne. "Diplomacy is the mask of cowards in the face of such insolence! Besides, do you doubt the strength of our armies? Are you suggesting that a handful of merchants will stand against the soldiers of Bengal?"

Yet, for a fleeting moment, Siraj's fingers tightened around the carved wood of his throne. Alivardi had always favoured restraint.

But restraint had led here - to humiliation. His jaw set, his resolve hardening.

Leaning forward, his fists clenched on the polished wood of his throne, Siraj declared, "We shall reclaim Fort William and bring it under our control. It will be a symbol to the world - European and local alike - that no one mocks the Nawab of Bengal. This is not just about the British. This is about every power, foreign or domestic, that dares question my authority. Let the French and Dutch watch and learn. Let our feudal lords and rivals remember."

The silence was absolute, broken only by Siraj's laboured breathing. He surveyed his court, his ministers frozen in fear and compliance. "Enough of talks! Prepare the army," he commanded. "We march on to Calcutta. The British will learn the price of defiance."

The courtiers, one by one, bowed their heads in agreement, their fear of Siraj outweighing any doubts they might have had. The die was cast.

Soon thereafter, Siraj-ud-Daulah set out with his formidable army, now 70,000 strong, determined to subdue Calcutta and bring its defiant merchants to their knees. They covered the 130 miles to Calcutta within ten days.

• • •

Hirajheel Palace, the seat of the Nawab of Bengal, stood on the banks of the Bhagirathi, its ivory-white domes and sprawling courtyards embodying the prestige of the dynasty it housed. A bastion of authority and grandeur, it held court in its vast halls, where jeweled courtiers and dapper diplomats shaped the fate of the kingdom. Yet beyond the marble columns and silk-draped chambers lay another world, hidden from the eyes of men - the zenana.

Secluded behind towering walls, the zenana was both haven and prison, its silken opulence masking the rigid confines of tradition.

Guarded by eunuchs and bound by custom, it was home to the Nawab's wives, concubines, and female attendants, whose lives played out in veiled rivalries and hollow triumphs. Through the jalis - intricately carved lattice screens - they glimpsed the palace gardens, the flickering lamplight of evening processions, the distant ripples of the Bhagirathi. They could watch, but never partake.

One afternoon, in a spacious chamber of the zenana, a few of Siraj ud-Daulah's consorts gathered, lounging on embroidered divans. Their jeweled hands played with silver hookahs and strands of pearls, the air filled with delicate fragrances and subtle undercurrents of rivalry.

"Jaan-e-Bahar will summon me tonight," Gulbadan said, adjusting her gold-trimmed veil with a smug smile. She was referring to the Nawab. "He seems… particularly allured by my company lately."

Nasira raised an eyebrow, her kohl-lined eyes glinting with amusement. "Allured, you say? He was with me just last night, and he seemed most pleased. Perhaps your interpretation of his attentions is overly optimistic, dear Gulbadan."

The others chuckled, their laughter mingling with the soft clinking of bangles. It was a well-worn game - flirtation, rivalry, and the ceaseless contest for the Nawab's favour. Gulbadan's smile tightened, but before she could reply, Rukaiya spoke, her voice lilting with barely concealed haughtiness. "Really, must we indulge in this?" she asked, reclining against a pile of cushions. "Nawab Sahib's affections are hardly a secret. This ruby necklace, for instance" - she tilted it into the lamplight - "from Persia no less, speaks volumes. One doesn't simply bestow such treasures without intimate affection."

The room grew quieter, the women exchanging guarded glances as the air of one-upmanship thickened. Lutf-un-Nissa sat with quiet poise in the corner, an ivory fan in her hands. Her simple yet elegant attire set her apart with an understated refinement. Gulbadan turned to her, her tone laced with a practiced sweetness. "Why so silent, Lutf? Surely you, too, have stories of Nawab Sahib's affections?"

Lutf-un-Nissa met her gaze with calm poise. "Nawab Sahib's favour is his to bestow," she replied softly. "I find no joy in comparisons."

The women fell silent, taken aback by her composed response. But the stillness was fleeting. Nasira tilted her head with an affected smile. "Such humility, Lutf," she said. "It's easy to forget beginnings, but I must say you wear these silks well."

Lutf-un-Nissa said nothing. Her past, though rarely spoken of, lingered in every room she entered. Sold as a child, Lutf was raised in the Nawab's household, her life shaped by servitude - until fate intervened. Begum Sahiba's - Nawab Alivardi's wife – had seen something in her, something worth shaping. She had taken Lutf under her wing, teaching her the graces and dignity fit for nobility. As she emerged into womanhood, she had caught Siraj's attention, and he had made her one of his Begums.

Lutf-un-Nissa let out a quiet sigh. She had seen moments of genuine sisterhood among the Begums, but too often, they surrendered to petty rivalries, debasing themselves in their own vanities.

Yet, despite these rivalries, the zenana was more than just a battlefield of egos. It was also a vibrant cultural haven, frequently hosting Hindustani music, Kathak dance, Persian and Urdu poetry recitations, dramatic performances, storytelling sessions, and grand celebrations of festivals like Basant Panchami and Holi. In these moments, the burdens of hierarchy and competition seemed to fade, if only briefly. Lutf-un-Nissa eagerly looked forward to such occasions.

And today was the cause for such an occasion. As the day give way to evening, the zenana, illuminated by the warm glow of hundreds of oil lamps, came alive with an air of festive anticipation. The rich aroma of sandalwood incense intertwined with the delicate fragrance of jasmine garlands draped over the curved teak pillars. Cushions embroidered with gold thread lay arranged in elegant semicircles, while silent-footed attendants glided through the room, offering silver trays laden with sweets and fragrant rose sherbets.

At the heart of the gathering sat Ustad Shamsuddin, the renowned musician from Lucknow. Clad in an immaculate white angarkha, the maestro sat cross-legged on a Persian carpet in the centre of the hall, his sitar resting gracefully on his lap. Bowing his head, he plucked the first note - so pure it cut through the stillness like a ripple on a moonlit lake.

Tonight, he would perform a raga - a traditional Indian classical composition, meticulously crafted to evoke a specific mood and suit the hour. The room fell utterly silent, save for the soft rustle of silk as the women leaned forward, drawn into the melody as if by an unseen force. The sitar's ethereal notes wove a tapestry of sound, each thread throbbing with emotion.

The alāp - the gentle introduction to the raga - unfolded like the meandering Ganges at dawn, steeped in longing. The jor - the second movement of the raga, where rhythm emerges - quickened, its steady pulse echoing the growing fervour that gripped the enraptured souls. Ustad Shamsuddin's fingers danced over the frets, coaxing a cascade of notes that painted images of moonlit gardens, riverbanks bathed in silver light, and the gentle sway of lotus-laden ponds. The music whispered of unspoken love, fleeting joy, and wordless sorrow.

Lutf-un-Nissa closed her eyes, her hand resting on her heart as if to steady the flood of emotions the music had stirred. Yet, beneath the beauty of the melody, she felt something else - an unease she could not name. The rising cadence, the trembling high notes, they spoke to her of something more than longing. It was as if the sitar itself was warning of shadows creeping at the edges of their world, a quiet storm gathering beyond the palace walls. She opened her eyes, her gaze lingering on the flickering lamps, their golden glow wavering with an almost restless energy.

As the final note quivered into silence, the women remained still, unwilling to break the spell of transcendence that had enveloped them. Many eyes glistened with tears, not of sorrow but of gratitude for the divine gift they had been bestowed with. Ustad Shamsuddin bowed humbly, his head low, as if he, too, were merely a vessel for a celestial force.

For a moment, the zenana was a temple, the music its prayer, and all within it were worshippers of the sublime. And yet, in the depths of Lutf-un-Nissa's heart, a whisper of unease remained, a subtle tremor in the stillness of the night.

• • •

Crouched behind the parapet with a musket trembling in his hands, David Pratt found all those dreams of glory felt distant, like a boy's naive fantasy. The sense of unease that had loomed over the fort for days had thickened into something suffocating. Orders were barked with growing urgency, officers paced the ramparts, and even the most seasoned veterans watched the horizon with grim expressions.

The first real jolt to his illusions had come just days ago, when he overheard a conversation in the garrison's mess hall. There had always been murmurs of war, but now the warnings carried hints of inevitability. The veterans spoke in hushed voices, their confidence wavering. Even those who had once dismissed Siraj-ud-Daulah as an inexperienced boy now spoke with caution, their bravado tempered by the growing unease.

Pratt had stationed himself along the outer defences when the first clear sign of trouble appeared. He observed a distant shimmer of movement along the horizon, like the ripple of a heatwave, that gradually sharpened into discernible figures and banners fluttering in the wind. A shiver ran down Pratt's spine. There was no mistaking it - an advancing army. The tension thickened through the fort as the news spread like wildfire, tightening its grip on every man in the garrison.

"God save us," muttered one of the artillerymen, watching the dust rise beyond the Maratha Ditch. A drummer boy stood frozen, his sticks limp in his hands.

"How soon do you think they'll reach us?" Pratt asked quietly, sitting beside a fellow soldier, Carter, who had a reputation for knowing everything before anyone else. Carter shrugged. "They're camped at Dumdum already. The scouts say they march at dawn. If Drake doesn't do something soon, they'll be at the Maratha Ditch before we know it."

Pratt looked at him, alarmed. "Surely the governor has a plan?" Carter leaned in, lowering his voice. "Aye, he has a plan – to save his own skin."

That night, the first cannon fire split the sky. Pratt was manning a post along the northern ramparts when the bombardment began. Cannonballs whistled through the air, slamming into the fort's walls with deafening force. Smoke from the burning Black Town curled into the sky, and the sound of distant screams reached their ears.

"Load faster, Pratt!" Sergeant Hargreaves barked, snapping Pratt out of his daze. "You think that musket's going to fire itself?"

"Yes, sir!" Pratt scrambled to reload, his fingers fumbling with the powder and shot.

By nightfall, chaos reigned inside the fort. The outer defences had crumbled, and the remaining defenders retreated to the inner ramparts. Supplies were running dangerously low, and the soldiers were almost dropping with exhaustion. Pratt sat slumped against a wall, his musket across his lap, when Carter dropped down beside him.

"We're finished, aren't we?" Carter said, his voice barely above a whisper, his usual certainty absent but not his awareness. Pratt shook his head, though he wasn't sure if he was denying Carter's words or reassuring himself. "We'll hold. We have to."

Carter gave a hollow laugh. "Drake's gone, mate. Took a boat under cover of darkness. A few officers went with him as well."

Pratt stared at him in disbelief. "He fled? He just… left us?"

"Aye. Abandoned the fort, abandoned his men, and abandoned every last civilian who trusted his leadership. No valiant last stand for him, only cowardice and disgrace."

There was no time to absorb the betrayal. The gates had been breached.

Siraj's sharpshooters, perched on the rooftops around the fort, picked off anyone who dared show themselves on the ramparts. Pratt saw men fall one after another, their bodies crumpling like rag dolls. By mid-afternoon, the enemy had breached the gates. Inside the fort, chaos erupted as defenders fought desperately, swinging muskets like clubs when ammunition ran out.

"Fall back! To the inner wall!" The sergeant's voice rang out, though it was barely audible over the din of battle. Pratt fought on, wielding his bayonet with a mixture of fear and desperation. He caught glimpses of his comrades doing the same, their faces grim and bloodied.

When the flag of truce was finally raised, Pratt dropped to his knees, his chest heaving. He felt no relief, only a suffocating mix of despair, humiliation, and a creeping dread of what fate awaited him. He watched in silence as the last embers of resistance at the fort flickered and died. The surrender had been swift, its inevitability crushing. His muscles ached from days of fighting, but it was the weight in his chest that truly overwhelmed him. Around him, soldiers and civilians alike stumbled through the wreckage of the once-proud fort, hearts heavy with trepidation. He was among them, yet he felt strangely apart, as if the events were unfolding in a nightmare he could not escape.

Bound with the other prisoners, Pratt was herded into the courtyard. The air hung thick with smoke and the acrid remnants of plundered homes and torched goods. From his place in the huddled mass, he caught a glimpse of Siraj ud-Daulah's litter as it was borne into the fort. The Nawab, a young man like himself, exuded an air of smug exaltation that made Pratt's stomach tighten with unease.

The victors showed restraint, even more than what the seasoned soldiers had expected – at first. No swords flashed, no muskets fired in vengeful rage. For a fleeting moment, Pratt dared to hope - perhaps they would be spared the worst. But the illusion shattered when a drunken soldier, defiant in his humiliation, pulled a pistol and shot one of their captors dead.

This act ignited a fury that surged through the victors like wildfire. The prisoners were herded together, driven by shouting guards into a small, dimly lit chamber. Pratt was jostled forward, the press of bodies suffocating him before they even reached the cell. The door slammed shut behind them with an eerie finality. Pratt craned his neck to catch a breath of the stifling air, his vision blurring as the heat and lack of space took their toll. Cries of panic rose around him, men clawing for space that did not exist. The single small window, meant to provide light and air, offered no relief to the packed mass of desperate humanity.

As the hours dragged on, Pratt felt the life being squeezed from him, one ragged breath at a time. His limbs grew heavy, his thoughts sluggish. Somewhere nearby, a man collapsed, his body slumping against Pratt's legs, but he lacked the strength to move him. The oppressive darkness began to swallow him whole, his mind slipping into fragments of memory and fading light.

He thought of home. He thought of a life that now seemed so distant.

By morning, when the cell was finally opened, the scene was one of utter horror. Bodies lay heaped together, the few survivors gasping for air as they stumbled out into the courtyard. Among the prisoners who did not come out was David Pratt. He had become one of the casualties of the infamous Black Hole of Calcutta, an incident that would be taught to British schoolchildren for generations as a moral bedrock for their dominion.

• • •

The Padma River shimmered in the late afternoon sun as Javed Hussain's bajra - the flat-bottomed boat for the elite - glided smoothly with the breeze. A banner bearing his crest fluttered above. Beneath a shaded canopy, Javed gazed into the horizon as the lush fields of his zamindari, on Bengal's eastern edge came into view. Far from Murshidabad's political intrigues and the strains of military command, this land, granted to him in recognition of his service, was a reminder of his aristocratic standing. Like many nobles in the Nawab's service, he was both a soldier and a landlord. And with each of his annual visits, the sight of this fertile land, abundant and thriving, filled him with a quiet, unwavering pride.

The steady beat of the oars was accompanied by the lively chatter of the boatmen, who spoke of the ongoing festivities. "The Durga Puja, huzur, is grander than ever this year," one remarked, smiling broadly. "I hear the whole village has gathered." Javed leaned slightly forward, resting a hand on the boatman's shoulder. "That is good to hear," he said. "And your family, Aamir - are they well?" The man beamed at the unexpected inquiry, nodding enthusiastically. "By your grace, huzur, they are happy."

Javed nodded, a faint smile caressing his lips. The Durga Puja on his estate was a tradition he had wholeheartedly encouraged. And not just for his Hindu subjects who celebrated it as a sacred event but for the entire village. He thanked the Almighty for Bengal's prosperity, which had nurtured a wholesome harmony among her people, particularly in his zamindari - a sense of oneness where differences of faith were no barrier to shared joy.

As the boat neared the jetty, Javed spotted a small crowd gathered in anticipation of his arrival. His ageing dewan, Harinarayan Sanyal - a thin, sharp-featured man with a ready smile - stepped forward to assist his master disembark. "Welcome, Sarkar! The village eagerly awaits your presence at the Puja. This year's idol is exquisite, and as always, the festivities have united everyone in joy."

The walk to the estate was alive with colour and sound. Villagers bustled about, some carrying offerings of fruit and flowers, others leading children dressed in their festive best. The rhythmic, booming beat of the dhak drums resonated through the air, blending harmoniously with the distant strains of a conch shell being blown at intervals. The gentle fragrance of incense drifted through the air, mingling pleasantly with the crisp early afternoon breeze.

The main courtyard of the zamindari estate had been transformed into a lively fusion of devotion and celebration. The life-sized idol of Goddess Durga stood resplendent at the centre. Her face was serene yet commanding; her ten arms, each wielding a weapon gifted by the other Gods, seemed to radiate divine justice. She loomed with majestic grace over her faithful lion, its powerful form poised mid-leap, claws extended and jaws parted in a silent roar. Beneath the fearsome beast, Mahishasura - the demon king who had been tormenting Gods and mortals alike – reeled in his final struggle, his expression frozen between defiance and despair, his weapon slipping from his grasp.

Around Durga, her celestial children - Lakshmi, Saraswati, Kartik, and Ganesha - completed the sacred tableau. The priests, who moved with practiced ease, waved incense sticks in slow, deliberate arcs, releasing spirals of fragrant smoke. From their lips flowed a steady stream of mantras that echoed through the courtyard.

The villagers, Hindus and Muslims alike, joined in the revelry with the same infectious enthusiasm. Some gathered in the grand courtyard, watching the priests perform their rituals. Others lined up to offer flowers and prayers before the idols, hands folded in devotion. Nearby, elders sat on woven mats, recounting tales of bygone festivals and legends around the pantheon of Gods and Goddesses in Hindu mythology. Children darted between them, trying to mimic the beats of the dhak on makeshift drums. Women in colourful sarees carried trays of prasad, distributing the sanctified offerings with affectionate smiles, while friends and neighbours exchanged warm greetings all around.

Javed took his seat of honour beside Harinarayan, soaking in the laughter and music that seemed to merge into a shared rhythm of pure joy. A small group of the village notables - landowners, respected elders, prosperous merchants - also gathered around them, sharing a quiet sense of togetherness as they devotedly observed the rituals.

Harinarayan leaned closer to Javed, his voice low but eager. "This year's harvest has been plentiful, Sarkar. The people have reason to celebrate." Javed nodded, his gaze lingering on the children laughing and playing near the flower-strewn altar. "It is as it should be," he said. "When the land provides, the people prosper. And when the people prosper, there is peace and happiness."

An elderly schoolmaster approached Javed hesitantly. He extended a reassuring hand. "Tarini Babu, how have you been? Are your students keeping you busy?" The old man clasped his hands together, a smile breaking across his weathered face. "By your grace, Sarkar, I am well. The village children still recite their lessons under the banyan tree, though some are more eager for their slates than others." Javed nodded, his gaze warm. "That is good to hear. And your grandson? The last time I was here, he was just starting to learn his letters." Tarini's face lit up with pride. "Ramu is learning quickly Sarkar, he has even started reading the Ramayana book in our house." Javed's smile deepened. "That is wonderful. You know better than me how a learned man is respected by all. But tonight, let us forget all else and enjoy the festivities - these moments with the community are what truly matter."

As the evening deepened, oil lamps were lit. The priests intoned the final chants of the evening's rituals. The dhak's beats softened and finally came to a stop. Presently, the crowd assembled at an open-air theatre within the estate, where a troupe of performers from a nearby village had begun to enact the tale of Prahlad and Hiranyakashipu. Seated on the ground, the gathering watched with rapt attention, hanging onto every word and gesture of the performers. The tension mounted as the tyrant king, Hiranyakashipu, blinded by arrogance, defied the divine and demanded that all worship him alone. Gasps rippled through the audience as, in the climactic moment, Narasimha, the half-man, half-lion incarnation of Lord Vishnu, emerged from the pillar in a terrifying roar and dragged the demon king to the palace threshold. As the mighty Narasimha tore Hiranyakashipu apart with his claws, the crowd erupted in exhilaration, cheering as everyone does when good prevails over evil.

As the play came to an end, Javed rose to leave, with the rest of the throng. Yet he paused for a few moments, his eyes lingering on the now dimly lit courtyard. A fleeting prayer of gratitude - for the land and its people - passed through his mind, yet a quiet unease gnawed at him. For something about the play had unsettled him in a way he could not quite place. The image of Hiranyakashipu - draped in royal finery, believing himself invincible - clung to his thoughts. His arrogance, his refusal to see reason, his blindness to danger until it was too late. Javed's mind rebelled against the comparison, yet the shadow of the young Nawab loomed large in his thoughts.

The world around him was shifting, unravelling under the weight of a ruler too proud to see the storm gathering on the horizon. Siraj ud-Daulah, like Hiranyakashipu, ignored counsel, dismissed warnings, and mistook defiance for strength. Javed had seen it in court, in the reckless way the Nawab provoked powerful enemies, believing himself invincible. The thought disturbed him. Would his hubris invite his own reckoning? And if it did, would Bengal be dragged to ruin alongside him?

Javed exhaled slowly, pressing his fingers together in silent contemplation. The play was only a story, yet its lesson refused to fade from his mind. Closing his eyes briefly, he murmured a quiet prayer to the Goddess standing in solitary vigilance in the courtyard.

"Mother, keep your gaze upon this land, as you always have. Let your hand remain steady over her people, that they may not stray into ruin."

• • •

Robert Clive, the Governor of Fort St David, in the Madras Presidency of the East India Company, was relishing one of his morning horse rides along the expansive beaches of the Coromandel Coast. The sea broke upon the shore in steady bursts, a cadence that filled the morning air. Clive galloped through the serene landscape, his horse's hooves striking the sand in steady rhythm. In the distance, palms swayed gently in the wind. These morning rides, a cherished ritual, left his mind invigorated and sharpened, ready to face the challenges of governance. But this morning, as he urged his horse forward, his thoughts were elsewhere. A dispatch had arrived from Bengal - urgent, troubling. He had read it before setting out, yet its implications still lingered.

His ride completed, the thickset man with sharp features and a stern expression returned to his residence, a sturdy European-style bungalow. After a quick bath, he settled for his light breakfast in the shaded veranda of his bungalow, where the soft morning breeze offered a fleeting respite from the intensifying heat. The breakfast table, elegantly set with fine Chinese porcelain and polished silverware, held a modest spread of freshly baked bread, tropical fruits, and steaming tea. He reached for his cup but hesitated, his gaze shifting beyond the veranda's edge. The sight of Indian servants, clad in simple white dhotis and turbans, moving about with quiet efficiency, the distant hum of Fort St David, and the seabirds crying overhead - all of it blurred against his thoughts. The news from Bengal gnawed at him, pulling him into the past, into the turbulent life of the 30 years that he had led so far.

And what a life it has been! A life of remarkable twists of fate, forged - as Clive quite unapologetically acknowledged to himself - by his audacity and unrelenting determination. Born into the modest comforts of Styche Hall in Shropshire, his early years were marked by a spirit quite ungovernable. Tales of his escapades still echoed in his memory. *"The terror of Market Drayton!"* his uncle had once teased him, shaking his head with a mix of exasperation and amusement.

"This boy will either hang or make his fortune!" his schoolmaster had once proclaimed to a snickering classroom. Clive smiled now, recalling the way it had set a spark in his chest. Fortune, indeed. And fortune had carried him here - to power, to influence. Yet now, his fate was once again at a crossroads.

Clive's journey to India began in the most unremarkable way imaginable. Sent as a junior writer for the East India Company in 1743 – 13 years ago - he was barely more than a clerk, consigned to the drudgery of tallying accounts. But India - unfamiliar, unforgiving India - had no warmth for a homesick heart. Alone in his dim room in Madras, staring at the relentless sun cutting through the shutters, he had grappled with despair.

"Why are you so glum, Robert?" one of his fellow clerks had prodded, trying to cheer him during a grim supper of rice and curry. *"I am in a land of riches and ruin,"* Clive had replied darkly, pushing his plate away, *"and I see neither path for me."*

There was even that one fateful evening, pistol in hand, staring at the walls of his quarters, wondering if his loneliness and despair might end with a single shot. But destiny had other plans, for his pistol jammed. Clive occasionally wondered - was that luck or providence? But it no longer mattered. What mattered was what followed. For Clive carved his own path.

The French attack on Madras in 1746 was his first real test. Amid the chaos, one man had taken note of him - Stringer Lawrence, the formidable commander of the East India Company's forces in India. When Clive first encountered him, the seasoned officer's piercing gaze seemed to weigh his worth in an instant. Now, as the city reeled under siege, Lawrence's voice came back to him vividly, rough and clear: *"Clive, are you a writer or a soldier?"*

"A soldier, sir," Clive had answered without hesitation, though at the time, he hardly grasped the full import of his own words. *"Then ride tonight. Get yourself to Fort St David, or die trying!"* And so he had

ridden - alone and desperate, slipping through French patrols under a moonless sky, his life hinging on every breathless gallop. That night, the clerk had died, and the soldier had been born.

Under Lawrence's mentorship, Clive found his calling in war. The siege of Arcot in 1751 had been madness, he knew, and yet it was his finest hour. He could still hear the voices of his weary, hungry men as they held the fort for fifty days. *"Sir, we can't hold another hour!"* his lieutenant had cried, blood streaked across his face. *"We hold until there's nothing left to hold."* Clive had replied, the words clipped, as if spoken by someone else. And they had held.

Victory at Arcot, victory at Srirangam - one after the other, his triumphs came like dominoes falling, leaving French forces reeling and Indian allies awed. After the victory at Srirangam, an Indian ally, a local commander, had clasped his hand with admiration. *"You are a lion among men, Clive Sahib. How do you fight without fear?" "Fear has its uses"*, Clive had replied with a knowing smile. *"It sharpens the mind, but it is courage that wins the battle."* And in Clive, courage was an unwavering trait that turned the tide of battles.

Returning to England in 1753, he had tasted wealth and recognition. The comforts of London society were pleasurable, yet strangely hollow. Politics, as he soon found, was a dull battlefield - filled with polite backstabbers in wigs and silks. An acquaintance at Westminster once sneered, *"Clive, India has made you bold, but do leave the sword behind when you enter the Commons."* Clive had chuckled, but something in him bristled. England was too small for his ambition. Too safe. Too tame.

His return to India in 1755 had felt inevitable. *"Duty calls, Margaret,"* he had told his wife as they said their farewells. She had clasped his hand tightly. *"Promise me, Robert, you will not be reckless in chasing your ambitions." "I promise to be careful, Margaret,"* he had said with a gentle smile. But as her eyes searched his, his inner voice whispered the truth - *I will only chase victory.*

Sitting now, gazing out across the sunlit veranda, Clive could not ignore the irony of his journey - from the unruly boy in Shropshire to a much admired leader of the East India Company. He had seized every opportunity fate had offered, carved his own fortune with grit and ruthlessness. Yet a quiet voice echoed in the back of his mind - a voice that whispered of unfinished business, of more lands to conquer and more victories to win.

And it was this voice that brought his wandering mind back to the urgent reality of the present. The dispatch from Bengal still lay on his desk. It held the report of the fall of Fort William and the city of Calcutta a month earlier.

Clive placed his teacup down with deliberate care. The battlefields of Bengal beckoned. A new test of his audacity. He had shaped his own fate before. Now, he would do so again. And this particular enterprise would begin with a council meeting of key functionaries of the East India Company in the Madras Presidency later in the day.

• • •

Although Calcutta was lost to the East India Company, by a twist of fate, an option to retaliate had presented itself for them. A flotilla of battle-ready warships, which included three regiments of Royal Artillery, had recently arrived at the port of Madras. Although Robert Clive was a senior officer in the fleet, it was commanded by Admiral Charles Watson, the commander of the entire British naval forces in the Indian Ocean. Their intention was to confront the French, not the Nawab of Bengal. Clive, however, saw an unmissable opportunity. Motivated by his vision for bold action and personal losses tied to investments in Bengal and Company stock, he would advocate strongly for a more aggressive response.

The council chamber in Madras buzzed with tense anticipation as the members gathered, most of them wearing a worried look. At one end of the long mahogany table sat Admiral Watson in his immaculate naval uniform. At the other was Robert Clive, his piercing and determined gaze fixed on the men before him. The Madras Council had convened to strategise British responses to the escalating French threats and growing unrest in Bengal.

George Pigot, the Governor of Madras, cleared his throat and broke the uneasy silence. "Gentlemen, we are here to decide the future of our operations in India. Bengal is lost, and the question now is whether we can afford to risk more. Monson, what is your view?"

Edward Monson, the cautious and seasoned Company merchant, adjusted his spectacles and leaned forward. "Governor, our situation is precarious. The French flotilla from Port Lorient is expected any day, and if it reaches the Coromandel unchallenged, we could lose Madras itself. I say we hold our forces here. Protect what we still have."

There were murmurs of agreement from the other council members. Henry Bradshaw, another influential voice, nodded emphatically. "Monson is right. Bengal's loss is unfortunate, but we cannot compound it with further recklessness. If we divert our fleet to Bengal and the French attack, it could spell disaster for the Company."

Governor Pigot interjected. "Bradshaw, are you suggesting we simply abandon our position in Bengal? That region contributes the most to our revenues. If we lose our influence there, the very financial viability of the Company could be at stake."

Clive, who had been silent until now, straightened. "Did you say disaster, Bradshaw? Gentlemen, Bengal is the Company's lifeblood. Calcutta is not just a trading post - it is our strongest foothold in India, a gateway to its richest province. To abandon it now would be to concede defeat, not just to Siraj-ud-Daulah but to every enemy we face. Now *that* is what I would call disaster."

Monson frowned. "Clive, you speak with passion, but we must be practical. Our resources are limited. What if the Nawab's forces overpower us? What if -"

Pigot raised a hand to silence him. "And what if they don't? What if we march into Bengal and reclaim what is rightfully ours? What if we restore not just our factories and privileges but our honour? Have you all forgotten the Black Hole of Calcutta? Innocent men who had surrendered - British subjects - suffocated to death in a barbaric display of cruelty! Shall we let that go unanswered?"

The room fell silent. Even Bradshaw, who had been so vocal moments ago, looked uneasy. The council members exchanged uncertain glances, torn between the risks and the rewards.

Admiral Watson, who had been listening intently, leaned forward. "Clive, my orders are to engage the French, not to meddle in local disputes. Monson is right. If I divert my fleet to Bengal, then who will protect the Coromandel? If the French choose this moment to strike, we may lose Madras itself. What assurances do I have that this is a fight worth committing to, given such a risk?"

Clive nodded, acknowledging the Admiral's concern. "You are right, Admiral. The risk is real, and I do not take it lightly. But consider this: if we allow Bengal to slip away, we lose not only the Calcutta Presidency but our entire standing in India."

He held the silence for a moment, allowing the weight of his words to settle. "The French are a threat, yes, but a temporary one. Bengal, however, is the true prize. Its wealth, its resources - once secured, it will give us the financial strength to reinforce our holdings along the Coromandel and beyond. A bold move now will secure our dominance for decades to come. If we dither, we may never get another chance."

Clive turned to Watson, his tone shifting to one of urgency. "Admiral, this is not just the Company's fight. It is about securing *British* dominance in trade. Your fleet is already prepared for war. With your support, we can ensure that Bengal remains in British hands."

Watson studied Clive for a long moment before exhaling. "The fleet will not move without guarantees. The Company must ensure adequate financial backing for any repairs and losses suffered during this campaign."

Governor Pigot nodded. "I am sure that can be arranged, Admiral".

Clive pressed home the advantage. "But Admiral, we need swift action. Every day that we delay emboldens our enemies and weakens our position".

Watson's eyes narrowed; his gaze locked onto Clive as he weighed the gravity of the proposal. The room held its breath. Finally, he nodded slowly. "I take your point, gentlemen. With the Company's commitment to provisions and reinforcements, you have my support, Clive. But this venture must not fail."

Clive straightened, his face a mix of triumph and resolve. "It will not fail, Admiral. Together, we will ensure that Bengal is ours once more - and that no one dares challenge British power in India again."

One by one, the remaining council members gave their studied agreement. The decision was made. The fleet would sail for Bengal up the Coromandel coast, and Clive would lead the charge to reclaim Calcutta.

As the meeting adjourned, Clive stood alone for a moment, gazing out of the chamber's window at the restless sea beyond. He felt the weight of the task ahead. His mind turned to the logistics before the campaign could begin – the need to secure funds, coordinate troop movements, and gather intelligence.

• • •

A faint breeze stirred the heavy drapes of the spacious study, carrying with it the distant hum of the Bhagirathi River. Mir Jafar, a senior commander of the Bengal army - and also its Bakshi, the paymaster - sat among his trusted lieutenants, who had gathered in his mansion. The air inside the chamber carried the scent of sandalwood and old parchment, now mingling with the spiced aroma of grilled meat and the faint bitterness of steeping tea. Murshidabad had settled into its routine after Siraj ud-Daulah's campaign in Calcutta, now renamed Alinagar. But within these walls, the weight of simmering discontent lingered.

The men were seated on cushions around a low table, the remnants of a light refreshment spread before them - silver plates bearing skewers of half-eaten kebabs, a small dish of dates, and delicate ceramic cups filled with steaming tea. They were all veterans of the Maratha conflicts, protectors of Bengal in those tumultuous times during Alivardi Khan's reign. But tonight, they were not warriors - they were men passed over by a ruler too callow to recognise their worth. For Nawab Siraj ud-Daulah had granted the governorship of Calcutta to Raja Manikchand, a court administrator who had not held a sword in his life.

Beneath the frustration of the men assembled lay something more - an understanding of the wound festering within Mir Jafar. He sat at the head of the gathering, reclining slightly, his fingers idly tracing the rim of his teacup. Denying him the governorship of Calcutta had been an open slight, one that burned deeper than he dared admit. And their stock was tied to his; if he remained cast aside, so too would they.

Ataullah Khan was the first to break the silence, as he turned to Mir Jafar. "It should have been you, Mir Sahib" he said, his voice edged with measured insistence. "Who in the Nawab's army has earned this post more than you? Who else has stood beside Alivardi Khan when Bengal bled, and held the borders when the Marathas stormed our lands?"

Mir Jafar did not respond at once. He picked up a date from the dish, rolling it between his fingers before setting it back down untouched. The sting of being cast aside had not stopped hurting - but to speak of it aloud was another matter.

"Manikchand?" Mir Asad scoffed. "A courtier, a man of ledgers and ceremonies. What does he know of war? What does he know of the English and the treachery that lurks beneath their supplication? The Nawab has placed Calcutta in the hands of a man unfit to defend it."

THE TRAITOR'S BARGAIN

Ataullah had just picked up a skewer of kebab, sliding off a piece of meat with his fingers before setting it back on his plate. He now leaned in slightly, his voice softer, almost conspiratorial. "And you accept this, Mir Sahib? That after decades of loyal and valorous service, you are to be passed over for a man who has never seen battle?"

"We all fought under your command, Mir Sahib," added Raja Ramnarayan. "You were Alivardi's most trusted general. Even the Marathas feared your name." He shook his head. "What greater insult could there be than to cast you aside for a court administrator?"

Mir Jafar let out a slow breath, as if weighing their words. His gaze shifted to the balcony beyond, where the city stretched out bathed in moonlight. Murshidabad, the palace - power, close yet distant. Finally he spoke, in a tone that betrayed the bitterness in his mind. "I have fought his battles, bled for his cause, yet the Nawab casts me aside like a worn-out scabbard. But he has made his choice, and we have to abide by that."

Ataullah's expression darkened. He set aside the skewer, his fingers idly brushing off the faint traces of spice. "And what if his choice weakens us all, Mir Sahib? Do you think he will stop at Calcutta? If Manikchand commands there, who will be next? Do you truly believe the Nawab will not replace those who have shed blood for Bengal with men who have only ever shed ink?"

Mir Jafar hesitated, his fingers tightening slightly against his teacup. A part of him wanted to dismiss their words, to insist that loyalty was all that remained. Yet another part whispered of humiliation, of doors shut in his face, of flatterers who murmuring into Siraj's ear while soldiers like him were left to fade into irrelevance.

Still, he shook his head, as though the very thought of defying the Nawab was dangerous to entertain. "Siraj values those who tell him what he wishes to hear," he said at last, his voice quieter now. "That is the way of rulers. What can we do but serve as we always have?"

Ataullah leaned forward. "Then perhaps it is time for the ground to shift beneath him."

Mir Jafar turned back to the city, his thoughts a tangle of uncertainty. The word they dared not say clawed at the edges of his mind. Yet, in the heavy silence, it loomed over them all.

Finally, he spoke, more to himself than to them. "A kingdom held together by flatterers and courtiers will crumble when the storm of war arrives. And when that time comes, who will stand to defend it?"

The men exchanged glances etched with frustration. They had come seeking a leader, but what they found was a man wavering on the edge of doubt.

· · ·

On a clear morning in October 1756, two months after the pivotal Madras Council meeting, the salty sea breeze carried the anticipation of an impending campaign. The harbour at Madras was alive with the bustle of activity, sailors moving about noisily as they heaved crates of gunpowder and rations onto five East India Company ships. Among them were 1,000 European troops and an equal number of Indian sepoys - the largest force the British had ever mustered in India. Their destination: Calcutta.

On the deck of the flagship, HMS Kent, Private Thomas Hawke gripped the railing, staring at the receding coastline. At nineteen, he had fled the monotony of a blacksmith's apprenticeship in England, trading soot and iron for the promise of fortune and adventure in the Company's ranks. But as the rigging creaked and officers barked orders, he felt something he hadn't expected - doubt. What did he truly know of the land they were marching to reclaim? Of the enemy who awaited them beyond the murky waters of the Ganges?

His gaze shifted to the quarterdeck. Robert Clive paced the deck, his mind fixed on Calcutta. He had studied its fall - the panic, the disorganised resistance, the disgrace of Governor Drake's retreat. There would be no such failure under his command. Siraj-ud-Daulah believed the British too weak to return, a mistake Clive intended to exploit. The assault had to be swift; a prolonged siege would only lead to retreat or worse.

Further along the deck, Admiral Charles Watson stood with his officers, reviewing naval preparations. His fleet would pound enemy positions and secure the waterways, while Clive would lead the land forces, Success depended on their coordination, and both men knew failure was not an option.

The voyage was long and unrelenting. The sea, once calm, soon turned restless. The sky darkened, and the winds grew stronger, forcing the ships to fight against towering waves. Though it never became a full storm, the relentless squalls tore at the sails, slowing their progress. The decks remained slick with rain, the air thick with the briny scent of seawater.

Hawke braced against the gunwale. He spat salt from his lips, stomach churning as the ship pitched. "If this is the sea in a temper," he muttered, clutching a rope to steady himself, "I'd hate to see her in a fury."

Beside him, Private John McBride, his usual smirk tight with strain, wiped water from his eyes. "Cheer up, Hawke. If we're lucky, there'll be rum waiting for us in Bengal."

When the winds finally calmed, the troops surveyed the damage - sails torn, supplies dampened, and worse, men already coughing from fever.

Days blurred into nights; the passage of time marked only by suffering. The air became thick with the stink of sweat, mildew, and the rot of damp wood. The ship's hold became a pit of sickness, filled with the hacking coughs of men, a few of them too weak to climb the ladder to the deck.

Then came scurvy. At first, just a few men - gums turning black, teeth loosening, fever burning their skin. Then more. Then dozens. Their bodies, once strong, shrivelled beneath ragged uniforms, their faces gaunt and hollow. The ship had set sail with warriors, but now, what remained were spectres of men, shadows of the army that had once stood tall on the docks of Madras. The low murmurs of suffering rose and fell beneath the relentless sound of the sea, and every morning, more bodies were wrapped in canvas and sent overboard, the splash no longer drawing notice.

Hawke sat hunched near the mast, staring at his own trembling hands. Had they always been this thin? His uniform, once stiff with starch, now hung loose over his frame. He caught his reflection in a puddle on the deck - sunken eyes, hollow cheeks, a face he barely recognised.

Clive stood above it all, watching the slow decay of his army with a cold, calculating gaze. He had started with 2,000 men. Now, he estimated, barely 1,200 remained fit for battle, and even that number dwindled by the day. Another few weeks, and they would be lucky to field half that. He mentally adjusted his strategy - he would have to move faster than planned, strike before his force became emaciated even further. There was no room for hesitation.

The Kent, along with two other ships, limped into the estuary of the Ganges, dropping anchor near the swamps just off her mouth. But the relief of reaching land was marred by the smell of decay that hung thick in the humid air. The men swatted at mosquitoes, but it was of little use. Malaria, or what the men mistook it as swamp vapour, had now become their foremost nemesis.

A few days passed, while the men waited for the stragglers in the fleet to catch up with them. Days of rationing foul-smelling water, of men too weak to stand, of nights spent listening to the muffled prayers of the dying. Rows of fresh graves lined the shore, dug hastily, filled even quicker.

Then came the order. They would move upriver - what remained of them. About half of those who began the voyage had already perished.

As the fleet inched toward Calcutta, the jungle pressed in, thick and oppressive. The river wound lazily through tangled mangroves, its waters swirling brown with silt.

The jungle appeared quiet - too quiet. The usual chorus of birds and insects had faded, as if the land itself held its breath. No chatter of monkeys, no rustling in the undergrowth - only a heavy, expectant hush before the storm.

McBride's voice was barely a whisper. 'This land isn't just wild,' he said. 'It's cursed. And men have met worse fate in the city beyond. Suffocating in the dark, crying out for mercy that never came.'"

Hawke did not argue. They had all heard the stories - men gasping for breath in the dark, crushed together until silence claimed them. Few dared to speak of it aloud. The promise of adventure had withered into something else, something unspoken, lurking beneath every step they took.

Yet as he glanced at Clive - calm, unwavering - he felt, for the first time in weeks, a glimmer of hope. Maybe they would take Calcutta after all.

• • •

When the first light of 2 January 1757 broke over the horizon, the hulking silhouette of Fort William came into view. The air was thick with anticipation as the squadron anchored.

Clive had spent the evening before in Admiral Watson's cabin, putting the finishing touches to their strategy. The admiral's ships would initiate the assault and soften the fort's defences. Under cover of the bombardment from the river, Clive's ground forces would strike with speed and precision. It was important not to allow the enemy time to organise a drawn-out resistance.

The ground forces disembarked. The approach to Fort William was fraught with tension. Hawke tightened his grip on his musket as the column advanced stealthily through the jungle. He could feel the sweat running down his back despite the cool air of the misty morning, his pulse quickening with each step.

"Stay sharp," a sergeant barked in hushed tones. Concealing themselves well in the jungle, the soldiers observed the fort carefully. Hawke noted with some relief that while its ramparts lined with the Nawab's defenders, they were not as many as he had expected. The enemy had not anticipated this assault.

With the troops in position, at the pre-appointed hour, Watson's fleet unleashed the first strike. The river came alive with the roar of cannon fire, as the British warships pounded the fort's bastions. Smoke coiled into the air, while stone and debris erupted from the walls.

The fort's defenders, though caught off guard, reacted with a deafening barrage. Musket and artillery fire erupted from the fort ferociously. The air came alive with the shriek of shot and the crash of cannonballs. Hawke ducked instinctively as the ground around him exploded in showers of dirt.

Clive's voice cut through the din. "Advance!"

The British line surged forward, bayonets levelled, boots pounding the earth. Officers bellowed orders over the roar of gunfire, driving the men onward. Hawke fired his musket, the recoil jarring his shoulder, but he barely felt it. He reloaded with practised hands, fingers slick with sweat and powder. Ahead, a Nawab's soldier crumpled from the ramparts, but more emerged through the swirling smoke.

The defenders answered fiercely. Musket fire cracked in rapid bursts, mingling with the shouts of men and the dull thud of bullets striking earth and flesh.

With a desperate cry, the Nawab's soldiers made a counter charge, swords flashing as they closed the distance in a frenzied rush. Hawke's pulse hammered as he levelled his musket, breath held. Then, above the chaos, came a commanding voice - sharp, unwavering.

"Fire!"

The British line erupted in unison, a storm of lead tearing through the charging ranks. Smoke billowed thick and acrid as bodies crumpled mid-stride, their advance dissolving into chaos well before they could reach the British line.

Clive, sensing the moment of collapse, pushed forward. His voice carried above the din. 'Press the attack! Do not give them ground!"

As Clive's men closed in on the fort, Watson's guns fell silent, the admiral having ordered a halt to the bombardment to avoid endangering the advancing troops. The battle was now left to the soldiers on the ground - their bayonets and muskets would decide the final outcome.

Clive gave the order for the final assault. The gates of the fort groaned under the relentless blows of a battering ram, wood splintering with each strike. With a final, thunderous crack, the gates gave way. Hawke charged alongside his comrades. The fort's defenders scrambled in the choking smoke, fighting desperately amid the chaos. A final musket volley cut through them, and the British forces poured in like an unstoppable tide.

Hawke's musket discharged one last time. Around him, the enemy soldiers faltered. Sensing the futility in any further resistance, they threw down their weapons, hands raised in surrender.

Hawke sagged against the wall, his breath ragged. The fight was over, and the defenders had been routed decisively. But his hands still trembled, muscles taut from the rush of battle. The acrid scent of powder clung to the air, mingling with the groans of the wounded. His heart pounded in his ears, unwilling to believe it was done.

As the East India Company's banners were raised over Fort William, a resounding cheer erupted from the British soldiers. However much emaciated with disease and depleted through death, they had reclaimed the most strategically important fort in India - and with it, the keys to the city of Calcutta.

After the initial euphoria had faded, Hawke paused at the threshold of an unremarkable chamber - unremarkable, yet infamous. The Black Hole of Calcutta.

His breath caught as he stepped closer, his fingers brushing the splintered doorframe. Here, in the suffocating darkness of this room, so many had perished - among them, his best friend of boyhood. David Pratt.

They had signed up together, lured by the same promises of adventure when the army recruiter came to their parish. But war had torn them apart, and fate had carved different paths for them.

A tear streaked through the grime on Hawke's cheek. He swallowed hard. Tonight, he would write to David's parents. They deserved to know that their son's death had been avenged.

The next day, Robert Clive officially proclaimed hostilities against Siraj ud-Daulah on behalf of the East India Company. Admiral Watson followed suit shortly thereafter, declaring war in the name of the British Crown. This marked a historic moment, as it was the first instance of a European entity formally declaring war against an Indian ruler.

THE GATHERING STORM

Within the inner sanctum of Hirajheel Palace, the Nawab's personal chambers lay behind grand teak doors, intricately carved with royal hunts and gilded motifs. Inside, silk tapestries embroidered with gold adorned the walls, while niches held jade vases and ivory figurines. Against the far wall stood a grand canopy bed. Beside it, the Nawab's ceremonial sword, its jewelled hilt glinting faintly, rested as if ever ready to defend his realm.

Siraj ud-Daulah paced the cavernous chamber, his steps restless and uneven. Now and then, he halted abruptly, raking a hand through his dishevelled hair, only to resume his frantic march. Outside, the night stretched on, pierced only by the shrill calls of insects and the distant howl of a jackal. But sleep eluded him, driven away by the storm of disbelief, rage, and fear that clouded his thoughts.

Reports had reached him of the British recapturing Calcutta and the destruction wrought at Hughli port, Bengal's vital gateway for trade and commerce. The audacity of these merchants astounded him. They were foreigners he had allowed to conduct business in Bengal, men whose manners and customs he had nothing but disdain for. Yet here they were, defying his authority and defeating his keepers. How had this humiliation come to pass?

But more than disbelief, it was paranoia that gnawed at Siraj. This was not merely a blow to his dominion but to the aura of fear upon which his rule rested. He knew his court teemed with traitorous noblemen who would seize any opportunity to see him fall. His spies were hard at work uncovering them. He had sworn that when the day came, he would make an example of the traitor, one so harrowing that it would chill the blood of every conspirator in Bengal.

His eyes drifted toward a sandalwood chest near the window, its carvings dulled by time. Once, it had held treasures of a different kind - stolen sweets, a wooden sword, a tiny figurine of an elephant his mother had gifted him. Now, it housed only scrolls, treaties inked in deception, and the heavy seals of state, each one a silent decree of duty. A tired smile flickered across his lips. How different life had been before power bound him in chains.

In those days, he had raced through the palace corridors with the reckless joy of a boy who knew no care, weaving between pillars, his laughter echoing across marbled halls. And always, always, there had been his grandfather - his watchful eyes crinkling at the edges, his voice firm but warm. How long had it been since Siraj had last heard that voice? Since he had last felt the reassuring press of Alivardi Khan's hand on his shoulder?

The memory came unbidden, sharp and golden. He had been no older than ten, lurking behind a lattice screen in the courtyard, stifling laughter as he clutched a clay pot brimming with coloured dye. His heart had pounded in gleeful anticipation as his grandfather strolled into view, deep in conversation with a minister. With a triumphant cry, he had flung the contents of the pot, drenching Alivardi in brilliant crimson. The minister had gasped in horror, attendants had frozen in shock. But Alivardi? The old man had merely wiped the dye from his beard, eyes twinkling with mirth.

"A fine ambush, my boy," he had chuckled, ruffling Siraj's hair. "But remember this - if you must strike, make sure it is at your enemies, not those who stand beside you."

The memory now felt like a cruel joke. Where was that laughter now? Where was the man who had always stood between him and the abyss? Gone, like the echoes of his childhood, leaving Siraj alone in a world that had grown cold and insidious.

He exhaled sharply and clenched his fists. Not all was lost. There was Mir Jafar - Alivardi's trusted commander, a man of experience and loyalty. Surely this was one man he could trust with his life. That thought brought him a measure of solace. The weight of the throne was his alone to bear, but at least, for now, he was not without allies.

The hours crept by, and Siraj finally sank onto the edge of his bed. His hand brushed against the hilt of the ceremonial sword, a stark reminder of the power he wielded - and the fragility of the throne it protected. For a fleeting moment, he wished he could cast it all away, trade his crown for a child's careless laughter. But time was a cruel master, and pining for the past could not shield him from the dangers that lay ahead.

As the first light of dawn filtered through the veiled arches, exhaustion finally overtook Siraj. His body slumped against the silken pillows, his mind too weary to resist sleep. Yet even in dreams, there would be no escape.

Somewhere, in the restless haze between wakefulness and sleep, he felt it - a sense of something slipping beyond his grasp. He reached for it, but it flowed past his fingers like water.

• • •

Jagat Seth Mehtab Rai paced the length of his study, his steps muffled by the soft Persian rug beneath him. The air was thick with the scent of aged parchment and sandalwood, the rows of ledgers stacked neatly on the teakwood desk. His silk robe, embroidered with fine gold thread, shifted with each deliberate step, the folds barely concealing the fullness of a man accustomed to comfort.

Mehtab's mind churned as he replayed the events of the morning - another demand from Siraj-ud-Daulah, blunt and heavy-handed, with no pretence of courtesies. The young Nawab, reckless and unpredictable, seemed intent on treating the Seth family's wealth as his personal treasury.

He had summoned Swaroop Chand, his cousin and deputy in the family's financial empire, to the study. "This cannot continue," Mehtab

Rai said, his voice tight with frustration as he stopped mid-stride. "Siraj grows more erratic by the day. He sent word this morning, demanding yet another atrocious sum - a so-called 'gesture of loyalty.'" He spat the last words with disdain. "Does he think we are financiers or his privy purse?"

Seated at a small teak table, Swaroop folded his arms, struggling to maintain his composure. "And if we give in today, what of tomorrow? What sum will be 'necessary' then? He will not stop until we are ruined, Mehtab bhai."

Swaroop exhaled, measured, deliberate. "Rulers have fallen for less."

Mehtab met his cousin's gaze. There was no dithering in it - only the quiet understanding of men who had held Bengal's wealth long enough to know that gold alone could not keep them safe. "Then we are agreed. He must fall."

With a brief pause, he continued. "But we must decide - who shall replace him?"

Swaroop leaned forward. "A ruler we can control. One who is ambitious enough to seek the throne, yet weak enough to need us."

"Mir Jafar," Mehtab said without hesitation. "He was once Alivardi Khan's trusted commander, yet Siraj treats him as a relic - passed over, humiliated. His resentment festers."

Swaroop considered this. "But he is a soldier, not a statesman. Once he takes the throne, will he not seek real power?"

Mehtab smiled slightly. "That is why he is ideal. He hankers for the crown, not the burden of rule. He will be a puppet who will be pulled around with strings by an unseen hand. And that hand will be ours."

Swaroop reciprocated his chief's smile. "Then he is the right choice."

Mehtab exhaled, his gaze steady. "And neither will this be the first time Bengal's fate has rested in our hands. We secured Alivardi Khan's throne when the moment demanded it, and we will do the same now. Power shifts, but it always finds its way back to those who control the purse strings."

Swaroop frowned. "But Siraj, for all his faults, still commands the loyalty of a significant faction of his army. Can we lure the nobles of his court into an alliance to overthrow him, with Mir Jafar as its face? Rai Durlabh, Yar Lutuf Khan, Javed Hussain - they all have grievances. Siraj humiliates them at court, appoints flatterers over them, and treats them with open contempt."

Mehtab waved a hand. "That is obvious. Rai Durlabh, once trusted, is reduced to a ceremonial role. Yar Lutuf Khan, a military commander, finds himself sidelined from key decisions. Javed Hussain, despite his years of service, is ignored. They despise him. But do they have the will to act?"

Swaroop hesitated. "I do not think so. They watch, wait, unwilling to be the first to move. Fear binds them as tightly as their hatred."

"Because they are divided," Mehtab stated. "Each sees the other as a rival. If one makes a move, the others will hesitate, fearing that power will simply shift from one hand to another."

"Besides, a failed coup means certain death," Swaroop murmured. "They know it, and none is remotely willing to risk that"

Mehtab nodded. "But that does not mean they are useless. We will not ask them to strike - only to lean in our favour. Their loyalty is fickle. If we ensure they simply abandon Siraj at the right moment, his forces will crumble before the fight even begins."

Swaroop considered this. "Then they must be brought into the fold."

"They will be," Mehtab assured him. "But who will provide the military might to topple the Nawab of Bengal? I see only one alternative - the British."

Swaroop exhaled sharply. "True. Their military strength is proven. They retook Calcutta with a fraction of Siraj's numbers, and their resentment toward Siraj is no secret. Their cannons and disciplined soldiers are the implements that we must leverage. All that is needed to bring down Siraj's unwieldy forces is a swift and decisive blow. And if by any chance they fail, it is they who will bear the consequences. We shall remain concealed in the background, our hands clean while the storm unfolds."

Mehtab inclined his head. "You are correct. They have the force, the resolve, and the incentive."

Swaroop's expression darkened. "But Mehtab bhai, the British do not fight and leave - they stay. They are not like the Marathas, who raid and retreat. Look at the Carnatic. They came as traders, yet through war and intrigue, they became kingmakers. They played one Nawab against another, backing their chosen rulers until their influence became permanent. With us also, they may decide they need no Nawab at all.""

Mehtab narrowed his eyes but allowed himself a small, knowing smile. "And yet, the men of the Carnatic were short-sighted. They let the British dictate terms, squabble over power like jackals, and in doing so, lost everything. But Bengal is not the Carnatic, and I am not some courtier scrambling for favour. This time, it will be us holding the reins."

His fingers tapped against the table. "They must see Mir Jafar as their only option - not as a tool for conquest, but as a guarantor of their trade and stability. We will make them believe Bengal is more valuable as a ledger of gains than a kingdom to govern."

Swaroop chewed his fingernails. "Then we bait them with what they understand - profit. As long as wealth flows, they will have no reason to reach for a crown."

Mehtab nodded. "Exactly. Through our figurehead on the throne, we promise them trade privileges - exclusive rights to Bengal's finest textiles, reduced tariffs on their goods, duty-free transit along the Hooghly - but always on our terms."

Swaroop studied him for a long moment before nodding. "Right. That should ensure they fight for us, but never against us."

Mehtab leaned over the table, tracing a finger across its surface. "Glad you agree. Now, we move in three phases. First, the nobles - weakening

Siraj's foundation by ensuring they stand aside when the moment comes. Second, Mir Jafar - securing his loyalty with the throne he is hungry for. Only then do we engage the British - through him - ensuring they see no path forward except with Mir Jafar as their chosen Nawab."

Swaroop exclaimed. "A masterful plan, Mehtab bhai. So the nobles weaken Siraj, Mir Jafar replaces him, and the British ensure it happens."

Mehtab's eyes gleamed with satisfaction. "I will handle the nobles myself," he said firmly. "A message from the Jagat Seth carries weight. These men must know their grievances will not go unheard. I will make them understand that Mir Jafar's rise will secure their positions, not threaten them."

He paused, turning toward his desk. "Swaroop, you will bring Mir Jafar into the fold. He must see us as his path to power - and know that his survival depends on our counsel."

Swaroop's voice dropped slightly. "But the risk is great, Mehtab bhai. If Siraj suspects even a whisper of this, we are finished."

Mehtab's expression darkened. "That is why secrecy is paramount. We approach no one directly - only through trusted intermediaries. Nothing is put on writing. And any man who wavers is cut loose before he can become a liability."

Swaroop inclined his head. "Understood. No promises, no oaths - only necessity binds those involved. Fear of exposure must be greater than any temptation to betray us."

Mehtab leaned back slightly, his gaze steady. "Until the moment it succeeds, this plan is like mist in the morning air - there, yet unseen. But once it thickens, it will never fade. It will choke out those who stand against it, leaving only the shape we have chosen for Bengal."

• • •

Anyone who knew Javed Hussain closely would swear by his unwavering sense of honour. But tonight, that honour felt less like a virtue and more like an iron shackle - pressing down, crushing him beneath the weight of impossible choices.

The day had been long, its events leaving a shadow that stretched into the night. Earlier, within the high walls of Murshidabad's palace, he had been approached - no, entangled - in whispers of treason. Rai Durlabh, like him a senior courtier and military officer in the service of the Nawab of Bengal, had chosen the setting well. A chamber, buried in the heart of the palace - its doors sealed, its stone walls absorbing every murmur. There he had laid the words before Javed like poison-laced silk.

"A man of your wisdom, Javed Miyan, must see what is coming. Siraj's reign will consume us all. His temper, his whims, his paranoia… they will raze everything we have built. You are not blind to it. You are not deaf to his rages. Think of your son, your lands, your people. Will you stand idly by and watch them burn?"

Javed had held his silence, his knuckles white against the carved wood of his chair. To speak too quickly was to condemn oneself. Treason was a fire that, once lit, could consume even those who sought to wield it.

Rai Durlabh had leaned in, his voice as smooth as flowing water. "You would not be the first in Hindustan to stand against an unworthy sovereign. Think of Sultan Ghiyasuddin Balban - how he rose to power. Not by birthright, but by necessity. When the weak and decadent Nasiruddin Mahmud sat upon the throne, he ruled in name only. It was Balban, his vizier, who truly held the reins of power. And when the time came, did the empire not flourish under Balban's rule, free from the incompetence of its figurehead? This is not betrayal, Javed Miyan. This is the duty of men who see beyond the blindness of kings."

Javed had said nothing. He had merely nodded and excused himself.

Yet the words clung to him, wrapping around his ribs like tightening iron bands. As he rode back to his estate at dusk, the world outside seemed distant - the rhythmic clatter of hooves, the golden ripples of the Bhagirathi in the dying light, the scent of earth after a long summer's day. Everything moved as it always had, yet within him, something had shifted.

By the time he reached his chambers, his hands were unsteady, his mind thick with turmoil. He poured himself a goblet of wine. A rare indulgence, but tonight, the weight of the conflict in his mind demanded it. One drink turned to two. Two became three.

And now, as the moon cast silver slants of light across the chamber, he sat slumped on his divan, the near empty goblet dangling from his fingers. The oil lamp guttered, its flame shrinking and flaring with the wind that slithered through the open balcony.

His gaze wandered - then stilled.

The mirror stood tall against the far wall, its polished glass reflecting the wreckage of a man. His robe had come loose at the collar, his turban lay discarded, and his eyes, glassy with torment, betrayed the war raging within.

Then the reflection moved.

Javed straightened, blinking against the haze of alcohol. But the man in the mirror was not merely a reflection - it was another presence, one that no longer shared his ruin. Its robe, loose and crumpled only a moment ago, now rested impeccably across broad shoulders. The discarded turban had reappeared, neatly wound, its folds precise. Where Javed seemed worn, the apparition stood poised, its shoulders squared with quiet authority, its gaze piercing, calculating - a man who did not doubt, but decided.

"You look like a man about to fall," the reflection said.

Javed's breath caught in his throat. He should have been alarmed, terrified even. Instead, he found himself speaking, his voice hoarse. "Who are you?"

The reflection smiled - a knowing, cynical curve of the lips. "I am the voice you have silenced."

Javed swallowed hard, gripping the armrest of his divan. "Then stay silent."

"I cannot," the reflection replied. "Not when your own mind screams for me to speak."

Javed exhaled sharply, rubbing his temples. "And what is it that my mind screams for you to say?"

The reflection's gaze did not waver. "That you should follow Rai Durlabh's direction."

Javed's fingers curled against the wood. "I am loyal. I will not betray my Nawab."

The reflection laughed, a low, bitter sound. "Loyalty? To whom? To the boy-king who squanders his rule in tantrums and tyranny? To the ruler who alienates his strongest allies and destroys the very men who secured his throne? Look around you, Javed - he is not a king, he is a storm waiting to break."

Javed's fingers tightened around the goblet, his knuckles bloodless. "It is not my place to decide who sits on the throne."

"And yet the throne decides the fate of all you hold dear."

The words struck like a blade. Javed closed his eyes, but the reflection's voice coiled around him like a serpent.

"Think of Sarfaraz. Your son, the apple of your eye. Do you think Siraj's tyranny will spare him? Do you think his unchecked rage will not turn on you, on him? If the coup fails, yes - you may die. But if you do nothing, you will live just long enough to watch everything you love and cherish be destroyed before your very eyes."

Javed shuddered. A memory surfaced - Siraj's men dragging a courtier through the palace halls, his screams ringing off the marble walls. Accused of treason on a mere whim, his lands seized, his family wiped out, his name erased.

That could be me. That could be Sarfaraz. He opened his eyes, staring at the reflection. His own face - yet not his own, for it held no hesitation.

"And what of honour?" Javed whispered.

The reflection's eyes darkened. "Honour? Honour is not blind servitude to a tyrant. Honour is ensuring that Bengal does not drown under the rule of a mad child."

Javed's breath was ragged now. His mind swam. His body ached as if caught in the undertow of an unseen current, pulling him deeper into the unknown.

The reflection leaned closer - though the glass did not shift, the presence felt real, near enough to touch. "You are not betraying Bengal, Javed. You are saving it."

Something inside Javed broke. His shoulders sagged, the last vestiges of resistance unravelling like thread pulled too taut. He turned from the mirror and sank back onto his divan, the wine goblet slipping from his fingers and shattering on the marble floor.

The apparition smiled in triumph, then unravelled like mist, its edges fraying into nothingness before entirely dissolving into the void. Javed's tormented mind surrendered to the blissful oblivion of sleep.

. . .

The sprawling estate of the Jagat Seth family gleamed under the late afternoon sun. The acres of meticulously manicured gardens, marble courtyards, and glistening water fountains were a fitting testimony to the wealth and prestige of its owners. But today, its splendour was amplified into a living tapestry of tradition and festivity, as the Seths hosted a grand celebration to mark the birth of a son in their extended family.

Presiding over the occasion with measured grace was Rameshwar Rai, the father of the newborn and a senior functionary of the Jagat Seth financial empire. Dressed in a flowing silk jama - long, flowing coat - embroidered with gold threads, he moved through the gathering with the practiced ease of a man accustomed to hosting the high and mighty. Every bow of his head, every measured word, was steeped in an awareness of the weight his family's name carried in Bengal's affairs.

From the grand archways of the entrance to the lush lawns, the estate bustled with activity. A vibrant elephant procession wove through the gardens. The majestic beasts were adorned with silk and gold, their trunks painted in intricate patterns of crimson and cobalt. Atop them sat dignitaries and family members, swaying with regal poise. As the procession passed under festoons of marigolds strung high between mango and neem trees, loud cheers accompanied the procession, mingling with the distant strains of shehnai.

On a raised platform near the garden pavilion, a troupe of performers captivated onlookers with a dazzling display of fire dancing. Flames curled and twisted through the evening air as the dancers moved in perfect synchrony, their brass anklets jingling with every step. The crowd watched in awe as one performer exhaled a plume of fire, illuminating the pavilions with a brief, flickering glow.

Amidst the revelry, the guests were not slow in exchanging words of admiration. "A sight worthy of the grandest courts of Hindustan," a prosperous merchant remarked. "The Seths have truly outdone themselves."

His companion, a visiting noble from Awadh, nodded in appreciation. "In my travels, I have seen few celebrations that match the splendour of Bengal's elite."

The merchant smiled, accepting a goblet of saffron sherbet from a passing servant. "And few that can rival its feasts either. Come, let us see what wonders the Seths' kitchens have prepared."

Near the central courtyard, long tables were laid with a lavish feast. Platters of fragrant biryani, slow-cooked nihari, and delicately spiced shahi paneer were set beside an endless array of sweets - gulab jamuns, laddoos, malpua, and sandesh sculpted into ornate floral shapes. Earthenware bowls brimming with mishti doi sat alongside silver trays of dried fruits and nuts. Crisply liveried servants glided through the crowd, balancing trays of saffron-infused sherbets, rosewater drinks, and goblets of imported wine, their deft hands ensuring not a single cup remained empty. For now, the guests indulged, as if fine food and rich wine could momentarily shield them from the shadows creeping ever closer.

Among the gathered guests, a French emissary and a Dutch trader stood near a marble fountain, their conversation laced with quiet amusement as they observed the grandeur around them.

"The British move like a tide," the Frenchman mused, swirling the dark liquid in his goblet. "They fall back, only to return stronger. Reclaiming Calcutta was not the end - it was merely a statement."

The Dutchman exhaled slowly, his eyes drifting across the revellers. "It is the way of power. If Siraj falters, others will decide his fate for him. And those gathered here tonight? They already weigh their loyalties, calculating where fortune will favour them next."

As the festivities continued unabated, the sun dipped below the horizon. The famed nautch girls from Lucknow, their beauty as legendary as their skill, stepped into the open air theatre under a canopy of lanterns. Their anklets chimed in perfect harmony with the lilting strains of the sitar and tabla, as they moved around with hypnotic grace, their richly embroidered lehengas - traditional Indian skirts - swirling like liquid gold under the lamplight. Their dance was more than mere entertainment - it was a living art, a tribute to the centuries-old fusion of grace, rhythm, and storytelling.

As the evening deepened into night, the sky erupted into a brilliant display of fireworks. Streaks of crimson, emerald, and gold blazed across the heavens. The bursts of firecrackers reverberated across the estate. Delighted gasps rippled through the crowd, momentarily replacing the hum of conversation. For this night, at least, revelry reigned, suspending reality in the glow of spectacle and celebration.

• • •

As all eyes turned skyward, the deep chimes of a stately grandfather clock echoed through the grand hall, marking the stroke of midnight. At this innocuous cue, a select few guests discreetly withdrew, weaving through the festivities unnoticed. Their destination lay in a secluded wing of the sprawling mansion that stood at the heart of the estate. There they assembled at a mahogany-panelled library. Within its confines, thick wooden doors and heavy velvet drapes over towering windows ensured absolute privacy, shielding their gathering from prying eyes and ears.

The festival had been a convenient façade, carefully arranged to mask the conspirators' gathering. Under its cover, they sought a solution to the oppressive rule of Siraj ud-Daulah while evading the Nawab's formidable intelligence network.

Assembled in the room, other than the host Jagat Seth Mehtab Rai, were Mir Jafar, Rai Durlabh, and Javed Hussain - all trusted commanders in the Nawab's army.

The chamber was cloaked in a subdued glow, the scent of aged parchment and smouldering incense lingering in the air. A solitary candelabrum cast flickering light across the walls, causing the shadows of the men to waver and stretch in the dim haze. Mehtab Rai, the banker whose fortune rivalled the coffers of kingdoms, reclined in an ornate chair, his eyes glinting like coins in the half-light.

Across the room, Mir Jafar sat stiffly, his fingers drumming against the armrest of his chair. His face bore the unmistakable shadow of resentment, a man wronged and nursing his grievance. "Alinagar," he began, his voice sharp with bitterness, referring to Calcutta's new name after the Nawab seized it. "I stood beside Alivardi Khan when the Marathas stormed our lands. I led men into battle, held the line when our borders burned, yet when the time came for the reward of the city's governorship, Siraj saw fit to pass me over. I deserved it, but instead, he grants favour to men who have never raised a sword."

Mehtab Rai leaned forward slightly, his eyes darting between the others present in the room. His voice, smooth and deliberate, cut through the air of grievance like a blade cloaked in velvet. "It is indeed unjust," he said softly. "Your military brilliance should have been rewarded. But Siraj - young, impetuous - sees only threats in the competence of others."

Rai Durlabh, whose political cunning was legendary, nodded slowly. "Siraj's tyranny is surpassed only by his paranoia," he murmured. "He alienates his allies, terrifies his subjects, and sees betrayal in every shadow." He exhaled, his expression darkening. "He has begun to mistake brutality for power. That is the mark of a ruler doomed to fall."

Mehtab Rai's voice was calm, yet edged with finality. "Then it falls upon us to ensure his reign does not outlast his folly. Siraj must be removed, and his downfall must be swift, irreversible"

Javed Hussain, seated at the far end of the table, shifted uncomfortably. His expression betrayed a flicker of unease, though he masked it quickly. "Replacing Siraj will not be easy," he said, his tone cautious. "However erratic he is, he still commands loyalty from key factions of the army and the court. His spies are everywhere. If he uncovers this cabal, his wrath will be swift and unforgiving. If we are to do this, we must have a plan where his downfall must be certain."

Mehtab Rai's lips curved into a faint smile, a calculated attempt at reassurance. "Which is why we must act decisively," he said, his voice smooth and steady. "Hesitation is only a recipe for failure. And we are not without assistance in this. The British are as eager as we are to see him removed. They loathe him, not just for his arrogance but for the blows he has dealt on their ambitions. Their military might, their cannons and disciplined forces, can tip the scales in our favour."

The room fell silent for a moment. Mir Jafar, seated stiffly in his chair, cleared his throat. "And... what would they demand in return for their help?" he asked, his voice hesitant. His fingers fidgeted with the edge of his robe, his eyes darting nervously between the others. "The British do nothing without a price."

Mehtab Rai steepled his fingers, his gaze settling on Mir Jafar with a mix of amusement and disdain that he carefully concealed. "A price, yes," he said, his tone almost patronising. "Perhaps certain trade privileges, concessions to their Company. But would that not be a small cost for the stability we can achieve under a more… capable ruler?" His eyes flicked meaningfully toward Mir Jafar, the implication hanging heavy in the air.

Mir Jafar stiffened, a sudden heat rising in his chest. He had heard whispers before - subtle feelers, vague allusions, murmurs from well-placed voices suggesting that he might be the one to replace Siraj. But those had been nothing more than shadows on the wall, hints without confirmation. Now, as Mehtab Rai's words settled over the room, the ambiguity vanished. This was it. This was real. His pulse quickened, and his heartbeat hammered against his ribs, though he fought to keep his expression composed. The air in the chamber suddenly felt heavier, pressing against him with the looming gravity of destiny. He took a slow breath, steadying himself. "If they help us overthrow Siraj," he said, his voice no longer hesitant but measured, assured. "Then I will negotiate with them. I will ensure their demands are reasonable."

"Indeed," Mehtab Rai said smoothly, his voice a gentle current carrying the flow of conspiracy. "You are the natural leader for this endeavour. With the British forces behind you and the support of Bengal's leaders" - his gaze briefly swept over Rai Durlabh and Javed - "there is no doubt you will be seen as the rightful Nawab, a striking contrast to Siraj's reckless tyranny."

Rai Durlabh allowed a faint smirk to cross his lips, though he quickly masked it with a cough. But Javed stiffened, the discomfort in his posture making it clear he shared little of Mehtab's confidence. "And if Siraj's loyalists rally? Or if the British overstep?" he asked, his voice low. "We may replace one tyranny with another."

"The people and the soldiers are weary of Siraj's recklessness," Mehtab Rai quickly interjected before anyone else could muster a response. "They will follow stability, not chaos. Mir Jafar is the ideal figurehead - someone they can rally behind." His emphasis on "figurehead' was subtle but deliberate, his gaze lingering on Mir Jafar, who seemed oblivious to the condescension.

Mir Jafar leaned forward, his grip firm on the chair's armrest. He was no longer merely a disgruntled general weighed down by past slights, no longer a bygone relic but a man stepping into his rightful place in history. Excitement and euphoria stirred within him, yet his voice remained firm and measured. "Yes, stability. Under my rule, Bengal will not only regain its strength but flourish. The people deserve a ruler who can guide them with wisdom, not recklessness."

Mehtab Rai inclined his head slightly, his expression one of measured approval. "Spoken like a man who understands destiny when he sees it," he said smoothly. "Bengal's fate rests on those with the foresight to shoulder its burdens and the resolve to shape its future. Power does not wait for the hesitant - it rewards those bold enough to claim it." His voice carried no urgency, no pressure - only the quiet assurance of inevitability.

Across the room, Rai Durlabh and Javed exchanged sharp glances, a silent understanding passing between them. The pieces had already been arranged, the game played long before Mir Jafar ever sat at this table. His agreement was not the turning point - it was the inevitable conclusion of Mehtab Rai's carefully spun web. The banker had masterfully guided every word, every moment of doubt, nudging Mir Jafar toward his fate while letting him believe he was seizing it.

Rai Durlabh leaned forward slightly, his fingers interlacing. "Discretion must be absolute. Siraj's spies are everywhere. Our messages must travel through intermediaries who have our utmost trust. Meetings will be few, and only where no stray ear can catch a whisper. And most importantly, when the moment comes, our movements must be swift. The first blow must be the last."

His gaze hardened as he continued. "No one beyond this room

will have full knowledge of our intent. Each will know only what is necessary to fulfill their role - nothing more. The fewer who see the entire design, the fewer chances there are for betrayal or folly. A single loose tongue could undo everything."

Mehtab Rai inclined his head slightly, his smile thin but approving. "A wise precaution, Durlabh-ji," he murmured. Then, with chilling finality, he added, "And rest assured, should a tongue loosen, it will never move again."

Javed's fingers dug into the armrest, his knuckles white with tension. The weight of the conspiracy pressed against his chest. The night had begun with quiet machinations, but now, it had taken the shape of something cold and utterly irreversible. The room felt smaller; the air thick with the unspoken finality of their pact. He was no longer a bystander to court intrigues but a man standing at the precipice of treason, his own silence binding him as surely as any oath.

As the room fell silent, Mehtab Rai's smile deepened. "Let us not waste time," he said, rising to his feet. "Janab Mir Jafar, prepare for discussions with the British. Bengal's future depends on our unity and resolve. And her throne waits for you."

As the others filed out of the room, Mehtab Rai lingered, his gaze fixed on the solitary candelabrum. A faint smile curved his lips as he reached out and pinched the flame between his fingers, snuffing it out in an instant. Darkness swept across the chamber, silent and absolute. He exhaled slowly, savouring the stillness. Power did not belong to those who sat on thrones or wielded swords - it belonged to those who pulled the strings, unseen and unchallenged. Let others fight, bleed, and bask in fleeting triumphs; he would remain in the shadows, where true dominion was forged, where fate itself was rewritten by unseen hands and whispered words.

· · ·

THE GATHERING STORM

A steady drizzle tapped against the wooden shutters of the council chamber in Fort William. The air was thick with the mingled scents of tobacco and old parchment. Three men sat at the polished oak table, each bearing an expression of varying resolve and intrigue.

Robert Clive leaned back in his chair, a faint smirk playing on his lips. Admiral Charles Watson, his uniform impeccably crisp, sat upright. Across from him, William Watts, the Company's Resident at Murshidabad, shifted slightly in his seat.

"Gentlemen," Clive began, his voice steady and authoritative, "we stand on the precipice of an extraordinary opportunity. The court of Siraj ud-Daulah is ripe with discontent, and high-ranking officials themselves seek our assistance to topple the tyrant."

Watson nodded thoughtfully. "Indeed," he said. "The man is no friend to the Company, and his reckless behaviour has already cost us dearly. Supporting a regime change could provide immediate compensation for our losses and ensure a friendlier disposition towards our trade."

"Not to mention the French and the Dutch," Watts added. "Siraj has shown himself willing to court them to our detriment. If we act decisively, we could secure trade privileges that will cement our dominance in Bengal and outpace our rivals."

Clive leaned forward, his elbows resting on the table, fingers steepled. "I see your points, gentlemen, but you're thinking too modestly. The overthrow of Siraj is not merely a means to secure trade concessions. It is the first move in a grander game. Mir Jafar, the man they propose as the new Nawab, is pliable. He craves power but lacks the strength to hold it without our support. We could position him as our ally, ensuring his rule remains dependent on us. And in return, we dictate the revenues."

A sharp intake of breath from Watts betrayed his surprise at Clive's boldness. Watson raised an eyebrow but said nothing, allowing Clive to continue.

"Bengal is the richest province in India," Clive pressed on, his voice growing more fervent. "Its wealth is vast - enough to recover our losses, strengthen our trade, and ensure we never again find ourselves at the mercy of an Indian prince. With Mir Jafar beholden to us, we control the treasury, the mint, the flow of goods and silver. Imagine Murshidabad's fortunes funnelled into our ventures, the Jagat Seths answering to us, the customs and duties of Bengal filling our coffers. This is not merely about restoring our standing; it is about securing an advantage so great that neither Siraj nor any other ruler will ever threaten the Company again."

Watson's lips thinned into a line. "Your ambition is… remarkable, Clive. But such a move is not without risks. What if this is a trap? Siraj could be setting us up to decimate our forces. Our troops, though superior in firepower, are vastly outnumbered."

Clive's eyes gleamed with resolve. "True, Admiral. I do not underestimate the risk. But does fortune not favour the bold? If we orchestrate this well, Mir Jafar and his allies will ensure our success by standing down their contingents during the showdown that we have with the Nawab's forces. We may have fewer men, but our superior artillery and discipline will carry the day. And once Siraj is removed, the true work begins."

Watts exhaled, rubbing his chin thoughtfully. "I see the merit in your plan, Colonel Clive. If Mir Jafar delivers on his promises, our victory is all but assured. But once he has the throne, what guarantee do we have that he won't turn against us? A desperate man swears loyalty to whoever paves his path to power, but a seated ruler may see less reason to honour his debts. What if, once crowned, he seeks to shake off our influence rather than bow to it?"

"He won't," replied Clive, his tone edged with certainty. "The lure of the throne and the promise of personal enrichment will keep him in line, but more than that, he will have no choice. He lacks the strength to rule without us - his army is divided, his court filled with men who seek their own gain. Without our backing, he is nothing more than a figurehead waiting to be toppled. And should he entertain any notion of defying us, he will soon learn that the same hand that places a man on the throne can just as easily remove him. A Nawab who serves at our pleasure will think twice before testing the Company's patience."

The room fell silent for a moment as the two men contemplated the audacity of the vision. Finally, Watson broke the silence.

"It is a gamble," he said, his tone measured. "But perhaps a calculated one. Siraj has made his enmity towards us clear. This may be the best chance we have to secure our position… and our future."

Clive's smirk widened. "Precisely, Admiral."

Watson leaned forward, his tone decisive. "Watts, as the Company's man in Murshidabad, you are uniquely positioned to oversee the correspondence and rendezvous with Mir Jafar and his supporters. Your task is to detail the plan and ensure that all conspirators remain committed to our cause. This groundwork is crucial for the success of our endeavour."

Watts exhaled slowly, the weight of the assignment settling upon him. He knew this was more than just correspondence - it was the careful weaving of a web where the consequences of exposure were too horrendous to even contemplate. There could be no missteps, no loose ends. He met Watson's gaze with a measured nod. "Understood, Admiral. I will draft a plan detailing every point of contact, every assurance to be extracted, and every contingency accounted for. And I will see to it that all correspondence and meetings are handled with the utmost discretion. "

Clive nodded approvingly. "Bravo, Watts. Laying this groundwork is pivotal. Send word to Mir Jafar's envoys immediately. He must know that our support is real - and that this operation, once begun, has no turning back."

Watson rose from his chair, signalling the end of the meeting. He cast a final glance at Clive and Watts. "We stand on the edge of fortune or folly. Let us hope this venture secures our standing, not our ruin."

As the men stepped out into the damp night, the chamber settled into stillness, the low candlelight wavering over scattered papers and empty chairs. Outside, the Hooghly River flowed steadily past the fort, the distant call of boatmen and the creak of moored ships drifting through the thick night air.

...

The moon hung low over the spired domes of Murshidabad, casting its silvery glow over the palaces that dotted the landscape. In a secluded corner of the bustling city, Khwaja Aratoon, a young man of lean build, adjusted his cloak as he prepared to deliver yet another message to the conspirators plotting to overthrow the Nawab of Bengal. Hidden in the folds of his robe was a scrap of parchment containing the latest message from the East India Company.

Aratoon was an Armenian agent for the East India Company at Murshidabad, overseeing the procurement, storage, and shipment of goods at the Company's warehouse. After the fateful meeting with Clive and Watson, William Watts did not take long to choose the intermediary for the exchange of correspondence with the cabal. Aratoon's ability to blend seamlessly with the local population set him apart, aided by his native looks, fluency in Bengali, deep knowledge of the city, unobtrusive movements, proven discretion, and daring. More importantly, he had no personal loyalties in this power struggle - his allegiance lay solely with commerce and survival, making him all the more trustworthy.

Before he set out for today's rendezvous, Aratoon had asked himself again why he was taking on such a dangerous assignment. If he were caught, there would be no trial, no negotiation - only the sharp steel of an executioner's blade. Did the generous compensation that he was receiving from Watts justify such a risk? And the answer was always the same - opportunity. The Company had rewarded those who proved useful, and Aratoon understood that in this world, fortune favoured those willing to take chances. He had spent years navigating the dangerous undercurrents of Murshidabad's mercantile world, forging relationships with men of power, be they Mughal nobles, Marwari bankers, or European traders. To be indispensable to the British meant securing his future, not only as a merchant but as a man whose influence could extend beyond the warehouse walls. If they emerged victorious, those who had aided its ascent would not be forgotten, and Aratoon intended to be among them.

Aratoon's route was well-rehearsed. Through shadowed alleys and past the ghostly bazaars, he made his way toward the dilapidated mansion that served as the clandestine rendezvous point. His footsteps were light, his senses sharpened by the ever-present risk.

The rendezvous had grown more perilous of late, though. Siraj ud-Daulah had grown increasingly paranoid, his spies rooting out informants, his men doubling their patrols. Only a day earlier, whispers in the bazaar spoke of arrests - men taken in the dead of night, never to be seen again. But Aratoon had chosen his route with such care that he believed the chances of encountering a patrol were slim.

Yet tonight, while Aratoon was navigating a narrow alley, he suddenly stopped dead in his tracks. A pair of sentries were patrolling the area, their torches cutting swathes of light through the darkness. Aratoon cursed under his breath; this was new. As he darted into the shadows of a weathered archway, he heard the clink of armour and the murmur of conversation. The sentries were drawing closer. Aratoon knew he had seconds to act.

Javed Hussain strode back and forth inside the mansion, his grip tightening around the hilt of his sword. The walls felt closer than before, the air thick with the weight of uncertainty. The coded correspondence with Aratoon was the thread holding the conspiracy together - but threads could snap. Every delay, every whisper of suspicion could unravel their fragile conspiracy.

He exhaled sharply, his patience fraying. 'Where is that Armenian fool?' he muttered, his gaze darting to the shuttered window, half-expecting danger to slip through before Aratoon even arrived.

From the corner of his eye, Aratoon spotted a cart laden with burlap sacks. He slipped behind it and yanked the top sack loose, revealing a stash of dried turmeric. He smeared handfuls of the pungent spice onto his hands and face. In moments, his robes were streaked with a grimy yellow. Swiftly, he retrieved the encoded message and tucked it beneath the loose stone at the base of the cart, pressing it firmly into the crevice. Satisfied it was well hidden, he pulled the cart forward, adopting the stooped posture of a weary labourer as the sentries approached.

"Who goes there?" The sharp voice of one of the sentries broke through the night. "Your humble servant, huzoor," he murmured, keeping his eyes lowered. "A poor spice seller trying to take my goods back to the warehouse. The traders in the market said they had no need for them."

The sentries moved closer, their flaming torches illuminating Aratoon's turmeric-streaked robe. One of them narrowed his eyes. "Why are you skulking around at this hour?"

"I beg your pardon, huzoor," Aratoon stammered, bowing deeply. "I meant no offence. I thought it better to clear the streets with haste rather than block the way during the day. If I've displeased you, please - let me make amends."

The sentries eyed him critically. "Step away from the cart," one ordered.

Aratoon complied immediately, his hands shaking as he stepped back. The sentries patted him down roughly.

"Empty," one of them grunted.

The other moved to inspect the cart, kicking the burlap sacks and scowling at the pungent smell. "Turmeric," he muttered, wrinkling his nose. "Move along, spice man, but if we see you again tonight, you'll wish you hadn't."

Aratoon bowed deeply, his voice trembling. "Thank you, huzoor.

May the Nawab's blessings be upon you."

He pushed the cart away, maintaining a steady pace until he rounded a corner. Once certain the sentries were gone, he darted back, swiftly retrieved the letter, and tucked it back into the folds of his robe, his heart pounding in his throat. Then, without hesitation, he slipped into the shadows once more. Only then did he allow himself a shaky breath.

Inside the mansion, Javed Hussain finally heard the faint knock on the back door. He opened it to find a dishevelled and grimy but triumphant Aratoon.

"You're late," Javed hissed.

"I nearly had to die for your letter," Aratoon retorted, retrieving the encoded parchment from his robe. He handed it over, his fingers still stained yellow. "Tell your Nawabzada-in-waiting," - a mocking reference to Mir Jafar - "that Siraj ud-Daulah is tightening his patrols. The noose is closing around all of us."

Javed's expression darkened for a moment, but as he broke the seal and scanned the letter, his features hardened with grim resolve. The endgame was approaching. The British were ready for the final negotiations with the cabal.

Aratoon slipped away. In time, once the dust of war had settled, he would command a far greater fortune than he did now. No longer just a warehouse agent, he would oversee lucrative Company contracts in Bengal, securing shipments of silk and opium for London's markets. His calculations had been correct - the British handsomely rewarded those who aided their ascent.

• • •

The merchant bowed deeply as Javed Hussain dismounted the steps of his estate. His weathered face bore the marks of long journeys, but his eyes sparkled with anticipation as he presented the fine-bred horse tethered beside him, its sleek coat glistening under the afternoon sun.

Javed circled the horse, his discerning gaze appraising its stature, gait, and temperament. He ran a hand over its powerful neck, the muscles taut beneath its velvety skin. "A remarkable specimen," he murmured, though his voice carried the weight of a distracted mind.

As the merchant extolled the horse's virtues, Javed's thoughts drifted to a simpler time, a time when the world's complexities had not yet burdened him. It was a memory of Sarfaraz, his only child and the apple of his eye. Javed had raised him alone after his wife had passed away when Sarfaraz was just a boy. He had never remarried, choosing instead to dedicate himself to his duty and to his son, to mould him into a man of integrity and honour.

As a boy, Sarfaraz had clung to Javed's side with wide-eyed admiration, eager to absorb the lessons his father imparted. One such lesson played vividly in Javed's mind, as he continued his inspection of the horse.

The sun had been high in the sky that day, and the dust of the training grounds swirled with every hoofbeat. Sarfaraz, not yet into his teens, gripped the reins tightly, his small frame swaying awkwardly in the saddle. "Steady," Javed had called out, his voice firm but encouraging. "Feel the rhythm of the horse. You must move with it, not against it."

Sarfaraz, his face flush with exertion, nodded earnestly. He was a quick and determined learner. When he finally managed a smooth trot, Javed had beamed with pride. "Excellent, my boy! You're learning the first rule of riding - trust. The animal must feel your steadiness, just as you must place your faith in its stride – this mutual trust is the essence of true riding."

After the lesson, as they sat together beneath the shade of a mango tree, Sarfaraz had remained quiet, his fingers idly tracing patterns in the dust. His brows furrowed, his young mind turning over the lesson. "But, Abba... trust can break, can't it? If someone is cruel to the horse, it will stop trusting him." He hesitated before looking up. "So... what if someone breaks our trust? Do we still have to stay with them?"

Javed considered his son's words, watching the way his small fingers carved uncertain lines in the earth. "Trust is fragile," he said gently. "Once broken, it is not easily mended. But there are bonds stronger than trust—bonds that do not shatter so easily." He paused, letting the thought settle. "Loyalty, my son, is one such bond. It does not depend on kindness or ease. It is a commitment, a duty that endures even when tested."

He met Sarfaraz's gaze, his voice steady. "For us, loyalty is not just personal—it is sacred. It is the thread that holds our world together, binding us to our family, our land, and above all, to our ruler."

Sarfaraz had nodded, his young mind grappling with the weighty concept. Yet his lips pursed as if the answer did not sit fully with him. "So if the ruler is not kind", he asked at last. "Should we still be loyal?"

Javed had hesitated, then replied with conviction. "Even then, my boy. Loyalty is not about the ruler's kindness but about the principle of fealty. To break it is to invite chaos."

Yet even as he had said it, a shadow of doubt had flickered across his mind. He had hurriedly pushed it away then, too certain in his own ideals to entertain questions.

The memory faded, and Javed found himself standing beside the horse, his hand still resting on its mane. A tinge of unease curled in his chest. How certain he had once been, how absolute his convictions. The world had seemed simpler then, its lines stark and unyielding.

Now the lines had blurred. What had once been an unshakable creed had become a burden he could no longer shoulder. The Nawab's tyranny had forged loyalty into a weight that pressed down upon the foundations of his conviction, weakening them with each passing day. His secret meetings with fellow noblemen, the clandestine alliances with the British, all pointed to a path that once would have been unthinkable.

He told himself it was for Sarfaraz - for a future where he would not inherit a world of fear and cruelty. But in the stillness of his own thoughts, another question loomed: Had he chosen this path for his son, or had he simply grown weary of the man he once was?

Javed's gaze drifted back to the horse. "A fine creature indeed," he finally said, his voice steady despite the storm within. In its eyes, he saw no doubt, no hesitation - only trust. How simple its world was, governed by instinct and certainty, untouched by the burdens of conscience and betrayal. For a fleeting moment, he envied the beast - the freedom of a mind untroubled by choices that cut at the soul.

As the merchant led the horse away to await further deliberation, Javed lingered, his gaze fixed on the horizon. Somewhere, the boy who had once asked about trust and loyalty had grown into a young man who still saw the world in absolutes, believing that honour and duty could stand unshaken against the weight of reality unaware of the quiet compromises that had already begun to shape his father.

Javed closed his eyes briefly, as if to ward off the thought. One day, Sarfaraz would learn the truth. When that moment came, would he understand - or would he see his father as the very man he had once feared becoming?

• • •

A covered harem palanquin was being carried through the streets of Murshidabad by four bearers. Its occupant was a Muslim woman covered head to toe in a black burqa, with only a slit for the eyes. *Clearly a woman of high birth*, thought the bearers to themselves, given the destination of the palanquin. They were taken aback a bit when the woman had hurriedly boarded the palanquin, as they observed her unusual height and rather unwomanly gait. They hardly cared, though – the man who accompanied the palanquin on foot, clearly a high ranking servant in the woman's household, had promised to pay them a generous gratuity after they completed their trip. Besides they felt relieved that they would not suffer the hassle of being stopped and searched by the gendarmes who seemed to have become increasingly vigilant of late. For a harem palanquin was sacrosanct – any man who dared to peer inside it risked severe retribution, both legal and divine.

Presently the palanquin stopped in front of a palace. At that point, the servants of the estate took charge of the palanquin and carried it to a chamber in the personal quarters of the master of the estate. Shortly thereafter an elderly man with a sharp, angular face framed by a well-groomed beard entered the room, dressed in a silk jama and an elegant turban. He answered to the name of Mir Jafar Ali Khan.

"Salaam, Watts Sahib", pronounced Mir Jafar in a hearty tone. The burqa-clad William Watts emerged from the palanquin, lifted his veil and made a deferential bow to Mir Jafar.

The meeting underway in Mir Jafar's residence was the culmination of weeks of secret parleys and coded messages between the plotters and officials of the East India Company. Its objective was to finalise the deal to overthrow the current regime. William Watts had been authorised by the high command of the East India Company in Bengal to negotiate the terms of the deal on their behalf.

The air in Mir Jafar's dimly lit chamber hung heavy with tension and intrigue. The muted glow of a brass lantern bathed the room in a subdued amber hue. William Watts sat on a cushion, his powdered wig looking rather out of place amidst the Persian rugs and ornate carvings that adorned the room. Across from him, Mir Jafar leaned forward, with an expression that spoke of a mix of caution and expectation.

"We stand on the brink of history, Janab Mir Jafar," Watts began, his voice calm yet laden with import. "Siraj-ud-Daulah grows reckless by the day. His tyranny – ruinous to both our interests - leaves us with no choice but to act decisively. The East India Company has the might to bring him down, but such an endeavour is not without cost."

Mir Jafar nodded, his heavily kohled eyes fixed on Watts. "We cannot agree with you more on the need for for Siraj-ud-Daulah to be removed. But for your assistance," he said, "What will be the cost, Watts Sahib? What does the Company desire?"

Watts allowed himself a small, calculating smile. "Victory, Janab, does not come cheap. After we bring down Siraj, the Company will have to be compensated - appropriately. First, a sum of twenty-eight million rupees must be secured."

Mir Jafar flinched visibly. That was a staggering sum – equivalent to the annual revenue of Bengal, and far beyond what had agreed with his fellow conspirators. His fingers tightened slightly on the folds of his robe as he leaned forward. "Watts Sahib," he began hesitantly, "This is an enormous sum. The treasury is already strained... perhaps... we could find a more reasonable figure?"

Watts did not respond immediately, only studying him with an impassive gaze. "Surely, Janab Mir Jafar, you do not expect the Company to risk its men and arms for anything less than what is due?" he said smoothly.

Mir Jafar hesitated, then exhaled. "Of course," he murmured, lowering his gaze. "Bengal's wealth is vast; it can be arranged." In his mind, he calculated - this was the price for the throne - which had, in recent days, consumed even his dreams.

"In addition," Watts continued, "we require a monthly payment of one lakh and ten thousand rupees to maintain our troops. The zamindari rights near Calcutta, a mint within the city, and a reaffirmation of duty-free trade for the Company."

Mir Jafar opened his mouth as if to protest but caught himself. The zamindari rights and the mint had not been part of their earlier discussions. He shifted uncomfortably. "A mint in Calcutta? That is... quite an ask," he ventured weakly. "It may cause discontent among my nobles -".

"That is your concern, not ours," Watts interjected smoothly. "A ruler must know how to manage his court. The Company requires its due compensation."

Mir Jafar wet his lips, his mind racing. The deal was shifting, its burden pressing down on him with increasing might. But to object, to haggle, would be to risk the British walking away from it. He meekly nodded. "Yes, of course. The mint, zamindari rights... they shall be done.

"And then there is the matter of Calcutta," proceeded Watts, steepling his fingers. "Compensation will be required. One million pounds sterling for the losses incurred during Siraj's occupation of Calcutta, and an additional half a million to recompense its European inhabitants."

This was daylight extortion. Yet Mir Jafar dared not protest. He exhaled shakily, offering a slow, reluctant nod. He realised he was conceding too easily - but what choice did he have? His ambition of ruling Bengal depended on British muskets. Such terms would be a severe drain on Bengal's treasury, but by then, he would be Nawab - and Nawabs had ways of bending fate to their will.

A heavy silence settled over the room. Mir Jafar's gaze wavered, his voice measured but laced with caution. 'And what,' he said slowly, 'does the Company offer in return?

Watts's smile widened, cold and calculated. "Superiority in arms, Janab Mir Jafar. The Company's artillery is unmatched in range and accuracy, our disciplined infantry drilled in European warfare. Bengal's forces are numerically superior, but they are disorganised - our ranks will hold firm where yours will falter." He let that sink in before continuing. "Furthermore, the Company will provide strategic coordination. Colonel Clive himself will lead the campaign, guaranteeing a swift and decisive victory. Your army need only remain passive at the opportune moment."

"Beyond the battlefield, the Company shall secure your throne. We will ensure the Marathas and the Afghans do not threaten Bengal under your rule. Trade will flourish under our protection, and the disorder that plagued Siraj's reign shall be a thing of the past. Your kingdom will stand strong, but only if we stand together."

Watts let the promise linger, allowing its weight to settle. Then, his tone shifted - measured, yet firm. "But we need to ensure, Janab Mir Jafar, that when the time comes, you are not the only one who stands aside. Rai Durlabh, Yar Lutuf - can you guarantee their compliance?"

Mir Jafar straightened, offering Watts a firm, reassuring nod. 'Rest easy, Watts Sahib. They are already committed. Their silence in battle will be assured."

Watts leaned back, satisfied. "Good. Between your and the other generals' neutrality, and the Company's strength, Siraj's army will collapse before the first shot is fired."

Mir Jafar said nothing at first. The weight of the pact settled over him, an uneasy blend of greed and fear twisting in his chest. He had fought beside Alivardi Khan, seen the ruin brought by the Marathas, and knew well how swiftly fortune turned against those who miscalculated. The British were powerful, but what if their appetite for control extended beyond mere trade? What if he was merely exchanging one master for another? And then there was Siraj - volatile, suspicious. If even a whisper of this plot reached his ears, retribution would be swift and merciless. His own family, his closest men, all would be dragged to their deaths. *This was the moment of no return.* His hand, resting on the armrest, grew still. He met Watts' gaze, his voice resigned. "Very well," he said. "The terms are agreed. Bengal will harness British might, and I as her Nawab shall provide Bengal the governance it deserves. Let Siraj face his fate."

Watts inclined his head, concealing the flicker of amusement that threatened to curl his lips. "Provide Bengal the governance it deserves," indeed. Did this old fool truly believe he would rule unchallenged? That the Company, after engineering a coup at such great cost, would simply hand him absolute power? Watts stifled the urge to chuckle. Mir Jafar was not a partner - he was a placeholder, a necessary tool in the grander design. The moment he outlived his usefulness, he would be discarded like a soiled chess piece. But for now, it was best to let him revel in the illusion of control.

A scribe was brought in who recorded the agreement in the presence of the two men. Mir Jafar affixed his signature on the it and took a formal oath on the Quran to fulfill his part of the treaty obligations. Watts was expected to carry the document back to Calcutta to be counter-signed by the authorised Company officials.

As the ink dried, Watts took a final glance at the aging general before him. A man who believed he had bought his future, unaware he had merely signed away his fate. He rose smoothly, bowing once more.

"May your reign be long and prosperous, Nawab Mir Jafar," Watts said, his voice measured, almost gracious. Then, without another word, he turned on his heel and strode into the night, carrying with him not just a treaty, but the keys to Bengal's destiny.

...

The banquet hall glittered with breathtaking opulence, lit by chandeliers adorned with countless lamps that bathed the room in a warm golden glow. Silken drapes of deep crimson cascaded from the vaulted ceiling. The polished marble floor, laced with veins of jade and lapis, glistened with a cool, shimmering glow. At the heart of the hall, a banquet table stretched lavishly, its surface adorned with jewelled goblets, delicate porcelain, and platters overflowing with the finest delicacies.

Nawab Alivardi Khan, regal in his flowing robes, presided over the banquet, his commanding presence undeniable. Around him sat his daughters, grandsons, and the begums of the palace. Conversation flowed freely, punctuated by bursts of laughter that blended with the soft clinking of silver cutlery against finely crafted dishes. Liveried servants moved gracefully through the room, carrying delicacies on exquisite. The air was thick with the heady aromas of saffron and rosewater.

Javed Hussain felt out of place amid this intimate gathering. Why had he been invited? The thought gnawed at him, yet no answer came. Outside, the night lay still and silent, broken only by the occasional cry of a night bird echoing through the darkness.

Javed gingerly reached for his goblet, but before he could take a sip, a sudden hush settled over the hall. The laughter faltered, and an uneasy stillness took hold. The flames of the chandeliers flickered erratically. Then, from beyond the palace walls, a chorus of jackals erupted, their wails rising in an unearthly crescendo. A cold prickle ran down Javed's spine. Something was wrong.

Then it came - a gale so sudden and violent it seemed to erupt from the very bowels of the earth, an unholy roar that shook the palace to its foundations. The stained glass windows exploded inward with a deafening crash, the shards scattering like malevolent stars. The gale tore through the hall, carrying with it an icy chill that cut through the flesh, colder than the most harrowing winter.

Javed sat frozen, his breath stolen by the unnatural tempest. The wind howled through the hall, but within its deafening roar slithered something else - a whispering presence, threading through the air like unseen fingers. Shadows flickered, twisting and writhing, their movements too fluid, too sentient. Then, impossibly, they coalesced - ever-shifting, yet unmistakably alive. Grotesque figures formed from the storm, their elongated limbs stretching, reaching, grasping, as if desperate to tear free from the wind itself.

The first touch was almost delicate - a phantom caress trailing along the diners' arms, their throats - before it turned to something far worse. The wraith-like figures moved with dreadful purpose. Their spectral fingers sank into the flesh of Javed's fellow diners, raking sloughs of it away with precise, cruel intent. The guests shrieked, recoiling, clawing at their own bodies as if they could rip away the unseen hands. They staggered back, slipping on spilled wine, their embroidered shawls and jewel-studded sashes clutched in desperation.

But the wind was merciless. It kept tearing away the regal flesh in ragged strips, like a monsoon tearing leaves from a tree. The melodious laughter of the Begums curdled into a cacophony of bone-rattling wails.

The phantom hands, relentless in their task, stripped the diners to stark, glistening skeletons. Rich garments hung in tattered folds on their glistening skeletal forms, their once-vivid faces warping into grotesquely grinning skulls.

And yet, even in death, they did not collapse. Slowly, deliberately, their heads turned as one, their hollow eye sockets, devoid of mercy or warmth. They turned towards Javed, accusatory and unblinking.

The gale ceased as abruptly as it had begun, its phantom forms unravelling into nothingness, leaving only a lingering chill. Silence hung in the air - but it was fragile, fleeting. Javed, shivering through the grisly spectacle, barely had time to catch his breath before the ordeal began anew.

A deep tremor rumbled through the floor. The chandeliers swayed violently, their crystals rattling - then, with a final shudder, they shattered into cascades of fine, glimmering sand. The golden goblet in Javed's grip crumbled instantly, dissolving between his fingers. The very walls began to unravel, collapsing into torrents of cascading grains. The grand banquet hall was disintegrating without mercy, transforming into a suffocating desert.

Javed flailed as the ground beneath him crumbled into shifting sand. Its relentless pull dragged him deeper with every frantic movement. The more he fought, the more it gave way, swallowing him inch by inch like a living grave. His lungs strained for air, every breath choked with gritty particles that scoured his throat and scraped against his teeth. He thrashed in desperation, his fingers clawing at the collapsing ground, seeking purchase on something – anything - but there was nothing. Only the endless, suffocating abyss of sand, indifferent to his struggle.

Above him, the skeletons gathered at the edge of the rising dunes, their hollow eyes burning with an unnatural gleam. They pointed at him with jagged, bony fingers, their movements unnervingly deliberate, as if savouring his descent. A slow, mocking laughter rose from their ranks, weaving into a cruel, spectral harmony that pulsed through the desolate expanse. Carried by the wind that hissed through their exposed ribs, their chorus of malice and retribution echoed through what had been the banquet hall moments ago.

Javed's gasps turned to desperate choking as the sand reached his chin, his vision blurring. The laughter swelled into an unbearable crescendo, until –

Javed woke with a start, the echo of that laughter still ringing in his ears. His body was slick with sweat. The darkness of his chamber felt thick, suffocating. His breaths came in ragged, shallow gulps, as if the sand still filled his lungs. He clawed at the sheets, his fingers trembling, willing the sensation of sinking to go away. Sleep was now a distant, unattainable shore - Javed lay on his bed, haunted by the vividness of the nightmare, a nameless omen pressing against the edges of his mind.

THE UNMAKING OF BENGAL

The morning mist hung thick over Fort William as Robert Clive stood at its gates, his sharp gaze fixed on the ranks before him. His troops stood at rigid attention, their freshly pressed red coats vivid against the pale dawn. The date was June 13, 1757. Today, they would march toward Murshidabad, where a decisive reckoning awaited with the army of the Nawab of Bengal, Siraj ud-Daulah.

Clive's eyes swept over his men - hardened Europeans, seasoned Indian sepoys, and artillerymen poised to drag their cannons through Bengal's treacherous terrain. He was not a man given to empty bravado. When he spoke, his voice carried no flourish, only the quiet force of conviction.

"Soldiers - a year ago, we were driven from Calcutta in disgrace. We have reclaimed it, but that was only the beginning. Our work is not done, for the man who cast us out still sits on his throne, believing we are few and weak.

"Let him think so." Clive paused, allowing the mist to swirl around them, his gaze steady as the weight of his words settled over the assembled ranks.

"He does not know that numbers do not win battles. He does not know the steel in our ranks, the fire in our muskets. His army is bloated with men who would rather flee than fight, commanders who would rather plot than lead."

"We do not need to kill them all - only to break them. And once they break, this land and its wealth will be ours.

"Stand firm, keep your powder dry, and when the time comes, fire true. Do this, and you will not only march into Murshidabad - you will own it."

A beat of silence followed, the mist curling around the motionless ranks. Then, with a crisp command, the ranks stirred to life. Drummers struck their cadence, boots thudded against the damp earth, and the great column began to move.

From above, the British column unfurled like an endless, winding serpent, cutting through Bengal's sweeping floodplains. At its head, Clive and his officers rode in measured formation, their figures distinct against the morning sun. Behind them, the infantry stretched in disciplined ranks - red-coated Europeans flanked by the sepoys, their turbans and tunics blending into the ochre earth. The artillery wagons trundled at then end, the oxen straining under the weight of their burdens.

Alongside them, a small flotilla of wood and bamboo boats drifted level with the march, gliding down the Bhagirathi River. Laden with food, ammunition, and supplies, the vessels served as the army's lifeline, ensuring the troops remained fed and armed as they advanced deeper into enemy territory. From above, a bird would see the entire force - men on land and boats on water - flowing with relentless purpose, like a disciplined tide gliding toward their destination.

The march was gruelling but mesmerising, mulled Private Thomas Hawke. He brushed the sweat from his forehead, his boots squelching in the muddy embankment as he trudged alongside his comrades. The floodplains stretched endlessly, dotted with glistening ponds and veined by meandering streams. The thick air carried the scent of damp earth and the faint sweetness of flowering grasses. Scattered huts with thatched roofs dotted the landscape, their mud walls streaked from the last monsoon, with wisps of smoke curling from distant cookfires. Bullocks waded sluggishly through the waterlogged rice paddies. On seeing the advancing army, the farmers prodding them ran away to a safer distance from where they stood gawking at the marching soldiers. The children bore less fear - they ran alongside the embankment, waving and shouting in excitement.

Private John McBride's voice, thick with the brogue of his Scottish Highlands, cut through the rhythmic trudge of boots and the creak of wagon wheels. "Seen anything like this back home, Hawke?" He and Hawke had marched, fought, and bled together in the campaign to reclaim Calcutta - a bond tempered by war and hardship.

Hawke chuckled, his lips curling into a weary grin. "If you mean endless mud and sweat, then aye. But not the parakeets. Can't say I've seen flocks like that screeching across the sky."

McBride shaded his eyes, watching the brilliant green birds dart between clumps of bamboo. "Like emeralds, those. Reckon they'd fetch a fine price back in Edinburgh."

"First we survive this march, then Murshidabad," Hawke said, glancing towards the front of the column where the officers rode in relative comfort. "Then we'll worry about birds and baubles."

The sepoys, accustomed to the terrain, moved with practised steps, their footing sure even as the earth turned to mud. The Europeans, in contrast, struggled through the marshes, their heavy boots sinking with each weary step, cursing the clinging muck that threatened to pull them down.

Hawke had noted, though, that the sepoys' ease in this land did not grant them ease among the ranks. They carried the heavier loads, cleared the paths, and were the first to be ordered forward when the need arose. Their British counterparts, though weary, marched with the privilege of lighter packs and safer positions.

"Do you think Siraj's lads will even wait for us?" McBride asked, his voice dropping to a wary murmur. "I hear there are tens of thousands of them. We are hardly three thousand… and less than a thousand, if you leave out the sepoys. They must be itching to make short work of us."

Hawke's grip tightened on his musket. "Aye, we are a measly lot against them - in numbers. But Clive has more than numbers on his side. We've trained for this. And don't forget those cannons."

McBride snorted. "Eight cannons against whatever monster guns

THE TRAITOR'S BARGAIN

the Nawab's packing? Brave words, Hawke."

Hawke's gaze drifted to a young sepoy a few paces ahead, his uniform damp with sweat, the weight of his musket and pack pulling his shoulders down like a yoke. The man stumbled, his ankle twisting in the mud, and for a fleeting second, it seemed he would collapse. Hawke swiftly reached out, steadying him with a firm grip. The sepoy straightened, casting Hawke a brief glance of unexpected gratitude before pressing on without a word. No officer spared him a glance; his suffering was expected, unseen. For a moment, Hawke felt a pang of shame. This man fought the same battle, marched the same endless miles, yet there was no glory waiting for him in Murshidabad - only another order, another burden. The redcoats would claim victory, but the sepoys would endure the toll.

A distance of 130 miles separated Calcutta and Murshidabad. The column was making good progress, at almost 15 miles a day. A few days into the march, Robert Clive sat atop his horse, surveying the column - British soldiers in their red coats and sepoys in their earth-toned tunics - plodding along the embankment. His forces were weary but disciplined, their ranks moving in steady rhythm, their bayonets catching glints of the fading sun. He had instilled in them the belief that discipline and firepower could outweigh numbers.

Major Francis Kilpatrick, his second in command, rode up beside him, adjusting his hat to shield his face from the glaring sky. "Our intelligence suggests Siraj's forces are near Plassey, camped along the Bhagirathi," he said. "Fifty thousand, as expected, but with conflicting allegiances. Their artillery, though, is formidable - French-supplied, heavier than ours, and plenty of it. If they set up defensively, we could find ourselves battered before we even close the distance"

Clive's fingers tightened around his reins. "Then we deny them that advantage. We must force them to move, to engage on our terms." He turned his gaze toward the horizon, where the distant fields stretched toward Plassey. "Their discipline is brittle. If we stand firm and keep our volleys steady, they will falter. And if they falter, their generals will hesitate."

Kilpatrick considered this, his brows furrowing. "So, we draw them out? Hold our ground, wait for the cracks to appear?"

Clive gave a curt nod. "Precisely. We use their own divisions against them. We do not charge recklessly - we wait, we punish any advance, and when they begin to break, we push. Hard."

Kilpatrick smirked. "Clever, sir. Turn their numbers into a weakness rather than a strength."

Clive's expression remained cold, calculating. "Precisely, Kilpatrick. War is won in the mind before it is won on the field."

The wind shifted, rippling across the flooded paddies. Somewhere in the distance, a lone jackal called - a thin, wailing note that faded into the dusk.

• • •

The afternoon sun cast long, golden beams across the Bengal countryside as Nawab Siraj ud-Daulah's small retinue made its way toward his grandfather's tomb. Inside the enclosed palanquin, the air was thick with the scent of jasmine from the cushions, yet it failed to quiet the unrest simmering within him. The rhythmic sway of the bearers' steps was steady, but his mind was anything but. His fingers absently traced the hilt of his dagger as his thoughts pulled him back to the war council that had gathered in the palace that morning.

"The British are marching toward Murshidabad," Siraj announced, his voice cutting through the murmurs in the council chamber. "We knew this day would come. Are we prepared?"

The room erupted in a flurry of voices. Some spoke of logistics, others of their forces' strength. Siraj's eyes swept across his assembled commanders and ministers - men who had fought under his grandfather, men he knew he should be trusting. Yet today, trust felt fragile.

Mir Jafar, standing at the head of the gathering, spoke first with conviction. "Nawab Sahib, their numbers are laughable - barely three thousand, marching under this cursed heat. We have twenty times their strength. The battle will be swift."

A murmur of agreement rippled through the chamber. Rai Durlabh nodded, his bejewelled fingers tapping against the armrest. "Their sepoys are mercenaries, their officers foreigners who know nothing of our land. Grant us your command, and we shall crush them before they reach Plassey."

But then, a lone voice cut through the growing enthusiasm.

"Nawab Sahib, I must caution you." Mir Madan, his most experienced general, stepped forward, his brow furrowed. "The British do not fight as we do. They rely on discipline, their guns, and battle formations. At Plassey, we will be on open ground. If we are not careful, their artillery will carve through our ranks before we even reach them."

A brief silence followed, broken almost immediately.

"Nonsense," Yar Lutuf Khan scoffed. "What are a few cannons against our cavalry? Our elephants will trample their lines before their gunners can even reload for a second shot."

"They can be beaten with ease" Mir Jafar added smoothly. "We have fought them before. We know their weaknesses. Do not let unnecessary fears cloud your resolve, Nawab Sahib."

The others nodded, voices rising in agreement. Siraj watched Mir Madan's expression tighten - he had wanted to argue, but against such unified certainty, he held his tongue.

Siraj had said nothing then, only nodded before dismissing the council. But now, as his palanquin rocked gently along the road, the memory of that moment clawed at his mind.

His commanders had seemed so sure. Too sure.

He pressed a hand to his temple as a dull ache throbbed beneath his skin. The voices of the council still echoed in his ears - their cockiness, the lone voice of caution drowned beneath them. Mir Madan was not a man given to panic, yet his concerns had been brushed aside unceremoniously.

Was it justified confidence that had silenced him? Was it an unfounded arrogance? Or something more sinister, a carefully woven lie?

He exhaled slowly, watching the fading light filter through the latticework of the palanquin. He needed his grandfather's blessing.

As the retinue reached Khoshbag, Alivardi Khan's final resting place, Siraj stepped out of the palanquin. The guards bowed low as he entered the mausoleum. The air was cool, and the dim glow of oil lamps cast shifting shadows against the marble.

Siraj knelt before the tomb, the stone cold beneath his touch. The faint light barely revealed the intricate inscriptions etched into its surface. He traced the name with careful fingers, as if seeking reassurance from the very letters carved in stone.

Alivardi Khan.

The man who had ruled Bengal with wisdom, with might. The man whose gaze had once measured Siraj and found him wanting.

A lump rose in his throat. He had been so sure then - so certain that his rule would be different, that he would carve his own name into history. He had laughed at Alivardi's warnings, waved them away as the fears of an old man too wary of shadows. "You see ghosts where there are none, Dada," he had said. "I will not live in fear of imagined enemies."

But now, as shadows of treason lurked within his own court, certainty had never felt so distant.

He pressed his forehead against the tombstone. A distant gust stirred the leaves beyond the mausoleum, and for a moment, it felt as though the words of his grandfather whispered back to him.

"As the prosperity of the state depends on union and cooperation, and its ruin on quarrel and opposition…"

Hadn't he fostered quarrels? Hadn't he driven men away with his temper, with his paranoia?

"If you take the path of quarrel and hostility, it is very likely that this state will decline so far from its good name that for a long period, grief and regret will prevail."

Grief and regret.

The words struck like thunder, unravelling his mind in a flash of revelation. Capricious. Despotic. Incompetent. Paranoid. Vengeful. Unstable. Extravagant. Rash. Tyrannical. Short-sighted.

Each word clung to him like a weight, bowing his head further until his breath brushed against the cold surface. How blind he had been. How foolish. His pride, his rage, his desperate need to be seen as strong - had it all been for nothing? Had he doomed himself from the very moment he took the throne?

His hands clenched into fists, nails biting into his skin. Not yet. It was not too late.

In a moment of humility, a virtue he did not remember embracing before, Siraj bowed lower, his fingers tightening against the cold stone as if seeking solace in its unyielding presence.

"Forgive me, Dada."

His voice was hoarse, barely above a whisper. "I have failed you. I have failed Bengal. The throne you entrusted to me - I have ruled it in folly and recklessness. But I swear to you, if I am granted this one chance - just one victory - I will change. I will rule with justice, with wisdom, with patience. I will be remembered as you are, not as a king who fell to his own arrogance, but as one who learned before it was too late."

He shut his eyes, his chest rising and falling in uneven breaths. He did not know how long he knelt there, but in the silence, he prayed - not just to Alivardi, but to the Almighty Himself.

Grant me this victory. Let me stand upon the battlefield not as a doomed ruler, but as one worthy of the trust that was placed in me.

The air was still. Somewhere in the distance, the faint echoes of a conch shell sounded, heralding the evening prayer of the Hindus.

Siraj exhaled and rose to his feet. His heart felt steadier, but the weight of uncertainty remained. Had his prayers reached the heavens, or had fate already sealed his downfall? He knew he would ride to battle with the uneasy resolve of a man who could no longer tell if redemption was within his grasp.

• • •

The British troops had been marching for nine days now. The heat had drained them, the rains had lashed them, and the sodden roads of Bengal had turned into a treacherous mire, clinging to their boots with every step. Yet they pressed forward, driven by the will of their commander and the promise of what lay ahead - loot, victory, and dominion over Bengal.

Presently they reached the abandoned town of Katwa, where the Bhagirathi River bent sluggishly through the floodplains, Clive's forces came to a halt. Intelligence reports had confirmed that beyond the river, in the village of Plassey, lay the Nawab's sprawling encampment. Clive knew that once they crossed, battle would be inevitable. But what truly unsettled him was the distinct possibility that they were marching into a trap.

Throughout the long days of the march, Clive had dispatched several urgent missives to Mir Jafar, seeking firm assurances of his cooperation in the coming battle. The responses, when they arrived at all, were maddeningly vague and evasive. Every hour that passed without clarity gnawed at Clive. Was the conspiracy real, or had the Nawab uncovered it? Was Mir Jafar truly waiting for the right moment, or was he stalling while Siraj prepared to crush them?

As the men settled into a temporary camp at Katwa, the last remnants of daylight faded beyond the river. Clive summoned his senior officers to council. The tent was thick with unease, the air heavy with the unspoken question that loomed over them all. To cross the river or retreat?

Clive stood at the head of the table, arms crossed, listening as Major Kilpatrick spoke first.

"Sir, if we cross, we commit to battle," Kilpatrick began, his brow furrowed. "The Nawab's forces are across the river in full strength. We are outnumbered twenty to one. If Mir Jafar has deceived us -" he exhaled sharply, shaking his head. "We will be swallowed whole."

Major Eyre Coote cleared his throat. "Sir, we have marched deep into Bengal with nothing but promises. Mir Jafar's evasiveness could mean he has been compromised, or worse, that he has betrayed us outright. If we cross and find ourselves alone against fifty thousand men, we shall have no retreat but the river at our backs. We cannot fight a battle with an escape route cut off."

Clive absorbed their words, his expression unreadable. For the first time in the campaign, doubt flickered across his face. The logic was sound - every report confirmed the Nawab's massive force, bolstered by artillery, cavalry, and war elephants. Their own force - 800 European troops, 2,200 sepoys, and eight cannons - was a puny fraction of that.

The tent fell into uneasy silence. Then Captain Fischer spoke, his voice low but firm. "We came for battle. But we also came for Bengal. If we turn back now, we abandon the riches of this land, and we return to Madras empty-handed."

Clive exhaled, running a hand over his chin. Then, slowly, he began to pace. He did not yet speak, but his officers had learned to recognise the signs - he was deliberating, weighing the course of action with a cold and ruthless calculation.

Retreat was not an option, Clive weighed. It would be the ruin of British ambition in India. If they turned back now, it could take years, perhaps decades, before another opportunity arose - if one ever did. In that time, the French, ever watchful, would tighten their grip on the subcontinent, exploiting British hesitation to strengthen their position. Without control over Bengal, the Company's influence, so carefully built, would wither, reduced to a mere trading body at the mercy of local rulers. This was their chance - perhaps their only one - to claim Bengal and all its wealth. To turn back now was to surrender it entirely, and that was not an outcome Clive was willing to accept.

"There is one advantage we must seize," Clive said, his voice sharper now. He pointed to the map spread across the table. "The mango grove. It runs along the battlefield, a natural line of cover that we can hold."

He looked at Kilpatrick and Coote. "If we position our artillery at the grove's edge, we gain protection from cavalry charges while still having a clear line of fire. The Nawab's elephants and horsemen will struggle to manoeuvre through the trees, forcing them to advance in disarray. Our troops can fire in disciplined volleys from beneath the shade, while their artillery - set in the open - will be exposed."

He leaned forward. "Siraj's forces will come at us in waves, hoping to overwhelm us with sheer numbers. But if we hold the grove, we force them into a bottleneck. We make them fight on our terms."

Finally, Clive turned back to them. His gaze was steady, his tone measured. "If we turn back now, we lose everything. The Nawab will see it as weakness, Mir Jafar will abandon us, and we will never get another chance at Bengal." He let the weight of his words settle. "We will cross."

Kilpatrick frowned. "Sir, if we lose -"

"Then we retreat." Clive cut him off sharply. "If by nightfall we have not won, we will break off, cross the river under the cover of darkness and the mango groves, and make our escape." His gaze swept the room. "But we will fight."

Silence settled over the tent. The officers exchanged uneasy glances, but one by one, they gave the smallest of nods.

The decision was made.

By dawn, the British were wading through the Bhagirathi River, their artillery ferried across on crude rafts. By the time the last of the baggage had been ferried across, the light had begun to fail. Night had fallen by the time they reached Plassey.

The ordinary troops lay exposed, spreading out across the open ground beneath the mango grove. Clive and his senior officers, however, found refuge in a hunting lodge, a modest but sturdy structure that once belonged to the Nawab. Clive observed with some satisfaction that the building stood on a slight elevation, overlooking the battlefield – thereby giving him a vantage point over the landscape, though little could be seen in the darkness.

Inside, by the dim glow of a lantern, Clive shrugged off his coat and turned to Kilpatrick.

"Make sure the men double-check their powder chests," he ordered. "I want no misfires tomorrow."

As Kilpatrick nodded and stepped away, Clive stood by the window, staring into the unseen distance where the Nawab's camp lay beyond the trees. He could hear faint voices, snatches of laughter, the restless braying of war elephants, the occasional clatter of armour as men moved about their posts. Were they aware that the enemy had arrived? It did not matter – come dawn, they will be.

Outside, the camp lay silent, save for the occasional murmur of men shifting in the night. Some whispered quietly, others lay motionless, staring at the starlit canopy above. A few clutched pendants or talismans, lips moving in silent prayers - to God, to fate, to whatever force might see them through the coming battle. The scent of damp earth and oil-blackened steel filled the air. None could truly sleep.

• • •

While the enemies of the Nawab were setting up camp at Plassey, on the other side of the mango groves, the air within Mir Jafar's tent hung heavy with the acrid sweetness of opium smoke. Reclining on a pile of silk cushions, his fingers trembled as he cradled the slender pipe. Each pull sent a wave of hazy calm through his jittering nerves, but the reprieve was fleeting.

Outside, the faint sounds of the Nawab's camp filtered through the tent - soldiers' murmurs, the occasional neigh of restless horses, and the distant beat of war drums meant to rally courage. But Mir Jafar found no courage in their rhythm, only a maddening reminder of the day to come.

The lure of the throne was irresistible, and Clive's envoys had spoken with eloquence and assurance. Their unwavering confidence in securing for him his rightful place as the ruler of Bengal had been headily intoxicating, feeding a thirst he had suppressed for years. Nawab Mir Jafar. The title sounded like destiny itself.

And yet, the spectre of failure haunted him. What if the British faltered? What if Siraj ud-Daulah triumphed despite the conspiracy? He could almost hear the crack of the executioner's blade, see his lifeless body discarded before a jeering crowd. Siraj's wrath would be unrelenting, and Mir Jafar knew firsthand the tempestuous Nawab's taste for cruelty.

He set the pipe aside, trying to steady his thoughts. The stakes were too high to leave to chance, and tomorrow's battle would demand subtlety. He would keep his troops back, as planned, watching from the sidelines under the guise of awaiting the decisive moment. Rai Durlabh and Yar Lutuf Khan would bear the brunt of suspicion if the betrayal failed.

But survival demanded more - it demanded erasure. Before dawn, he would ensure that every letter, every message exchanged with the British was reduced to ash. As for the envoys who had carried them, either their loyalty would be secured by gold, or they would be silenced by the edge of a blade. If Siraj triumphed, there would be no proof of treachery, no paper trail leading to his door. He would stand before the Nawab, hands empty, feigning loyalty, insisting he had merely waited for the right moment to strike.

His thoughts drifted to Clive's last message, delivered by a trusted envoy. The Englishman had promised victory, his words as blunt and assured as a commander dictating terms to destiny itself. No cautious assurance, no mention of risk - only the certainty of a man who had decided the outcome.

Mir Jafar reread the letter, searching for hesitation. None. No room for doubt, no contingency for failure. It should have reassured him. Instead, it chilled him. A man so sure of victory makes no plans for defeat, and if Clive was wrong, Mir Jafar would bear the horrible consequences.

Did Clive truly grasp what he was walking into? Siraj's army outnumbered the British many times over - cavalry, war elephants, artillery strong enough to tear through their lines.

A cautious man hedged his bets. A wise man left himself an escape. Clive had done neither. He had written as though the battle was already won.

For the first time, Mir Jafar wondered if he had chosen too soon - if, in his hunger for power, he had placed his fate in the hands of a man who did not know when to be afraid.

A gust of wind stirred the tent flap, sending a chill through the humid night. Mir Jafar pulled his shawl tighter around his shoulders, his gaze falling on the brass lamp flickering weakly on the low table. He thought of the soldiers outside, loyal to him for now, but how many would remain so if Siraj's forces turned the tide?

He closed his eyes, sinking into the silk cushions, yet rest would not come. The cacophony of doubts and calculations rattled in his mind, however much he tried to shut them out. If Clive was right, Bengal would be his. If he was wrong, survival would depend on how well he played his next move. Sleep eluded him, and in the restless dark, he could not tell whether the pounding in his chest was the echo of victory or the prelude to ruin.

• • •

As dawn broke on 23 June, the weary troops rose to the sight of the Nawab's forces stretching across the field. Stomachs churned at the sheer scale before them - tens of thousands of soldiers stood in disciplined ranks, banners snapping in the breeze, weapons gleaming under the rising sun. War elephants, their scarlet-draped forms towering over the ranks, swayed in formation.

From the flat roof of the hunting lodge, Robert Clive scanned the horizon, unease settling in his chest. The sight was overwhelming - cavalrymen, swords flashing, trotted alongside massive cannons, while vibrant standards whipped against the wind. The cacophony of war drums and shouted orders created a surreal, almost theatrical scene.

"A pompous and fabulous sight," Clive muttered under his breath, his heart sinking a little at the scale of the challenge. He estimated the strength of his enemy. His calculations were close to the actual figures of thirty-five thousand infantry, fifteen thousand cavalry, and fifty-three French-trained artillery pieces. A gigantic war machine that stood ready to crush his modest force. Behind him, the Bhagirathi River curved like a noose, cutting off retreat.

Yet as his gaze shifted to his own lines, his nerves steadied. He knew that his guns, though fewer, were highly mobile and effective. His officers had positioned them with precision, in a staggered, flexible defensive position. The gunners were well drilled in swiftly adjusting to changing conditions on the field. His eyes flicked back to the enemy's guns, noting how they were scattered across the battlefield, their placements rigid and disconnected. The sheer weight of the massive cannons, hauled by slow-moving oxen, meant that once fired, they could not be easily adjusted to shifting threats. Furthermore, the evident lack of coordination among the artillerymen would make it difficult for them to concentrate fire effectively. He allowed himself a flicker of satisfaction - an edge, however small, was still an edge.

Clive held back his forces, keeping them in a defensive formation near the mango grove, refusing to engage rashly against the overwhelming numbers before him. Instead, his artillery, positioned under Major Kilpatrick, stood ready at the front, prepared to swiftly respond to the shifting tides of the battle. Kilpatrick rode down the line, his voice carrying above the distant din of war drums. "Focus fire on their cavalry and artillery crews! Keep them from regrouping - make them feel our presence!"

By mid-morning, the first cannonade erupted from the Nawab's camp. Smoke thickened the air as the ground trembled beneath the ceaseless barrage. Explosions sent dirt and limbs flying, tearing through Clive's ranks. The sepoys fell back under the onslaught, scrambling for cover as men collapsed around them. Clive, assessing the mounting losses, ordered a retreat to the muddy riverbank that bordered the mango grove. There, crouched beneath the shelter of earthen embankments, his men steadied themselves, rifles clutched tight, waiting for the storm to pass.

The battle raged on, Siraj's artillery hammering the grove, turning trees into splinters and tearing up the earth. The British, pinned down, endured the relentless pounding, their resolve tested with every blast. Clive's mind raced, searching for an opening, a chance to turn the tide.

Then, as noon approached, the skies began to shift. The oppressive heat gave way to a darkening horizon, and thunder rumbled ominously. Within moments, the heavens opened, unleashing a torrential monsoon downpour.

"Keep the powder dry!" Clive's voice rang out from the roof of the hunting lodge, echoed by the sergeants as tarpaulins were hastily thrown over the ammunition supplies. The sepoys worked quickly, their movements precise despite the deluge. Across the field, Siraj's forces were not as fortunate. Their cannons sputtered and fell silent, the exposed powder rendered useless by the relentless rain.

"Now," Clive murmured, his gaze sharpening as he saw the moment unfold. The battle was far from over, but the monsoon had gifted him an opening. If he acted swiftly, the advantage could be his.

THE UNMAKING OF BENGAL

...

The downpour stopped as suddenly as it had started, leaving the battlefield soaked in mud. Siraj-ud-Daulah, watching from the shaded confines of his command tent, peered toward the British position beyond the mango grove. Their guns had fallen silent. Surely the downpour had done its work - surely their powder was as ruined as his own gunners' had been.

He spun toward Mir Madan, the valiant commander of the Nawab's cavalry of five thousand battle hardy horsemen, urgency hardening his voice. "Mir Madan, now is the time. Send in the cavalry. Cut them down before they rise."

Drums rolled across the Nawab's lines as the order spread. The cavalry surged forward first, hooves churning the sodden ground, their riders' swords flashing in the afternoon sun. Mir Madan rode along the front, a shining example of gallantry for his men. Behind them, ranks of infantry pressed onward, banners rippling as officers bellowed commands. At their centre, war elephants, their tusks capped in iron, lumbered toward the enemy. The fearsome war machine looked set to smash through the British lines.

Then the British guns roared.

A thunderous volley erupted from the mango grove, the air splitting with fire and iron. Round shot tore into the advancing cavalry, shattering bones and hurling men from their saddles. The war elephants let out piercing screams - some collapsing mid-stride, others rearing and trampling soldiers in their panic.

The charge faltered as riders veered wildly to avoid the mangled bodies of their comrades. Infantrymen hesitated, watching cavalrymen tumble into the mud. The elephants, now uncontrollable, turned in terror, crashing into the very men they were meant to protect.

From his vantage point, Clive watched with grim satisfaction. His gunners, their powder kept dry under tarpaulins, had struck with lethal precision. Along the artillery line, Kilpatrick shouted, "Keep the fire steady! Break them before they reach our lines!"

The relentless barrage shattered what little cohesion remained. Officers barked frantic orders, but panic spread like wildfire. The cavalry broke, their riders yanking at reins in vain, surging backward into the advancing infantry. Soldiers scrambled to form ranks, but the stampede crushed bodies and formations alike. Some fled in desperation, while others, trapped in the cascading retreat, were trampled or cut down where they stood.

Yet amid the turmoil, Mir Madan spurred his horse forward, undeterred by the crumbling charge around him. His voice rang above the din, fierce and commanding. "Forward! With me!" Some of his cavalry, shaken but not broken, answered, wheeling their mounts to follow his lead. Hooves pounded through the mud, spraying filth as they drove ahead. The British guns thundered again, their iron payload tearing through the charge. A cannonball ploughed into the riders at his flank, sending men and horses sprawling, while another burst of grapeshot cut through the ranks behind him. Still, Mir Madan rode on.

In the distance, Siraj ud-Daulah watched in horror as the grand assault he had envisioned dissolved into disorder. His army was breaking apart like a sandbank before a flood. Elephants screamed as they turned, trampling men beneath them. The cavalry collapsed in on itself - riders thrown, banners trampled in the mud. The proud formation had become a tangled mass of bodies and confusion.

• • •

Subedar Javed Hussain stood at the edge of the battlefield, his heart pounding as the carnage unfolded before his eyes. His fingers curled around his sabre, but he did not unsheathe it. He could feel the weight of his men's stares - warriors who had ridden beside him through skirmishes and campaigns, men who had trusted his leadership without question.

Yet now, in the moment of reckoning, they stood motionless, held back by his command. The betrayal he had been drawn into felt like iron shackles around his limbs, but he knew there was no turning back now.

His entire force watched with horror and disbelief as the battle turned against their own side, as brothers-in-arms were gunned down in waves. The invincible war machine they had once believed in was collapsing before their eyes, yet they did nothing.

One of his lieutenants turned to him, voice thick with desperation. "Subedar saab, we must go in- our men are dying out there!"

Javed did not look at him. His jaw tightened. "Stand firm."

"They're relentless," muttered another, shifting uneasily beside him. "Saab, we cannot stand idle while -"

"Hold position!" Javed snapped, his voice a whipcrack that silenced them. His men looked to him for guidance, their faces a mixture of fear and confusion. To them, his order to hold back seemed like restraint, a tactical pause. But as the charge disintegrated before their eyes, unease crept in.

A soldier's grip faltered on his sword hilt. Another took a half-step forward before hesitating.

Javed said nothing. He could not.

Then the final blow fell.

A sudden gasp swept through his ranks. Near the battered frontlines, Mir Madan, ever the warrior, refused to waver. Even as the British cannon roared again, he raised his sword high, his voice ringing above the din. "For Bengal! Forward -" The words were cut short as the iron shot struck, shattering his breastplate, hurling him from his saddle.

Yet even in ruin, he fought against fate. With bloodied hands, he pushed himself up, eyes burning with the fire that had made him Siraj's most valiant commander. For a moment, it seemed as if he would rise again, as if defiance alone could keep him standing. But his strength failed, and he slumped forward, his fingers clawing into the sodden earth, as though trying to hold onto the battlefield itself.

His horsemen, who had followed him through fire and storm, faltered. Some turned back in despair. Others stood frozen, unable to comprehend that the man they had believed to be unbreakable - the one who had led them through fire and storm, defying death at every turn - now lay motionless in the mud.

Javed felt his gut twist as the weight of his actions settled over him. Mir Madan had charged headlong into death, bound by loyalty, honour, and the belief that Bengal could yet be saved. And yet here he stood, watching - while men who had fought and bled for that cause were being torn apart.

• • •

From his distant vantage, Siraj stared, transfixed by the sight of Mir Madan's broken form. The commander who had once been his shield against fear, the warrior he had trusted to stem the tide, was gone. A hollow dread gripped him, his breath hitching as panic gnawed at his resolve. His gaze snapped to the one force that had not yet engaged - the thousands under Mir Jafar.

Mir Jafar, his most senior commander - the man who had sworn loyalty before God and court – led fifteen thousand fresh troops, their banners still, their swords undrawn. They had not fired a shot, had not lifted a blade.

Siraj turned sharply, his voice breaking through the din of battle.

"Mir Jafar!" he bellowed, his throat raw. "Advance! Strike them down before it is too late!"

Mir Jafar did not move.

For a long moment, the aging general remained silent, his expression unreadable. Slowly, he turned his head toward the battlefield. The British guns still roared.

Then, without a word, Mir Jafar and his men began to move - not forward, but away.

Siraj watched in stunned disbelief as the banners that had once stood firm now fluttered in retreat, their bearers marching in the opposite direction. His stomach turned to ice.

Treachery. The realisation struck like a blade.

He opened his mouth, but no words came.

Siraj's frantic gaze swept the battlefield - desperate for salvation, for some corner of his army that still stood with him. And then he saw them.

Javed's men.

They stood motionless. Not advancing, not retreating. Just watching.

His heart pounded against his ribs. The betrayal was total.

And in that moment, Siraj understood - he was not losing this battle to Clive. He was losing it to those who had sworn loyalty but now turned their backs on him.

Yet he made a last-ditch attempt to stem the tide. He turned wildly to his remaining men. "We must hold! Rally the men!"

But his words fell into a void - there was hardly anyone left to rally. What had once been a proud army had become a wavering mass of terrified soldiers, some still gripping their weapons, others simply staring in helpless silence. The will to fight had already died in most.

Then, the final breaking point.

The British charged.

From the mango grove, Clive's forces surged forward, steel glinting, driving into the disorganised remnants of the Nawab's troops. The first ranks shattered, men dropping their muskets and fleeing before the enemy even reached them. But not all ran.

A handful of loyal officers still held their ground, sabres flashing, voices raw as they bellowed commands. A few sepoys hesitated, torn between duty and fear - but they were too few to stem the rout. The redcoats swarmed over them in a relentless wave, their bayonets striking with precision. One by one, the last defenders fell.

The rout was complete.

Siraj's eyes darted between the fleeing soldiers and the advancing redcoats. His fingers trembled at his side. This was his battle. His war. His honour. A sudden, reckless urge gripped him - he could die here, sword in hand, as a Nawab should.

But then a hand seized his arm. His bodyguard. "We must go, Huzoor! Now!"

His legs moved before his mind could protest. Cowardice, honour - what did it matter if he was dead?

They pulled him toward a waiting camel, its reins held by a trembling servant. Siraj hesitated for a fraction of a second - he, a Nawab, fleeing his own battlefield? But behind him, the British gunfire grew louder, the screams of his men more desperate.

With a final, shuddering breath, Siraj threw himself onto the camel's back.

The handler snapped the reins, and the beast lurched forward. Siraj clutched the saddle as it galloped away from the field, away from the ruin of his rule. Behind him, he could hear the final death throes of his army - shouts, gunfire, the last stand of those too slow or too proud to flee.

By the time he looked back, the battlefield was no longer his. It was swarming with redcoats and their sepoys. The last of his troops were scattering into the countryside, some tossing aside their weapons, others trampled in the wild retreat.

Plassey was lost.

Bengal was lost.

And he, Siraj-ud-Daulah, was running for his life.

• • •

Robert Clive, directing the battle from the hunting lodge roof, rode forward, triumphantly surveying the devastation. Over forty enemy cannons lay abandoned amid shattered muskets, trampled banners, and the broken bodies of men who had stood firm only hours ago. Hackeries and carriages, laden with supplies, lay scattered.

Clive's losses were minimal: twenty-two dead, fifty wounded.

An officer approached, saluting. "Sir, the enemy camp is in complete disarray. They're retreating beyond pursuit."

Clive nodded, unreadable. He had gambled - and won. Victory had come not just from steel and powder but from deception and betrayal. A small breath escaped him, not quite relief, not quite satisfaction. But there was no time for reflection - only consolidation.

"Good," he said. "But let no one rest. Secure the cannons, gather supplies, and claim every inch of this ground by nightfall. Siraj must reclaim nothing."

He allowed himself a moment's reflection. Bengal was now within the Company's grasp, its fate sealed in a muddy grove near the Bhagirathi. But victory was only the first step - the greater challenge lay ahead: to rule, exploit, and hold Bengal in an iron grip.

Clive remained mounted, his gaze sweeping the battlefield. The air reeked of spent powder and blood. The dead lay where they had fallen - some contorted in agony, others face down in the mud, muskets still clutched in stiff fingers. The wounded groaned and writhed, some calling for water, others too far gone to speak. His men worked swiftly, dragging captured cannons toward their lines and scavenging abandoned supplies. Beyond the smoke-cloaked horizon, the last remnants of Siraj's army had melted away. This ground - soaked in blood and victory - belonged to the British now.

As the sun dipped, Major Kilpatrick rode up, uniform streaked with mud. "The work is nearly done, sir. Our men have secured the guns, and the camp is being scoured."

Clive exhaled, voice quiet but firm. "Good. We have Bengal in our grasp. But holding it will take more than muskets. Battles are won on the field – but kingdoms are kept with coin and calculation. And that war is only beginning."

Without another word, he turned and rode back to camp, his mind already beyond the battle. By morning, the machinery of British control would be in motion.

• • •

The next morning, the battlefield bore the weight of the prior day's carnage. The air hung thick with the stench of blood, burnt powder, and the sickly-sweet rot of bodies left too long under the Bengal sun. A swarm of vultures picked at the flesh of the fallen. Soldiers moved between the dead, looting rings from fingers that had stiffened in death's grip. Nearby, British officers gathered under makeshift tents, tallying the spoils - silver-hilted swords, silk garments from abandoned tents, and coin purses taken from the slain. Greater riches awaited in Murshidabad, but for now, they took what the battlefield yielded.

Meanwhile at his tent, Clive read aloud a letter, addressed to Mir Jafar, that he had just drafted. "Victory is yours, not mine," he declared, his voice measured, almost generous. Kilpatrick observed the performance with a mix of admiration and cynicism. It was a masterstroke of disingenuousness, designed to flatter the fragile ego of the traitor they were about to enthrone - bestowing power upon a man who had bartered away his freedom to grasp it.

Later that morning, Mir Jafar arrived at the camp, his nerves visibly frayed, his posture sagging under the weight of his own betrayal. As the camp guard turned out in his honour, he startled like a spooked deer, his wide eyes darting between the soldiers, searching for reassurance. His gaze flickered to Clive's officers with the desperate wariness of a man who knew he was at their mercy. His steps faltered as he approached, sweat beading at his temple despite the morning's breeze. He had placed his bet, but standing before them now, he could not shake the creeping realisation that his life and freedom no longer belonged to him.

Kilpatrick watched from a distance, his expression dark with contempt. *This is the man we are to call Nawab?* A snivelling traitor who had bartered his honour for a throne he had neither the courage nor the strength to seize on his own, too timid to meet the eyes of his new masters. He had grovelled before Siraj, and now he grovelled before Clive - forever bending to the strongest hand. There was no steel in his spine, no defiance, only the pathetic hope that submission might spare him from the fate he deserved.

Yet now, necessity demanded a veneer of respect, and Clive played the part with aplomb. He greeted Mir Jafar with a calculated warmth, saluting him as the new Nawab of Bengal. Kilpatrick marvelled at his commander's ability to suppress his private disdain. Mir Jafar, for his part, offered a low bow. "I am in your debt, Clive Bahadur", he said. "Bengal stands with you." The tremor in his hands belied the forced steadiness in his tone.

Clive studied him for a moment, then spoke, his voice calm but deliberate. "The days ahead will require swift action, Nawab. It would be wise to hasten to Murshidabad and take your place without delay. The capital must see its ruler ascend with certainty, and the treasury must be secured before disorder stirs."

He let the words settle before adding, almost as an afterthought, "Major Kilpatrick will accompany you to ensure all proceeds smoothly." The message was clear - henceforth, the Company would shadow his reign, and every step he took would unfold beneath their unyielding gaze.

Kilpatrick observed the flicker of realisation in Mir Jafar's eyes - the throne had come at a price far beyond gold.

The march to Murshidabad began at first light. Mir Jafar was borne in an ornate palanquin, flanked by British officers on horseback, their red coats stark against the dust-choked road. Behind them, Company soldiers marched in disciplined ranks, bayonets glinting in the morning sun, while sepoy regiments followed in formation. Kilpatrick rode close, a silent reminder that Mir Jafar's claim to power rested not on birthright or loyalty, but on the Company's steel.

As they neared the capital, word of their arrival spread swiftly. Traders and townsfolk lined the streets, whispering, their eyes darting from the mounted officers to the distant dust cloud trailing the artillery train. They had seen rulers rise and fall, but never one who arrived flanked by foreign soldiers, his throne secured not by victory or lineage, but by the decree of merchants from distant lands.

The great gates of Murshidabad stood open, but the palace beyond was a hollow shell. Once a seat of restless energy - where courtiers debated, emissaries pleaded their cases, and dancers twirled to the strains of the shehnai - it now lay eerily silent. Siraj ud-Daulah had fled days prior. The women and remaining members of the Nawab's household had been taken into custody, their fate uncertain, their future no longer their own.

Mir Jafar's palanquin slowed as it entered the courtyard - the same ground where Siraj had stood mere days ago, reviewing his troops before marching to Plassey. Now, the air hung heavy with subdued resignation, broken only by the measured tramp of British boots. Where once the halls had echoed with urgent deliberations and the bustle of attendants, only hushed murmurs remained, as if the palace itself recoiled from acknowledging its new master.

The formalities of the ascension proceeded in careful, orchestrated order. As Mir Jafar lowered himself onto the masnad – the throne, a surge of exhilaration coursed through his veins. The gilded cushions beneath him were no longer the distant dream of an ambitious commander but a tangible reality he had dared to dream about. For a fleeting moment, he allowed himself to revel in it - he was the Nawab, the ruler of Bengal, seated where his illustrious predecessors had ruled before him.

Yet the moment soured as his gaze flickered across the hall. Beyond the silk-draped courtiers and murmuring nobles, the crimson coats of British soldiers stood like a scar upon the ceremony. Their presence, silent yet commanding, coiled around his triumph like an iron chain. His hands did not grip the throne's arms with a ruler's certainty; they rested there with the wary touch of a man who knew his seat was borrowed, not claimed. He had the throne, but as the British bayonets lined the hall, the sceptre in his hand felt weightless - Bengal's fate no longer his to command.

. . .

In the small hours of the morning after the battle, Siraj ud-Daulah slipped into the outskirts of Murshidabad, a fugitive in his own capital. His clothes were torn and soiled, his forehead streaked with dried blood. Beside him, two loyal retainers rode in grim silence, their eyes scanning the darkened streets.

Exhaustion clawed at him, but his mind refused to still, churning with the impossible truth - defeat, not at the hands of a mighty foe, but by an army laughably so small. But nothing unsettled him more than the betrayal. Mir Jafar - his most trusted commander - had turned against him, his false oaths of loyalty now a bitter taste on Siraj's tongue. His own men, men who had eaten at his table and marched under his banner, had handed him over to the British without a fight.

The camel that had carried him from the battlefield had been left behind on the city outskirts - too conspicuous, too slow. He had abandoned it in the shadows of an alley, slipping onto a waiting horse. Now, as he tightened his grip on the reins, a cold, creeping terror coiled around his gut. His heart pounded as he glanced over his shoulder, every shadow along the silent streets a lurking assassin or informer.

There was no safety here. Murshidabad had become a hunting ground. And he was the prize now, a hunted animal. He knew what happened to fallen rulers. When they found him, there would be no mercy, no escape – only a swift and brutal end.

As the party approached the palace gates, his thoughts grew darker.

The grand walls that once symbolised his power now felt like looming tombstones. As he dismounted, one of his retainers stepped closer, his voice barely above a whisper. 'Do not stay long, Huzoor,' the man urged. 'The city is not safe for you.' Siraj held his gaze for a long moment but said nothing.

Entering the palace, Siraj moved swiftly through the dimly lit corridors. The familiar scents of incense and the polished floors beneath his boots brought no solace. As he reached the private quarters, he hesitated for a moment. Lutf un-Nissa would be there. She always was. The thought of seeing her favourite consort both soothed and tore at him. How could he look into the eyes of the one person who he knew still believed in him, who revered him, despite everything?

He pushed open the heavy door and stepped inside. Lutf-un-Nissa rose from her place beside the cradle, where their infant daughter stirred with a soft gurgle. Draped in grace, she moved with quiet, deliberate poise. When her eyes met his, there was no reproach, no hesitation - only concern and an unshaken devotion that cut through the despair closing in around him.

"You're safe," she said softly, her voice steady despite the worry beneath it. "For now," he murmured. "But the palace is no longer a refuge. They hunt me like a dog." His once-unshakable confidence wavered, the words catching in his throat. For a moment, he looked away, as if afraid to let her see the man he had become.

Lutf stepped closer, placing a gentle hand on his arm. "Then we must leave," she said, her calmness a striking contrast to his turmoil.

Siraj looked at her, his hardened expression softening. She had always been his anchor, the one person who saw beyond the Nawab and into the man. "Pack what you can carry. We leave at nightfall."

Hours later, cloaked in the shadows of the palace's deserted corridors, they slipped through a hidden passage, the baby in Lutf's arms. Every step felt like an eternity. At last, beyond the palace walls, two loyal boatmen awaited them at the riverbank, their faces tense with urgency.

The boat rocked gently as Siraj stepped in first, then reached for Lutf. She clutched the baby close, her black burqa concealing her features. The child stirred but did not cry. Siraj settled beside her, adjusting the coarse angarkha he had hastily donned.

One boatman pushed off, the other taking the oar. The river stretched before them, ink-black and endless. To anyone watching, they were no more than a merchant's family.

The river's course would take them northward, then west, towards Bihar. Siraj knew the Ganges would carry them steadily away from the reach of his enemies, beyond the tightening noose of the British and Mir Jafar's men. The river's shifting banks, sandbars, and hidden inlets provided cover, while the vast floodplains and scattered villages were indifferent to the affairs of Murshidabad's palace. If he could reach Patna, he might yet find allies among those still loyal to the old order, men who had served his grandfather.

Lutf glanced at Siraj, his face pale and etched with worry. She knew he carried the weight of his defeat like a wound that would never heal. But to her, he was still the Nawab, the man she adored and idolised. She had witnessed his kindness toward her and his unwavering strength, even as the palace hummed with whispers of his debauchery and cruelty.

"Nawab," she said softly, breaking the silence. "We will survive this. You will rise again." He turned to her, his eyes shadowed with melancholy. "No Lutf, I've lost everything. The throne, the army… Bengal itself." "You haven't lost us," she said, her voice steady. "And as long as we are together, there is still hope."

Two days passed in a haze of exhaustion and gnawing hunger, bereft of a single morsel of food. When they finally reached a secluded riverbank, the group disembarked. It was midday, and their only thought was to prepare a simple meal of khichri - rice and lentils.

However, at that instant, a fakir appeared. The ascetic's face was withered with age, and he bore an aura of worldly renunciation. He greeted the family warmly, then turned to Siraj with a knowing smile.

Lifting a hand, he gestured just beyond the riverbank. "Miyan, you have travelled far and must be weary. My cottage is but a few steps away, nestled under that old neem tree. Come, rest before you resume your journey. I have food and water to share."

Siraj hesitated, his instincts warning him against trusting strangers. But the promise of rest and food was too tempting to ignore. Besides, he reckoned that the longer they remained hidden from prying eyes, the safer they would be.

The cottage was small, its thatched roof weathered by time, but offered a respite from their arduous flight. For a fleeting moment, Lutf un-Nissa felt an aching longing, for a life untouched by bloodshed and betrayal. She imagined herself and Siraj as simple peasants, tending to a quiet existence, where their daughter could grow up laughing in the sunlight instead of hiding from fate. Exhausted, Siraj drifted into a deep sleep the moment he lay down.

The tranquillity did not last long. A sudden, ominous sound - footsteps, loud and deliberate - shattered the stillness. Lutf-un-Nissa's heart clenched. She reached for Siraj, but he was already awake, eyes wide with apprehension. For the briefest second, he looked at her - the look of a man who knew he had reached the end. Then he bolted to the window. Figures moved outside, their silhouettes unmistakable in their flaming torches - soldiers, armed to the teeth.

"No…" Siraj breathed, gripping the edge of the wooden frame.

The fakir stepped forward. His lips curled into a smirk. "Janab Nawab, on second thoughts, you will find far better food in Murshidabad than in this poor man's hut." He had known that Mir Jafar's men had been scouring every corner of Murshidabad and beyond for the fugitive - and was now brimming with anticipation, eager to claim the rich rewards that awaited him.

Siraj's hand moved instinctively to his ring. The ornate jewel caught the glow of a torch, its insignia unmistakable. Realisation struck him - this was no mere ornament. It was a proclamation of his identity. In his haste, he had forgotten to remove the ring.

He did not move, did not speak. The lash of betrayal, so familiar, should not have hurt anymore - yet it did.

Lutf-un-Nissa held their daughter tightly as the soldiers broke in, her eyes darting to Siraj. For a moment, his shoulders hunched, his face ashen. His wide eyes flickered with the raw terror of a man who had spent days looking over his shoulder. The torches cast jagged shadows across the walls, the clang of the soldiers' heels pounding in his ears. His breath came quick, shallow - then slowed. Fear still clawed at him, sinking deep, but something else rose to meet it. His fists clenched. His spine straightened. Let them come. His jaw set, his eyes burned, and as he stepped forward, it was not a hunted man they faced, but a king who would meet his fate unbowed.

Lutf un-Nissa saw the change in him, and her grip on their daughter tightened - in silent resolve. He was still the Nawab, still the man she would follow to the ends of the earth, even as the world closed in around them.

Siraj, the fallen Nawab, let his gaze linger on his sleeping daughter, committing every delicate breath, every curl of her hair to memory. A hollow ache settled in his chest - not just for her, but for Lutf-un-Nissa, for the life that had been wrenched from him. His hand hovered near her, a gesture unfinished, a farewell unspoken. The guards seized his arms, yanking him toward the waiting carriage. He did not resist, but as the doors closed behind him his throat tightened. They had taken his throne, his city - but this, this was the deepest wound of all.

. . .

The room was bare. A single lamp burned weakly in the corner, its light barely penetrating the darkness. Siraj sat cross-legged on the cold floor, his wrists bound, his robe torn and dust-streaked. The silence around him pressed in, broken only by the faint murmur of voices beyond the closed doors.

Then, the latch shifted. The doors groaned open.

Miran entered, his presence like a blade slicing through the still air. He was dressed in dark silks, a jewelled dagger at his waist, his expression one of smug triumph. Behind him, a hulking man stepped forward - his thick arms bare, his face impassive, a curved sabre glinting in his grip.

Siraj knew.

He did not flinch, nor did he plead. His gaze met Miran's – hard, filled with disdain,. A smirk tugged at his lips, contempt laced in his voice.

"A traitor's son comes in his father's stead. Where is Mir Jafar? Does he not have the courage to look me in the eyes?"

Miran chuckled, his fingers brushing the pommel of his dagger. "My father is the Nawab now, Siraj. He has no time for ghosts." He leaned in slightly, lowering his voice. "He sends those he trusts to do what must be done. That is why I am here."

Siraj exhaled sharply, a bitter smile twisting his lips. "Trust? Isn't that a bit rich from a man whose father understands trust as betraying his master and crawling into bed with foreign merchants? No, Miran. He sends you because even the most wretched dog needs someone to carry out its dirty work."

He rose slightly, his voice dripping with mockery. "Your father's throne is built on the blood of this land, propped up by foreign merchants who will abandon him the moment he no longer serves their purpose. The people will never acknowledge a man whose crown is stained with cowardice and betrayal. And history - history will despise him, and you, as abominable traitors."

Miran's smirk faltered, just for a moment. Then he snapped his fingers. The butcher stepped forward, lifting the sabre.

Siraj closed his eyes for a moment. Then he spoke. "A moment of prayer."

Miran hesitated, then nodded. "Pray, then. It will change nothing."

Siraj bent forward, his forehead touching the ground. His lips moved in silent supplication, whispering to the Almighty.

"Forgive me, Allah, for those I failed to protect - my loyal soldiers at Plassey, who bled while treachery hollowed our ranks. Forgive me for trusting jackals disguised as men. Forgive me for the pride that clouded my judgment, for the cruelty I allowed in moments of fear, for the harshness that drove good men away. Watch over Lutf-un-Nissa, and my daughter… if they still breathe. And if justice exists beyond this world, let it find those who mock it in this one."

Then, he rose. He met the butcher's gaze.

"I am ready."

The room fell into a tense stillness. Even the executioner hesitated, waiting for a signal. Miran's face remained expressionless, his eyes hard. Then he nodded, cold and unflinching.

The first strike landed across his shoulder, cleaving deep. Siraj staggered, the pain searing through him, but he willed himself to remain standing. The second blow crashed against his chest, forcing a harsh gasp from his lips. His legs trembled, but he refused to fall, his gaze steady, defiant. The third strike tore through his ribs, and this time his knees buckled, sending him crashing to the cold stone floor. Blood pooled around him, seeping into the cracks. Darkness swiftly crept over his vision, his consciousness fading like a dying ember, until all that remained was the hollow silence of his final breath.

He butcher wiped his blade clean with a casual swipe of a sodden cloth.

Miran stepped over the body, surveying his handiwork. A slow, satisfied smile curled his lips. Then, without another glance, he turned and strode out.

Outside, the night was calm, as if the world had already moved on from the fallen king.

After Siraj's demise, both Mir Jafar and Miran sought the hand of the famed beauty Lutf-un-Nissa. Historical accounts record her response to these proposals: "Having ridden an elephant before, I cannot now agree to ride an ass." She lived out her years with quiet dignity, supported by a meagre pension from the British. But in death, she reunited with Siraj, buried beside him in Khoshbag. Souls who could only be together for a brief moment in the living world now found togetherness in eternal bliss in the afterlife.

• • •

The main thoroughfare of Murshidabad, its wide, stone-paved road lined with shops and residences, usually bustled with life. But today it had been overtaken by a grisly spectacle, watched with utter shock and dismay by a throng of people who had spilled into it.

Before them, the procession advanced with brutal indifference. Siraj ud-Daulah's corpse, bound with ropes, was dragged behind a horse-drawn carriage, the body bouncing lifelessly over the uneven road.

Adjacent to the thoroughfare lay a lush and well-manicured maidan. Here, atop majestic elephants, the nobles of the new regime sat in morbid triumph. Javed Hussain sat among them. He wholeheartedly loathed this gruesome and debasing spectacle, but he had no choice. To refuse to attend would risk alienating himself from the new regime, perhaps even jeopardising his own safety.

Javed's hands clenched tightly around the silk-draped edge of the howdah, the canopied seat perched atop the elephant's back. His stomach churned with a bile of disgust. He felt the weight of revulsion from the commoners below. Some in the crowd turned their faces away, unable to bear the sight; others stood frozen, their wide eyes glistening with unspoken condemnation. Even those who had cursed Siraj for his tyranny now seemed aghast at the indignity of this act, at the wanton desecration of a Nawab's mortal remains.

Javed's eyes darted toward his fellow nobles, sitting atop their respective elephants that were draped in richly embroidered robes of silk and velvet, their turbans adorned with plumes and gems that sparkled in the sunlight. Mir Jafar, the newly minted Nawab, sat nearby, his expression one of cold vengeance, while the other courtiers watched with a mixture of morbid curiosity and quiet satisfaction.

Javed, however, felt none of their composure. Each jolt of the carriage dragging Siraj's lifeless body felt like a lash across his conscience, each moment a reminder of the chains binding him to this hideous new regime. Moreover, to him, the spectacle seemed to reveal a hidden fragility in Mir Jafar's rule - a power so insecure it sought to debase the fallen rather than assert dignity in victory.

As the carriage rolled on, Javed could feel the crowd's quiet discontent growing. He longed to turn away, to close his eyes and shut out the gruesome reality, but he knew it was futile.

...

It was in the midst of a busy bazaar in Murshidabad. Merchants hollered their wares, children darted between carts laden with silk and spices, and the air carried the mingled scents of cardamom, sweat, and the musty dampness of the Ganges nearby. But amidst the crowd, a lone figure tottered unsteadily - his once-rich robes, faded and patched, hanging loosely on his gaunt frame. His beard jutted out in wild tufts, and his eyes - oh, his eyes - darted about, glassy and unfocused, yet burning with some inscrutable fire.

"*Sab laal hai,*" (All is red) the man muttered, his voice low and rasping, as though the words clawed their way out of him. "*Sab laal hai… sab laal ha*i!" Each repetition grew louder, more fevered, until it became a chant that startled passersby. A group of idle boatmen leaned on their oars and exchanged amused glances. A spice merchant chuckled and nudged his apprentice. "Poor fool, he's seen too much, lost too much". Children followed him at a distance, giggling and mimicking his gait and cry. "*Sab laal hai! Sab laal hai!*"

But the man did not stop, his chant a relentless mantra punctuated by a hoarse, bitter laugh. "*Sab laal hai,*" he muttered one final time, his voice soft now, barely audible. And then, as though the weight of his words had drained the last of his strength, he sank to his knees in the middle of the street, head bowed.

The pitiable man was Omichand, a name that had once been uttered with the deepest of regard among Murshidabad's merchant class. His connections spanned far away provinces, and his wealth rivalled that of minor princes. Omichand had always been a man who played the long game, his fortune built not only on trade but on his uncanny ability to navigate the treacherous waters of political intrigue.

The chant faded in his throat as memory reclaimed him for a brief moment.

Omichand had uncovered the plot to topple the Nawab, where promises of wealth and power were traded like trinkets. Although he did not intend to join the scheme, he saw a chance to wield his knowledge of it as leverage.

Omichand confronted William Watts at the British factory. "You will tell Clive," he said, his voice silky yet menacing, "that I know of the conspiracy. If my loyalty is to remain assured, I must be compensated - five percent of the spoils." He leaned forward, his eyes gleaming. "Consider this as the price of silence, Watts Sahib."

Watts' expression betrayed no emotion. "Five percent, you say?"

"Yes," Omichand replied, his smile tight. "A mere token of gratitude for my discretion."

Soon thereafter Watts relayed the demand to Clive. Seated at his desk in the dim glow of an oil lamp, Clive smiled faintly. "Five percent. A small fortune, to be sure." he said. Then, leaning back, he added, "But we shall give him his treaty."

Watts frowned. "You mean to meet his demands?"

Clive's gaze sharpened. "No, Watts. He will get only a worthless paper".

And so, two documents were prepared: the genuine treaty on white paper, signed by Admiral Watson and Mir Jafar, which made no mention of Omichand's cut; and a second, forged version on red paper, which did.

"Here it is," Watts said, sliding the red treaty across the desk to Omichand. He picked it up with trembling hands, his eyes scanning the text, his expression softening into a smirk of satisfaction.

"So, it is agreed," Omichand said, reclining in his chair. "You may proceed with your plans, and my silence will be assured."

Watts forced a smile. "We are grateful for your cooperation."

After the events of the Battle of Plassey unfolded like clockwork, Omichand arrived at the Company's headquarters. His face was flush with anticipation of the immense wealth that would soon flow his way, the spoils of war he had so cleverly secured.

Clive greeted him, his expression neutral. "Ah, Omichand. You've come for your reward."

"Yes, and I trust the terms of the treaty will be honoured," Omichand said confidently.

Clive gestured to an attendant, who handed Omichand a document - the white treaty. As Omichand read, his smile faltered, then disappeared entirely.

"This… this is not what we agreed upon," he stammered.

"No, it is not," Clive said, his voice laced with mockery "You see, Omichand, the red treaty was a forgery. A necessary ruse to ensure your silence."

Omichand's hand shook as he clutched the paper. "This is fraud," he hissed. "You've cheated me - lied to my face and made a mockery of our agreement. Is this the honour of you British"?

Clive's gaze hardened. "Spare me your outrage, Omichand. You sought to blackmail us. Consider yourself fortunate you have not paid a greater price."

The revelation shattered Omichand. His dreams of wealth turned to ash. Struck by the dashing of his ambitions and the outrageous duplicity, his mind unravelled with devastating swiftness.

And that is when "*Sab laal hai*" was born, only Omichand's fevered mind knowing whether *laal* meant the blood spilled at Plassey, or the red ink of a treaty that never existed.

• • •

After the overthrow of Siraj-ud-Daulah, the women of his household were imprisoned in the Jinjira Palace, situated on the banks of the Buriganga River. A few months into their captivity, about seventy Begums were herded down the palace steps. For the first time since their imprisonment, they had stepped into the open air. A gentle breeze carried the river's sweet scent as a stately bajra awaited, its lacquered wood gleaming in the morning sun.

Some hesitated at the threshold, wary of sudden kindness, their instincts sharpened by betrayal. But among them were a few who allowed themselves a fragile hope - young women who murmured of possible exile, of being sent to another palace, another life. A mother held her child close, whispering reassurances she barely believed.

The boatmen stood ready, their faces bereft of any expression, as they guided the women aboard with quiet efficiency. The Buriganga stretched vast and silent, its waters smooth as glass under the morning sun.

The bajra set off with gracefully, its oars cutting through the river's tranquil waters. It soon reached a remote stretch of the river. Nearby, another bajra floated lazily - its hull inlaid with ivory, its canopy embroidered with gold thread, and silk pennants fluttering in the breeze - an unmistakable vessel of someone accustomed to power and luxury. Reclining on its deck was a young man, no older than twenty-five, swathed in the finest silks. A goblet of wine rested in his hand, his eyes locked onto the incoming bajra - as though it were a stage, and he its expectant audience.

The bajra carrying the Begums came to a gentle halt, the oars stilling as the boatmen exchanged subtle glances. Their movements were quiet, commonplace - as if tending to the routine upkeep of the vessel. One by one, they approached the hull, their hands stealthily removing concealed plugs that allowed water to seep in.

A faint ripple spread across the wooden floor, darkening the silk hem of a Begum's robe. A thin stream curled around Ghaseti Begum's ankles. She frowned, shifting slightly. Someone else murmured about dampness beneath them, but the air was still warm, the boat still steady. A boatman, adjusting an oar, murmured without looking up - 'Just river spray, Begum Saheba. Nothing to worry about.'

The boatmen, their task complete, furtively slipped into the water and swam away to safety. The dampness crept higher. The women pulled their feet up onto the cushions, some muttering about the state of the boat, others wrapping their shawls more tightly around themselves. Then the first gasp came. 'The water… it's rising.'

Within moments, as realisation dawned, the air was filled with the hysterical shrieks of the noblewomen, none of whom - befitting their station – knew how to swim. The bajra tilted under the surge of water. The Begums began to flail wildly, their delicate hands slapping against the cold, unyielding water as it rose with cruel inevitability. Eyes wide with abject terror stared into the murky depths of the water.

One by one, their struggles grew weaker. As the water began surging into their lungs, their piercing screams dissolved into wet, choking gasps. Presently the voices disappeared altogether, replaced by the slow gurgle of the river reclaiming its own. Moments later, the Buriganga lay still once more, its surface smooth and sunlit, as if nothing had ever disturbed it.

As the macabre scene had begun to unfold, Miran - the young man - had leaned forward from his vantage point, his lips curling into a smile of sublime satisfaction. The Begums' cries reached him as an ethereal melody. He savoured their terror with relish, the choking sobs and frantic splashes playing out like a dark concerto composed solely for his amusement. Their suffering was his entertainment, their despair a reflection of his newfound power.

The sarang – head boatman – approached the youth deferentially – "Shall we return, Janab?" "Yes", he answered laconically, then hissed to himself "Now that takes care of the Alivardi's full litter."

It was Miran who had overseen the hunting down of Siraj and organised the parading of his corpse. Now he took upon himself to systematically wipe out the house of Alivardi Khan. And drowning of Siraj's harem was only the more merciful of deaths he dispensed.

But fate delivered its own reckoning. Not long after, during a military campaign, a fire - reportedly sparked by lightning - ripped through the top of Miran's tent, consuming him in flames. Many called it divine retribution. Others whispered of an earthlier cause – that the fire was orchestrated by a concubine, whose sister had perished on that doomed bajra, and who had waited for vengeance.

It had happened, after all, on the very anniversary of the drowning.

• • •

Javed Hussain sat on the edge of a chair in the grand hall of his mansion. The room felt colder than it should have been, with the faint sounds of servants going about their duties drifting in from beyond the doors.

Footsteps echoed in the corridor, steady and deliberate, growing louder until Sarfaraz emerged in the doorway. Not yet past his teens, he carried himself with a maturity that belied his years. For Javed, Sarfaraz was not just his son; he was Javed's sole light in an increasingly dark world. He was the embodiment of hope, a reason to endure. And as the boy stood there, framed by the soft glow of the hallway lanterns, Javed briefly saw the child he once lifted onto horseback, laughing, fearless - before the world became grey.

"Abba," Sarfaraz said, his voice low but unflinching, "Is it true?"

Javed's gaze shifted to meet his son's, and in that instant, the man who had once been a proud noble looked older, his shoulders drooping under the weight of guilt. He knew what his son meant without needing further elaboration. There had been murmurs - betrayal had led to a Nawab's blood being spilled. And now, those murmurs had reached his son's ears.

"Sit, Sarfaraz," Javed said, gesturing to the chair opposite him.

"I'd rather stand," Sarfaraz replied, arms crossed, his eyes shadowed not just by disbelief, but by hurt. "Is it true that you betrayed the Nawab? That you turned against him in the hour of need?"

Javed took a deep breath, his chest heaving as though the act itself was arduous. "Yes," he admitted finally, his voice cracking like dry earth beneath an unbearable weight. "I did."

The words hung in the air, heavy and suffocating. Sarfaraz stepped closer, his hands clenching into fists at his sides. "Why?" The single word felt like a demand, sharp and unforgiving.

Javed rose to his feet, his tall frame towering over his son, yet he looked smaller, diminished. "The Nawab was a tyrant," he said, his tone defensive. "His reckless decisions, his disregard for wise counsel - it was tearing the province apart. I believed…I believed I was saving Bengal from further ruin."

"You believed?" Sarfaraz's voice rose, disbelief etched into every syllable. "What of loyalty? What of honour? You took an oath to serve the Nawab, to stand by him through storm and siege. And yet, when he needed you the most, you turned your back on him?"

"Loyalty to a tyrant is no virtue, son," Javed countered, his voice trembling. "It was not an easy decision. Do you think I do not carry the burden of this every waking moment? That I do not see the shadows of my betrayal everywhere I look?"

Sarfaraz shook his head, stepping back as though the words themselves were poison. "It is not just the Nawab you betrayed, Abba. It is yourself. And now you have betrayed me." His voice softened, but it carried the sting of a blade. "The man I respected, the man I aspired to be, is gone."

The room fell silent. Javed reached out a hand, trembling and desperate, a part of him aching for the days when that same hand steadied Sarfaraz's grip on a bow, or tousled his hair after a ride. But Sarfaraz turned away. "You may justify your actions however you wish, but in my eyes, you are no longer the man I once looked up to."

"Sarfaraz, please," Javed whispered, his voice breaking.

But his son did not stop. He walked out, his footsteps echoing through the hall as they faded into the distance. Alone, Javed sank back into his chair, his head in his hands. The estate's grandeur mocked him as he was consumed by shame and by the ghost of a boy who had once looked at him with nothing but pride. For a man who had once thought he could bear the weight of the world, the loss of his son's respect was a blow that utterly crushed him.

• • •

The heavy drapes of the durbar hall failed to keep out the oppressive heat of the Bengal summer. A few months had passed since the battle, but the air still hung thick with tension and uncertainty. Mir Jafar, seated on his elaborate throne, looked every bit a shadow of the mighty Nawabs of old. His turban sat slightly askew, his eyes bloodshot from yet another night dulled by opium fumes. He shifted uncomfortably as the British delegation approached, their bearing marked by quiet confidence and an undisguised sense of authority.

Francis Kilpatrick strode to the centre of the hall with measured precision, his boots striking the marble floor with the certainty of a man used to command. Since the victory at Plassey, Kilpatrick had been entrusted with overseeing Company interests at court. But his uniform, crisp and understated, bore the quiet severity of military authority rather than the flamboyance of a court envoy. He nodded stiffly, flanked by two Company aides who stood silently behind him.

"Nawab Sahib," Kilpatrick began, his voice steady, clipped, and unmistakably firm, "I trust you are well this morning."

Mir Jafar's lips moved, but the words were barely audible. "It finds me well enough," he muttered, avoiding Kilpatrick's gaze.

Kilpatrick did not bother with further pleasantries. "We come on a matter that concerns the stability of the region. The Company has borne considerable cost in maintaining troops to secure Bengal. It is only reasonable that the arrangements be revised to reflect those efforts."

Mir Jafar's eyes flickered nervously toward his diwans and ministers, who stood in uneasy silence along the sides of the hall. Rai Durlabh stepped forward cautiously.

"The treasury is already strained," he began carefully. "The payments already made to the Company for troops and fortifications have left little for administration. Perhaps the burden can be -"

"Burden?" Kilpatrick's tone sharpened, eyes narrowing. His gaze remained fixed on the Nawab. "The greater burden lies with those who secure your borders, Nawab Sahib. Without our regiments, that throne would already be dust."

Mir Jafar's head drooped, his fingers toying with the tassels of his robe. "What… what is it you ask?" he murmured.

Kilpatrick's expression did not shift. "First, an extension of zamindari rights to the Hooghly corridor, and to the districts of Burdwan and Midnapore. These changes will enable more efficient revenue management under joint administration."

A murmur rippled through the court. Rai Durlabh's face darkened, but he stepped forward once more. "The zamindars will resist, Nawab Sahib. These regions are vital to the kingdom's revenue, and surrendering them will weaken your hold on the land."

Kilpatrick's jaw tightened. "Resistance will be dealt with. Company forces stand ready to ensure compliance."

Mir Jafar's voice was almost inaudible. "And… and is that all?"

Kilpatrick took a half step forward, his tone softening only slightly. "Fifteen lakhs - for fortifications in Calcutta and other key locations. Maintenance and expansion are necessary to secure trade and deter threats."

One of the younger ministers, Syed Azam, stepped forward, his face taut with suppressed frustration. "This is extortion!" he said boldly. "The treasury is depleted, the people are starving, and yet you demand more? Have you no shame?"

Kilpatrick turned to Azam, unshaken. "And have you no sense of scale, Minister? Without our presence, you'd have no coin left to count. Call it what you will - reality doesn't negotiate."

He turned back to the throne. "Lastly, we must request an increase in the annual contribution for the upkeep of Company troops stationed throughout Bengal. Rations, equipment, allowances - all must be accounted for. The current arrangement of twelve lakhs no longer suffices; twenty lakhs will now be required to ensure their continued readiness."

Mir Jafar's hands trembled as he clutched the arms of his throne. In a faltering voice, he murmured, "How can we bear such a cost any longer?"

Kilpatrick's face remained expressionless. "Better to pay with silver than blood. This arrangement ensures peace - for now."

Azam opened his mouth to retort, but Rai Durlabh laid a calming hand on his shoulder and shook his head, a silent plea for caution.

"We have no choice but to… agree," Mir Jafar said, his voice trembling. "The Company's support is… indispensable."

Azam's face twisted in disgust. "They will bleed us dry! Have we no pride left?"

Mir Jafar's gaze dropped to the floor, his voice barely audible. "Pride does not provide shelter, Azam. Nor does it keep swords at bay."

Kilpatrick gave a curt nod. "Wise words, Your Excellency. The Company is pleased with your wisdom and foresight. Rest assured, your cooperation will not be forgotten."

As Kilpatrick and his aides turned to leave, Mir Jafar sank lower in his seat, his gaze fixed on the marble floor, while the gilded lions carved into his throne stared ahead with a resoluteness he did not share. Azam stormed out of the hall, his footsteps echoing in the sombre silence. The courtiers stood frozen, caught between the weight of their shame and the fear of their foreign overlords.

But it was not only the Nawab's authority that was crumbling - beyond these walls, in the markets and villages, the people of Bengal were already beginning to feel the weight of this submission. The price had been named, and Bengal would pay it - in silver, in hunger, and in creeping despair.

THE CHAINS OF CONQUEST

Two years have passed since the guns fell silent at Plassey, but Bengal has found no peace. What followed was not rule, nor even conquest - it was collapse. The markets of Murshidabad still stood, but their grandeur was fading into rot. Streets once walked by proud traders now echoed with the footsteps of the dispossessed. Crops still ripened in the fields, but they no longer belonged to the farmer. The province that had once dazzled the world was being hollowed from within, its lifeblood siphoned day by day.

Even Richard Wickham - the private English trader whose commerce knew no scruples - found himself startled by the depths of greed the new regime had stirred within him. He had stationed himself in the bustling river town of Rajshahi - where the land was rich, the silk trade thriving, and oversight scarce. The mansion he had claimed bustled with activity: sepoys drilling in the courtyard, clerks tallying accounts, porters hauling away bolts of silk and sacks of rice. It was less a political order, he often smirked from its veranda, than an anarchical void - one in which men like him could gorge without limit.

Wickham had paid the East India Company handsomely for the privilege of unfettered access to Bengal's riches. Dastaks - those invaluable passes exempting goods from taxation - were his most prized possessions, each sealed with the Company's imprimatur. The Company also sold him the protection of sepoys, and with these investments, Wickham became a force unto himself. These privileges - the dastaks, and even the sepoy escorts - were in direct violation of the treaty Mir Jafar had signed with the Company before Plassey. But Bengal was now awash with private traders armed with both.

But while traders like Wickham amassed fortunes under this new order, the lives of Bengal's artisans - men like Ramlal - were being quietly crushed beneath its weight.

Ramlal was a skilled weaver, heir to a lineage that had perfected the intricate art of silk weaving over five generations. His forefathers had woven dreams into thread, creating fabrics so fine they seemed to shimmer with a life of their own. The craft was their livelihood, and their pride. Their modest home, perched at the edge of the bustling market, stood as a quiet testament to generations of diligence - simple, well-kept. Life had been tranquil, if not lavish, for the weaver's clan - until men like Wickham arrived in the region.

Today, the tranquillity felt like a distant memory. Ramlal sat cross-legged on the worn floor of his dimly lit workshop, enveloped by the rhythmic creak of his loom. His fingers, once steady and confident, trembled as they tied off the final thread. The fabric before him gleamed faintly with golden threads and intricate patterns drawn from centuries of tradition. It had taken three months of backbreaking labour, each thread meticulously placed, each motif crafted with care - a creation fit for kings, and born of quiet devotion.

Yet, outside the workshop, the air was thick with unease. Wickham's sepoys stood like hungry predators, their muskets slung casually but menacingly over their shoulders. The sight of them alone was enough to turn the strongest resolve to ash.

The door creaked open, and Wickham, the English trader whose name had come to evoke fear itself, strode in, his polished boots clicking against the uneven stone floor. His eyes, sharp and calculating, scanned the workshop before settling on Ramlal and the roll of silk.

"I hear this is your finest work," Wickham said, his voice smooth, laced with the faintest edge of disdain. He stepped forward, lifting the roll of silk with an affected grace. Holding it to the light seeping through the window, he let the golden threads glint faintly in the haze. For a fleeting moment, his gaze lingered - appraising, not admiring - before he handed it off to a clerk with casual disregard.

"It'll fetch something," Wickham remarked dryly. "Five rupees."

Ramlal's heart sank. "Five rupees? Sahib, this silk took me three months. It is worth fifty!" His voice, though deferential, carried a creeping desperation.

Wickham's smile grew colder, his eyes narrowing. "Five rupees," he repeated, his tone as unyielding as steel. Beside him, one of the sepoys shifted, the bayonet at the end of his musket catching the light and Ramlal's eye. Ramlal lowered his gaze, his hands clenched into fists, but he knew better than to argue further. The roll of silk was taken away. In its place, a handful of tarnished coins clattered onto the floor at his feet, tossed carelessly like crumbs to a stray dog.

Wickham turned to leave, pausing near another loom, his gloved hand trailing across the threads. "I'll have the rest of these by tomorrow," he said over his shoulder, his voice as sharp as the edge of a blade, "for the same price."

But Ramlal was not alone - beyond his loom, the same machinery of coercion was grinding down Bengal's once prosperous merchants, one ledger entry at a time.

The marketplace was Wickham's next destination, a hive of activity where the town's richest merchants conducted their trade. Today, however, the bazaar's usual energy was muted. The merchants had been herded into a dimly lit warehouse, their age-old wealth and influence being mocked at by the threat of Wickham's sepoys. The air inside was thick with the smell of damp wood and sweat, and fear hung in the room like an unwelcome guest. Crates filled with valuable goods - dyes, muslins, spices - were laid out on long tables.

Wickham stood at the head of the room "These are now yours," he declared, his voice echoing off the warehouse walls, "at the price I have set." He gestured to the crates, his expression betraying no emotion.

One merchant, a portly man whose gold rings now seemed to mock his helplessness, mustered the courage to protest. "At these rates, we'll bleed with every sale," he said, his voice taut with desperation. "No buyer will match what you demand - we'll be ruined before the year is out!"

Wickham's gaze turned icy, his lips curling into a cruel smile. "Then treat it as a contribution to the greater good. The Company appreciates your generosity." A snap of his fingers brought a sepoy forward, his bayonets gleaming in the flickering torchlight. The merchant, his bravado crumbling, nodded hurriedly, his hands shaking as he signed over the demanded sums. One by one, the other merchants followed suit, their faces taut with indignation and dread as they signed agreements that would hollow out their fortunes.

By the time Wickham emerged from the warehouse, his pockets jingled with coins that had once belonged to the town's wealthiest men. He strode through the bazaar with a swagger, his clerks trailing behind him like vultures feasting on the remains of a carcass. Behind him, the merchants sat slumped over the tables, their expressions a mixture of despair and impotent rage. Their livelihoods now lay in ruins, just like the villages Wickham had passed on his way to the bazaar.

Through it all, Bengal's once-proud officials watched helplessly as their authority crumbled. Wickham, like countless others, refused to pay even the meagre taxes still required, brandishing his dastaks like charms of invincibility. Their protests went unanswered; the East India Company no longer listened to men without power. Private sepoys patrolled the roads, enforcing the will of traders who now ruled like feudal lords. And Wickham was only one of hundreds - private profiteers armed with Company privileges, hollowing out Bengal's economy like termites devouring timber, leaving behind only a fragile shell.

By 1760, Wickham's fortune had soared - and so had his infamy. His name became a whispered curse. Yet in his mansion, he stood unmoved, a ledger in hand, watching the sunset over the river. The columns of figures before him were not records of suffering, but marks of triumph - each rupee a conquest, each tally a victory. Whether Bengal would forgive him, or history condemn him, never entered his mind. The wealth was his. And in a world ruled by force, he was king.

The jewel of India, once famed for its peace and prosperity, now lay fractured and fading. Anarchy ruled the streets, poverty seeped into every corner, and under the shadow of British dominance, Bengal's golden age slipped quietly into history.

∴

The midday sun bore down mercilessly upon the streets of Murshidabad, casting long, wavering shadows on the dust-ridden thoroughfares. Sarfaraz moved through the market, but its once-proud vibrancy now frayed at the edges. The spice merchants still called out, the weavers still unfurled their fine muslins, but there was something hollow beneath the spectacle – a despondency that clung to the air like damp silk.

He had wandered further than intended, his thoughts weighed down by his father's silence in the face of the growing shadow of the British. Javed Hussain, who had once stood for honour, now felt like a stranger to him. It was in this state of troubled reflection that Sarfaraz nearly stepped past the hunched figure crouched in the shadow of a ruined archway.

The man was skeletal, draped in tattered cloth that had once been a fine robe. His sunken eyes, dull with hunger, flickered with a momentary glint of recognition. "Babu… do you not know me?" The voice was cracked, the words barely escaping his parched lips.

Sarfaraz halted, his gaze narrowing as he took in the man's features. Then it struck him like a blow - this was no common beggar. This was Karimullah, the famed artisan who had once been commissioned to weave for the zenana of Nawab Alivardi Khan himself. Sarfaraz had once watched those hands turn thread into wonder, his muslins so fine they were called 'woven air.'

"Karimullah?" The name left his lips in disbelief. "How did this -?"

The man let out a rasping chuckle, devoid of mirth. "How does any of it happen, Babu? The Company's traders have no need for artisans like me. They flood the market with cheap imports, impose crushing tariffs on our cloth, and demand commissions that strip us of all profit. They tax our looms, our dyes, our thread - until there's nothing left to live on. When we can no longer meet their impossible terms, they seize our livelihoods. My debts swallowed me whole. My family..." His voice broke. "I sent them away. Better they face hunger far from me than witness what I've become."

Sarfaraz's stomach churned. He had heard stories of the Company's brutal control over Bengal's commerce, but here, before him, was its living consequence. Karimullah had once been honoured in noble courts, his work coveted by the wealthiest patrons. Now, he begged for scraps in the streets.

The shame that had already festered within Sarfaraz now grew unbearable. His father's name was still whispered in the halls of power, his family still had a place among the city's aristocracy, yet this - this was the fate awaiting all who could no longer serve the Company's profit.

Karimullah's gaunt fingers fumbled at his side, drawing out a tattered scrap of cloth. He held it up - a fragment of embroidery, its delicate patterns barely visible through layers of filth. "I made this for the Nawab's palace," he murmured. "It was meant for queens. Now it rots with me."

Sarfaraz felt something inside him shift. It was not anger, nor pity - it was something heavier. A realisation. His name, his bloodline, meant nothing if it chained him to a world complicit in this suffering. To stay in his father's house was to remain among those who dined in comfort while men like Karimullah wasted away.

He knelt before the man and pressed a silver coin into his trembling palm. "Even though this is not enough," Sarfaraz said, his voice quiet but firm, "I cannot go on pretending not to see."

Karimullah's lips parted as if to respond, but Sarfaraz was already rising - his thoughts a storm of shame, grief, and revulsion. He did not know what lay ahead, only that he could no longer remain in his father's world. By sundown, he would walk away from the mansion and take shelter among the villagers - seeking not answers, but distance from a life that now repulsed him.

. . .

The scent of freshly made sweets and the rhythmic hum of Baul songs filled the air as Thomas Hawke strode through the bustling Poush Mela, his steps instinctively lighter than his usual soldier's march. He looked strikingly different today, dressed in an elegant kurta-pyjama, the fabric light against his skin in the mild winter sun. By his side walked Gulabi, her deep brown eyes sparkling with a mix of curiosity and quiet confidence, a vivid red sari draped over her slender frame. She adjusted the edge of her pallu modestly, though her gaze stayed locked on the vibrant festivities ahead.

Gulabi had come into Thomas's life just weeks before, a union born less of formality and more of quiet companionship. She was a bibi - an unofficial partner to a British officer in a relationship often unacknowledged by law or society - who had chosen him as much as he had chosen her. Her name, meaning "rose," seemed to suit her well - a beauty not loud in its proclamation but impossible to ignore. With her dusky skin and flowing black hair tied loosely, she exuded an air of grace that matched the calmness she brought to Thomas's often turbulent existence.

Thomas, for his part, had come to appreciate more than just her beauty. It was the way she moved through life with a gentle resilience that mesmerised him - the way she balanced tradition with her own quiet defiance. It was she who had suggested they attend the Poush Mela, her enthusiasm infectious as she described the festival's colours, songs, and stories that were as old as the land itself.

The couple moved through the throng of visitors, hand in hand, their fingers intertwined with an easy intimacy despite the stares of the locals. Gulabi's sari blended seamlessly with the hues around her, but her choice to walk beside him, rather than behind as custom often dictated, quietly unsettled the familiar order. Thomas caught glimpses of frowns, sidelong glances, and rare, knowing smiles - but none of it seemed to touch their shared contentment. Still, beneath that contentment, a quieter truth stirred - he was a soldier of the Company, a foreigner in a land his country now ruled, and she, a local woman without legal standing in their union. Their bond defied the roles written for them, but could never entirely escape their shadow.

As she moved ahead - laughing, bartering, brushing her hair back in the wind - Thomas felt the faint ache of something fragile. He wondered how long this little world would hold, how long before a posting, a transfer, or the blunt machinery of the Company tried to pull them apart. He did not speak the thought aloud, but it sat beside him, quiet and persistent, like the dust that clung to their clothes. And even then, he knew: he would not let go easily.

A troupe of Bauls, their ektaras in hand, sang songs of divine love and the impermanence of life. Gulabi paused, her eyes lighting up at the familiar melody. "They sing of Radha and Krishna," she explained softly to Thomas, her voice lilting like a melody itself. "Their love - timeless, forbidden, and never meant to last in the world of rules."

Thomas nodded, her words weaving into the vibrant tapestry of the fair, though something in them caught behind his ribs.

"Timeless and forbidden," he murmured, offering a faint smile. "We understand that better than most."

She said nothing at first, only looked at him. Then, as though choosing the moment over the weight beneath it, her fingers tightened gently around his. "Perhaps we do."

They wandered through stalls of brightly dyed textiles, handcrafted toys, and clay figurines. Gulabi showed him how to barter with the vendors, laughing as Thomas's attempts in broken Bengali earned him an extra sweet or two. She led him to a cart selling pithas, traditional rice cakes, and insisted he try the soft, syrup-soaked delicacy. He closed his eyes as the sweetness melted on his tongue, and when he opened them, her laughter warmed him more than the sun overhead.

For a moment, amidst the chaos of the mela, the two of them stood still, their world shrinking to just the space they shared. Thomas reached out to adjust the pallu of her sari that had slipped slightly from her shoulder. "This suits you," he said, his voice low, almost reverent.

"And you," she replied, brushing an invisible speck of dust from his kurta. "You look like you belong."

As the evening descended, the fairgrounds were illuminated by oil lamps and flaming torches, casting a golden glow on the faces of the revellers. Thomas and Gulabi found themselves seated on a woven mat near a bonfire, listening to a storyteller recounting tales from the Mahabharata. Thomas, though unfamiliar with the epic, found himself enthralled, his understanding deepened by Gulabi's whispered explanations.

In that moment, surrounded by the culture and rhythm of Bengal, they were not a soldier and his bibi, not a foreigner and a local. They were simply two souls, content in each other's company, immersed in a world that felt, for now, like it belonged entirely to them.

. . .

The harsh sun blazed over the dry, empty fields, casting long shadows of skeletal trees that seemed to mock the once-prosperous village. Sarfaraz stood among the peasants, his hands blistered and calloused from months of tilling the hardened soil. He had traded his silken robes for coarse cotton, his jewelled turban for a sweat-stained headscarf. Yet no physical discomfort could rival the torment within his heart.

The son of Javed Hussain - his very name was a wound, a constant reminder of his father's betrayal at Plassey. The shame burned quietly but relentlessly, scarring the ideals he had once cherished. In leaving the estate, he sought more than distance from his family's legacy; he sought to cleanse himself of the shadow it had cast over his soul.

He had chosen this village with care. Isolated, poor, and far from his family's lands, Mirganj lay a few hours ride from the town of Rajshahi. No one here knew him personally, but his name carried weight, and not the kind that earned welcome. The villagers had initially eyed him with suspicion. To them, he was an interloper, a privileged aristocrat whose kind had always profited from their labour. At first, they refused his help. When he reached for a plough, a farmer snatched it away. "We don't need your pity, babu," the man cursed, turning his back. Another villager spat near his feet. The message was clear - his kind had never toiled, never suffered. Why should they believe he was different?

But even in their anger, they could always use another pair of hands - especially a young man willing to sweat. So they let him work, if only in silence.

His first days were a blur of clumsy efforts and quiet humiliation. He tried to help with the irrigation trench but misaligned the channel, causing water to pool uselessly at one end. Another time, he attempted to stack harvested grain but piled it too high and uneven, and the bundles toppled into the mud. But he learned quickly - watching the others, copying their movements - and soon, his hands worked with the same steady rhythm as theirs.

Sarfaraz's humility and diligence began to wear away the villagers' distrust. He ate their coarse bread, drank the brackish water, and worked alongside them from dawn to dusk. And slowly, eyes that had once narrowed with scorn began to hold something else - curiosity, and in time, respect.

It was Birju, the blacksmith, who first softened. "Maybe he's not like the rest," he murmured one afternoon, watching Sarfaraz haul firewood without complaint. Then came Gauri, the widow whose son Sarfaraz had carried on his back through waist-deep floodwaters when the storm broke the embankment - she placed a fresh roti in his palm during a midday break and said quietly, "You work like you were born here." Even Raghu, the same farmer who had once snatched the plough from his hand, began nodding curtly when they passed each other in the fields. Each small shift stitched a thread of belonging.

But was this redemption or escape? Sarfaraz told himself he was atoning for his father's sins, but in the dead of night, another thought gnawed at him - had he failed just as much? He had walked away from Javed Hussain in anger, but what had he done to right the wrongs? Was he truly different, or just another man running from his past?

As the months wore on, Sarfaraz immersed himself in the lives of the peasants. He listened to their grievances, felt the crushing weight of the taxes imposed to fund the British demands. He saw how the fields yielded too little to satisfy the collectors, how the regime demanded revenue regardless of crop failure or calamity. Yet beyond sharing their despair, he began to inspire. His unshaken conviction that their lives could - and must - be changed lit a spark in the hearts of the oppressed. They began to see him not as a fallen noble, but as one of their own, willing to sacrifice privilege to stand and suffer beside them.

One evening, as the peasants gathered beneath the banyan tree, their faces gaunt and eyes hollow from hunger, Sarfaraz spoke. His voice, though tinged with sorrow, carried a rare fire.

"I was blind," he began, his gaze sweeping over the crowd. "I didn't see the pain of this land. I didn't understand the suffering of its people. I believed honour lay in lineage, in titles and wealth. But I see now - true honour lies in justice, in standing with those who have been wronged."

The crowd listened quietly. Some nodded, others lowered their eyes, as if his words had stirred something long buried. He was naming their truth. Sarfaraz pressed on.

"I have seen the children cry themselves to sleep on empty stomachs. I have seen the elderly toil until their bodies give out. This is not the world we were meant to inherit. This is not the world we must leave for those who come after us."

A peasant woman, her face lined with years of hardship, spoke up. "What can we do, babu? We are nothing against them."

"You are not nothing," Sarfaraz replied, his voice rising with conviction. "You are the lifeblood of this land. They feed on your labour, grow fat on your suffering. If we stand together, if we refuse to bow any longer, they cannot ignore us."

The crowd was silent, the weight of his words settling upon them. The simmering anger Sarfaraz had sensed in the fields now began to take form, a flicker of hope sparking in their weary eyes. He saw it - a cautious, almost imperceptible shift. They were beginning to believe.

Later that night, a few of the younger men lingered beneath the banyan tree after the others had gone. They asked quiet questions - about what could be done if the grain failed again, if the taxes rose further, if someone simply could not pay. Sarfaraz did not yet have answers, but unease was rising in him like smoke from a smouldering ember. How long could they endure? How long before silence turned to refusal? He listened. And in their voices, he heard something new - not just fear, but the stirrings of defiance. For the first time, they were imagining the possibility of saying no.

As the villagers dispersed, Sarfaraz remained under the banyan tree, the cool breeze carrying the scent of earth and despair. He was no longer merely a man fleeing a broken legacy. He was Sarfaraz - accepted, trusted, and beginning to feel the weight of what might come next.

Something had shifted. The old silence no longer held. The questions had begun - not just around him, but within.

• • •

The early morning air carried the scent of damp earth and distant smoke as Richard Wickham fastened the buckles on his riding boots. His leather coat, rich and black, gleamed faintly under the waning sunlight streaming through the veranda of his sprawling estate. In the nearby stables, his attendants saddled his horse in silence, their movements steady and rehearsed.

James Wickham, his younger brother, stood a few steps away, his hands clasped behind his back. He had arrived in India only weeks ago, still adjusting to the stifling heat and the peculiar rhythms of life in this foreign land. His clothes - stiff with London tailoring - felt rather out of place in the dust of Rajshahi. But it was not the heat nor the dust that unsettled him this morning. It was his brother's words.

Richard tightened the reins, a smirk curling on his lips as he turned toward James. "You see, dear brother, we do not just trade here. We shape this land as we see fit. Indigo - it is a marvellous thing, wouldn't you agree? It brings untold profit, far more than any grain or rice ever could. That's why the peasants have to grow it - and nothing else."

James hesitated before answering. He had spent the past few days listening to the murmurs among the locals, had seen the pinched faces of farmers whose lands had been stripped of rice and wheat to make way for the indigo crops. He had heard the cries of men and women, their backs raw with lash marks - punished when their bundles of indigo were deemed too light.

"I have heard talk in the villages," James said carefully. "That your trade has left many starving. That fields once full of grain now hold nothing but stunted indigo plants. That debts bind these men tighter than chains ever could."

Richard let out a bark of laughter, cold and dismissive. "Talk?" he repeated, climbing onto his horse. "The whining of witless peasants who've trapped themselves in contracts they scarcely understand. Debt keeps them bound to us - it's the key to our profits. Tell me, James: Do you wish to make money, or would you prefer to waste your sympathy on men destined to lose everything?"

James' jaw tightened. "Surely there must be a way to profit without driving them to ruin?"

Richard sneered. His horse shifted beneath him, sensing its master's impatience.

"And what would you have me do? Pay them fairly? Let them decide what to grow?" He shook his head.

"Do that, and you will never make a fortune here. No, James, in business, sentiment is a disease. The only thing that matters is profit. And if you cannot stomach that, then perhaps India is not the land for you."

The words settled between them, hanging in the still air like the fine dust stirred by the morning breeze. James said nothing. His brother spurred his horse forward, hooves kicking up earth as he rode toward the indigo fields.

Later that day, in the village of Mirganj - where Sarfaraz's presence had begun to stir a fragile sense of hope - a group of peasants gathered beneath the banyan tree at the village's edge, as dusk bled into twilight. Their voices were low - a mix of anger, fatigue, and resignation - as they tried to make sense of their shared suffering.

"What kind of life is this?" muttered Abdul Karim, his gaunt face barely visible in the dim, fading light. "Our stomachs are empty, our land is no more ours, and our children grow weaker every day."

"It's no life," added Hiralal, his once-sturdy frame reduced to skin and bones. "The land we once farmed for rice now gives us nothing but debts we can never repay, and crops that can't even feed our families. The sahibs have tricked us into these contracts, and now we are bound to a life of suffering."

Abdul's wife Amina, her frail hands clutching a bundle of firewood, spoke softly, her voice tinged with desperation. "If only someone would stand up against this. Someone strong enough to lead us. We could rise together, like the villagers in those old stories."

Hiralal scoffed, bitterness cracking his voice. "And who would lead us? Who dares stand against the Sahibs and their sepoys? This isn't like the stories, Amina. This is real. Their muskets speak louder than our hunger."

The group fell silent, the oppressive truth settling heavily over them. In the distance, a child's cry echoed.

At that moment, the sound of distant hoofbeats echoed faintly in the still air, growing steadily louder. The oppressive quiet of the village braced itself, the dread of what was to come settling in like the chill of an unwelcome wind.

Then, almost as if summoned from that very fear, Richard Wickham's form took shape - rising on horseback from the dust like a looming spectre, his eyes scanning the crowd with a predator's calculation. As he dismounted from his horse, his sepoys fanned out behind him, muskets gleaming with silent menace. At once, the villagers stepped back, entrenched fear overriding any embers of defiance, their whispers swallowed by the silence that clung to his presence.

Wickham, his rich leather coat almost mocking in its starkness against the farmers' tattered garments, reined in his horse in front of Abdul. Abdul knelt on the parched earth, his family - Amina and their three small children - standing huddled and quivering before their hearth. His trembling hands clasped before Wickham as he pleaded, his voice cracking, "Please, sahib. We tried… we worked day and night, but the indigo crop failed. The rains… they did not come. We have nothing left."

Wickham leaned slightly in the saddle, eyes narrowing as he gave a crooked smile. "Nothing left?" he echoed, voice like dry leather. "You still have land. You still have a roof. You still have that pretty hearth behind you." His gaze flicked to Amina. "Don't insult me, Abdul. There's always *something* left to take."

Amina clutched her children tightly, her eyes brimming with tears. "We will pay, sahib," she cried out. "Give us time. Our son is strong - he can work in your fields. Please don't take our land."

Wickham's polished boots kicked up a cloud of dust as he walked toward the hut. "Time?" He chuckled darkly. "You've had time. Too much of it. My generosity has limits." Turning to his sepoys, he barked,

"Confiscate the land and everything in that hovel. The man will learn what happens to those who fall back in their payments."

The sepoys stormed into the house, overturning the meagre belongings - a broken cot, a clay water pot, a worn quilt. The villagers gasped as the soldiers dragged out Karim's only cow, the family's lifeline for milk.

Abdul remained on his knees, but lurched forward, clutching at the hem of Wickham's boot with shaking hands. "No, sahib! Not the cow - it's all we have! My children need its milk, please!" His forehead touched the dust. "Take me instead! Beat me, hang me, do what you must - but don't take the last thing keeping them alive!"

Wickham's lips curled in disdain. "You should have thought of your children before you pressed your thumb to a contract you couldn't honour." With a flick of his leg, he jerked his boot free of Abdul's grip, as if shaking off something foul.

A sepoy stepped forward and shoved Abdul's shoulder with the butt of his musket. "Out of the way, old fool," he muttered, brushing past him toward the cow.

Sarfaraz Hussain had been tending to the far edge of the fields when the cries pierced the stillness. He came running, just in time to see Abdul shoved aside like a sack of waste. Fury flared in his chest. Without hesitation, he forced his way through the crowd and burst into the clearing.

"You vultures think this land is yours to bleed dry?" he shouted, voice ringing out like a slap. "You take our crops, our labour, our lives - and now even the cow that feeds his children? *Have you no shame?*"

No sooner had the words left his mouth than a sepoy stepped forward and slammed the butt of his musket across Sarfaraz's face. He crumpled into the dust.

Before he could rise, Wickham approached, his sneer stretching wider as he took measure of the diminutive man before him. With slow, deliberate cruelty, he uncoiled his whip and brought it down across Sarfaraz's back.

The crack of leather on flesh echoed through the clearing. The villagers recoiled in horror.

Wickham let out a low, mocking laugh. "Learn your place, boy," he spat. "Next time, you won't be left breathing."

The villagers stood rooted, paralysed in their fear of Wickham's wrath. Some muttered prayers; others turned their faces away, unable to bear the unfolding sight. But more eyes were on Sarfaraz now. A young woman took a step forward before her husband gripped her wrist. An elder muttered something under his breath that sounded like an old prayer - but it ended in a curse. And somewhere in the back, a hand clenched around a sickle.

As the sepoys hauled the cow away and began marking the land for repossession, Amina sank to her knees, clutching her children tightly.

Wickham mounted his horse, casting a final glance at the broken family huddled in the dust. "Let this be a lesson to all of you," he announced, sweeping his gaze over the villagers. "Grow indigo. Pay your debts. Or face the same fate."

With that, he rode away, leaving behind a stunned village and a silence thick with grief and simmering rage.

As the dust settled from the retreating hooves, Sarfaraz lay still for a moment, his breathing ragged, his nose bloodied, his back stinging from the lash. But in his heart, something had shifted. The time for idle talk was gone. The villagers needed to rise - not with pleas, not with bent backs, but with fire in their veins. And *he* – Sarfaraz Hussain - would lead them.

• • •

Javed Hussain stood at the prow of his bajra, the river's rhythmic lapping doing little to calm his troubled thoughts. The sky was a pale grey, the air heavy with the Bengal delta's humidity. As the boat neared the jetty of his zamindari, a familiar unease tightened in his chest. This annual journey, once a moment of quiet satisfaction - a time to survey his lands with the pride of able stewardship - had become a bitter ritual, a reminder of the suffering that had unfolded under his watch.

Stepping off the bajra, Javed's ornate nagra shoes sank slightly into the soft mud of the riverbank. His retinue followed in silence, their expressions mirroring the grim anticipation in their master's eyes. The village ahead, once bustling with life and activity, now greeted them with the hushed air of withering decay.

The hum of industry - clattering looms, steaming dye pots, the brisk chatter of merchants - had faded into memory, replaced by an oppressive void. Fields that once bore rice and lentils in plenty now showed only despair: cracked soil stretched like the withered skin of an aging hand. The river's proximity mocked the village, its waters glimmering just out of reach, a cruel reminder of abundance no longer theirs. Stray cattle, ribs visible under taut skin, wandered aimlessly in search of fodder.

The weight of desolation pressed against Javed's chest. "Let us proceed," he said to his retinue, his voice laced with sorrow. They moved along the narrow path, their steps crunching against dry, brittle earth. The village heart revealed a scene so stark it made the strongest avert their eyes.

Abandoned huts - with thatched roofs caved in and walls blackened by mildew - seemed to hunch in submission. Artisans' workshops, once the village's pride, were now silent tombs. Skeletal looms stood in corners, their threads replaced by spiderwebs and dust. Rusted tools lay scattered across cracked benches. Half-woven fabric hung limply. Pots lay shattered, baskets unravelled, grinding stones forgotten. Children's laughter had vanished; in its place, gaunt faces peered from behind broken shutters, hollow eyes filled with fear and hopelessness.

A small group of villagers emerged cautiously as the entourage approached. Among them was an old farmer, his back bent from years of toil and his face lined with hardship. "Malik," he greeted Javed, bowing low. "Forgive us for the state of the village. We've done all we could. But the land has been made to turn against us."

Javed's throat tightened at the quiet desperation in the man's voice. "What has happened here?" he asked, though he feared the answer.

The farmer's voice wavered as he spoke. "The new regime's taxes are unrelenting, malik. They leave little behind of what we produce. The firangi traders cheat us of fair prices, and the sepoys... they take what they want by force. Many have fled, and those of us who remain... we barely survive."

He hesitated, glancing briefly at the other villagers before continuing, "Some of us have been talking, malik - not just about how we suffer, but about how long we can keep enduring. What we might have to do, if things do not change.

He lowered his eyes again. "You have always been just. We still place our hope in you."

Javed opened his mouth, then closed it. The farmer's words lingered, heavy in the thick village air. His gaze swept over the ruined landscape - cracked earth, crumbling homes, hollowed lives.

At last, he nodded solemnly. "Gather the villagers. I will hear what you have to say."

In a clearing near the village shrine, a small crowd formed. Men, women, and even children stood huddled together, their faces etched with fear and desperation. Javed sat on a simple wooden stool. Just as he raised a hand to invite them to speak, his eyes settled on an old man near the back - leaning on a staff, his frame more fragile than he remembered.

"Tarini Babu?" Javed asked gently.

The old schoolmaster gave a slow nod. "Still here, Sarkar. Though the banyan tree feels emptier each year."

Javed's voice lowered as he looked toward him. "And Ramu?"

Tarini's gaze fell. "Taken to the indigo factory two monsoons ago. He writes letters sometimes. Says the work is hard, but at least he writes."

A quiet weight settled on Javed's shoulders. The old man's words carried more truth than any report ever could.

Javed turned back to the crowd, his expression set with a quiet grief.

One by one, the villagers poured out their grievances – the impossible demands of the Company, the ruin of their harvests, and the daily humiliations they suffer at the hands of traders and sepoys alike. The voices blended in a low murmur of pain - until one rose above the rest. "Malik," a young weaver pleaded, his voice cracking with emotion, "we beg you, relieve us from this burden. We are like your children, and you have always been just. Save us from this misery."

Behind Javed, Abid - one of the younger retainers - leaned toward another and muttered under his breath, "They always find something to blame. Bad harvest, bad rains, bad rulers. It's the same tale every year."

Javed turned sharply. "You think this is a tale? This is what it looks like when greed rots the land and leaves its people hollow."

The retinue fell silent. Abid lowered his gaze, chastened, as Javed looked back to the villagers whose hollow eyes had not once looked away.

As the villagers' cries grew more desperate, Javed's despair deepened. He saw the trust in their eyes - not only that he was just, but that he could still set things right. They did not understand how little power he truly held now. His hands were tied - by choices made in the past, by a betrayal that had brought devastation to Bengal.

He looked at the young weaver again, then at the crowd - worn faces, open wounds, all watching him with something more painful than blame: hope. He drew a breath.

"I hear you," he said quietly. "And I cannot promise what I cannot deliver. But I swear to you - your cries will not vanish into silence."

A murmur passed through the crowd - not relief, not yet, but something softer than despair.

After the villagers had taken their leave, Javed wandered alone across the lawn of his estate, the evening shadows long and soft. Their faces haunted him, their pleas echoing in his mind. His wealth, his position - all felt hollow in the face of their suffering.

Across the courtyard, the remnants of the old theatre stage lay in disuse - planks warped, the bamboo canopy collapsed. Once, it had echoed with the tale of Prahlad and Hiranyakashipu, told to thunderous cheers from a village united in faith and celebration. Now, it lay in silence. Javed looked at it for a long time, the ghost of Narasimha's roar still faint in his ears.

And in the silence, the ghost of Siraj ud-Daulah rose unbidden in his mind - not the erratic ruler they had feared, but the young man whose blood had soaked the soil that now refused to yield grain. Javed bowed his head. Whatever peace he had once hoped for was lost long ago.

. . .

Later in the day, Javed Hussain sat in the dimly lit study of his haveli. The cries of the villagers still echoed faintly in his ears, like a bruise beneath thought - dull, persistent, and impossible to ignore. Across the desk, Harinarayan Sanyal, his trusted dewan, sat with ledgers spread before him. He had aged rapidly over the last few years. The numbers in the ledger were damning.

"Javed Sarkar," Harinarayan began, his voice steady but grave, "I fear the situation is more precarious than even I had anticipated. The zamindari's revenues have been gutted. The poor harvest has left tenants destitute, and the Company's agents - the so-called traders -have drained what little reserves we had with their relentless demands."

Javed frowned, leaning forward. "I had sensed it during my tour. The villagers are desolate, and I fear we are losing their trust. Yet, we are squeezed from all sides - by their hardship and the Company's greed. What options do we have?"

Harinarayan adjusted his spectacles, his expression thoughtful yet burdened. "Sarkar, there are paths we can take, but none is easy. To save the zamindari, we must act decisively and employ a combination of measures. Allow me to outline them."

Javed gestured for him to continue, his jaw set in grim resolve.

"First, we could take on debt," Harinarayan began. "Loans are a double-edged sword, but they could provide immediate relief. The larger banking houses in Calcutta, as well as prominent moneylenders, might extend credit, though the terms would be harsh. Alternatively, local moneylenders are less stringent with formalities, but I wouldn't recommend that as their rates are exorbitant and their demands swift. Whoever we source our debt from, we would need to pledge parts of the zamindari as collateral, particularly the fertile lands they find most valuable. Failure to repay would be catastrophic, but the influx of funds could stabilise us in the short term."

Javed sighed deeply, the enormity of the risk weighing on him. "I do not relish placing our lands in jeopardy, Harinarayan-ji. What else can we do?"

The dewan turned to another ledger. "We could sell some of the less productive lands near the forest boundary. These tracts yield little but require significant resources to manage. A sale would inject much-needed capital, which could be reinvested in irrigation or relief measures for tenants. However, such a step would require careful negotiations to ensure we receive fair value."

Harinarayan further continued. "And then there is a third option. We could request a deferment of rents directly from the Company's agents. They are the ones now wielding real power over revenue collection, even though the Nawab remains the nominal authority. But this would come at a price - they may demand concessions in kind, a higher share of future yields, or even more intrusive oversight into our zamindari. The choice is fraught with risks, Sarkar."

Javed nodded slowly. "And the tenants? Can we not ease their rents to alleviate their suffering?"

Harinarayan sighed with melancholy. "A reduction in rents would be a noble gesture, Javed Sarkar, and it could foster goodwill among the people. However, given the state of the zamindari's finances, I do not see that as practicable."

Javed turned toward the window, his voice low but strained. "Then what good are we, Harinarayan-ji, if we cannot protect them?"

The dewan said nothing. His eyes lowered, his silence heavy with agreement he could not voice.

Javed rose and paced the room, his hands clasped behind his back. "So, you suggest a combination? Debt for immediate relief, land sales for medium-term stability, and possibly even requesting a deferment of rents to ease the immediate pressure on our finances?"

"Precisely, Sarkar," Harinarayan replied. "If chosen judiciously, these options form a balanced approach—one I believe can pull us out of this precarious situation."

Javed stopped his pacing and turned to face the dewan, his face resolute. "Prepare a plan, Harinarayan-ji. Detail how these measures can be implemented with minimal risk. We cannot afford missteps."

The dewan inclined his head. "As you command, Sarkar. I will have a comprehensive proposal ready by tomorrow. Together, we shall navigate this storm."

As Javed returned to his seat, the oil lamp cast a wavering glow, its flame bending with the draft. The road ahead remained steeped in uncertainty, and though Harinarayan's counsel offered structure, it was not comfort Javed felt, but the burden of choices he could no longer postpone.

• • •

Under the dense canopy of the sprawling banyan tree, the band of rebels stood in tense silence, their crude weapons clutched tightly in their hands. - rusted sickles, sharpened bamboo poles, iron rods, and farming knives; one man gripped a broken musket with no bayonet. The flaming torchlights in their hands cast wavering shadows across hardened faces - farmers, artisans, and labourers who had once bowed to their oppressors but now stood ready to fight. Sarfaraz Hussain moved among them, his voice calm but commanding as he issued final instructions.

Under his leadership, the villagers had already struck at revenue convoys, raided British storehouses, and overrun a police outpost deep in the countryside. But tonight's strike was different, it would cut deeper. It was a direct challenge to the zamindars, the local pillars of British rule, whose silence and scorn had bled the villagers dry.

"The zamindar's granaries are filled with grain stolen from our people," he said, his sharp gaze sweeping over the assembled fighters. "Tonight, we take it back. Move swiftly, strike hard, and retreat at the first sign of trouble. Our strength is in the shadows."

A young man, Rafiq, barely in his twenties, stepped forward hesitantly. "But, Sarfaraz bhai, what if they're waiting for us? What if they've set a trap?"

For the briefest moment, something tightened behind Sarfaraz's eyes - a flicker of the very doubt the boy had voiced. He felt it coil in his chest, sharp and familiar. But he could not let it show. Not now.

His gaze held steady, his voice calm but firm. "Then we move like water. If they've set a trap, we find the cracks. Trust your instincts. Trust each other. That's how we survive - and win."

Gauri tightened the cloth around her knife. "We've survived worse," she muttered. "At least this time, we strike under the cover of night."

The rebels did not follow Sarfaraz because he was louder or braver. They followed because he had shown them another way - a way to fight and still live. He had no uniform, no title, just a plan that made sense. Hit fast. Disappear faster. Use the land, use the night, trust no one who might think you are expendable.

As the moonlight filtered through the trees, the rebels advanced silently toward the zamindar's estate, nestled amidst thick groves of mango trees. Sarfaraz led from the front, fear thudding in his chest, resolve holding his stride firm. The scent of ripe mangoes mixed incongruously with the tension of the moment. He motioned for the group to stop as they reached the estate's perimeter, a high stone wall partially obscured by foliage.

"Kumar, Abdul chacha" he whispered, pointing to two wiry men, "scout ahead and signal if it's clear."

The two men nodded and slipped into the shadows. Minutes passed like hours before they returned with a thumbs-up. Sarfaraz gestured for the others to follow, and they moved swiftly but quietly toward their target.

The granary loomed ahead, its imposing wooden doors secured with a heavy iron lock. Sarfaraz turned to an older man carrying a rusted crowbar. "Mohan kaka, your turn."

Mohan nodded, his hands trembling slightly as he pried at the lock. The sharp creak of iron against wood made several rebels glance nervously around. Finally, the lock gave way with a resounding snap.

"Take only what we can carry," Sarfaraz instructed. "Leave the rest for the others to find later."

Suddenly, a sharp whistle pierced the night.

"An ambush!" someone in the party cried out in desperation as Company sepoys led by a British officer burst from their hiding spots, muskets raised. One sepoy - barely more than a boy, his torn sleeve flapping as he shouted in Urdu - fired blindly before a stone struck him down. Chaos erupted as gunfire shattered the stillness of the night.

"Retreat! Into the trees!" Sarfaraz bellowed, brandishing a staff he had fashioned from a sturdy branch. The rebels scattered, their rudimentary weapons no match for the sudden gunfire. Sarfaraz stayed at the rear, urging stragglers into the shadows. A musket ball tore past him, grazing his shoulder - a flash of heat, then pain. He stumbled but kept moving, weaving through the undergrowth.

Behind him, screams rang out – some bullets had found their mark. He turned briefly to see Abdul - the farmer who had lost everything to the indigo planter Wickham - collapse to the ground, clutching his chest.

The ragged group reached the safety of a secluded clearing, their faces pale, breaths laboured. But two men did not make their way back. Several more bled quietly into the grass, unsure whether they would last the night.

Sarfaraz moved quickly, dropping to his knees beside the nearest man. "Press here," he told one rebel, guiding his shaking hands to a wound in the man's thigh. He tore a strip from his own tunic, wrapping it tight around another's arm.

"Keep them awake," he urged. "Talk to them. Stop the bleeding first, prayers can come later."

His shoulder still burned, but he pushed the pain aside. The others were watching, and in moments like this, even hope needed tending.

A boy no older than fifteen sat beside his wounded brother, holding his hand tightly, whispering a lullaby their mother used to sing. Sarfaraz watched them, something sharp catching in his throat.

Tonight, they had suffered a setback. Some had even paid the ultimate price. But in the hollow left by failure, something remained - a refusal to let it be the end. And in that moment, with dawn still far off, that had to be enough.

• • •

The echoes of the muezzin's call still lingered in the air as Javed Hussain and Mozammel Khan stepped out of the Katara Masjid.

The grand mosque now bore marks of sullen neglect - its once-pristine white walls dulled with grime, its courtyard littered with stray leaves that no caretaker bothered to sweep. The fragrance of fresh jasmine, once a familiar companion to the faithful, had long since faded, replaced by the pungent staleness of unwashed bodies.

Mozammel adjusted his cap, his expression grim as they descended the stone steps into the street. Now beggars lined its edges, their thin hands outstretched, pleading for alms.

Mozammel broke the hush first. "Do you remember, Javed? We once stood here, right after the Jumma prayers, the city's heart still beating strong, merchants haggling in the bazaars, poets reciting verses in shaded courtyards."

Javed let out a bitter chuckle. "That was a different world, my friend. A world where we still believed in honour, where we still believed we had a say in our fate. Now look at us - pawns in a game we never truly understood."

Mozammel sighed. "The masjid was fuller then. The people, hopeful. The city, alive. Look at it now." He gestured around them.

Javed's expression darkened as he glanced at a group of British officers loitering near the bazaar entrance, their eyes scanning the crowd with the arrogance of conquerors. "I believed we were ridding Bengal of tyranny," he muttered. "Instead, we have shackled it to foreign masters."

Mozammel nodded. "Mir Jafar's court is a mockery of governance. His throne is built upon the blood of his lord, and now even the Company sees him for the fool he is. They use him, just as they used us."

Javed clenched his jaw. "And what of the people? The sepoys have turned to looting for their wages, traders are crushed under impossible taxes, and famine lurks at our doorstep." He paused, his voice quieter but no less pained. "At least under Siraj, the land was still our own."

Mozammel shook his head. "That is the cruelty of our fate, my friend. We did not know what we had until it was gone. Now, the British feast on Bengal's riches while the Nawab prances about in his silks, free of care to the ruin around him."

Javed let out a long breath. "Rebellions blaze like wildfires

– Midnapur, Purnea, Patna," he said, his voice edged with both despair and a strange, distant resolve. "Yet none of these uprisings are strong enough to reclaim Bengal as a whole. We need someone to unite us, someone who can rally all of Bengal against the British."

For a moment, despite the sorrow in his heart, he felt a flicker of secret pride - whispers had reached him of one of the rebellions being led by none other than his son, Sarfaraz. Ghost of Mirganj, they called him. Though father and son had not spoken in years, Javed had heard tales of Sarfaraz's courage, his defiance against the Company's chokehold. A fire kindled deep within him, though he dared not let Mozammel see it - he could not afford for such pride show, especially when word of Sarfaraz's actions could attract unwanted attention.

Mozammel placed a firm hand on his friend's shoulder. "Perhaps the winds will shift again. Perhaps another will rise, someone with the strength and wisdom to reclaim what was lost. And when that time comes, we must be ready."

"A leader," Javed murmured, eyes distant. "We can only hope he comes before there is nothing left to save."

The two men continued walking in silence. A tailor, his shop nearly empty, sat cross-legged at his doorstep, stitching in the fading light. A frail child clung to his mother's shawl as she haggled for a few grains of rice.

Then came the sound- distant at first, but growing louder - the steady beat of drums, the tinkling of anklets, the laughter of men untouched by ruin. Their gaze flickered toward a palanquin passing in the distance, its gold-threaded curtains shielding the figure within. A procession followed - musicians, dancers, and attendants bearing silver trays piled high with delicacies. The scent of rosewater and musk clung to the air.

Javed let out a dry chuckle, shaking his head. "And there he goes - the man who sold a kingdom for a throne. The treasury bleeds dry, the soldiers go unpaid, yet Mir Jafar parades himself like a prince of fables."

Mozammel's lips curled in disdain. "A Nawab who lacks both wisdom and honour. He feasts while famine devours the land. He adorns himself in pearls, while whispers of mutiny spread through his own ranks. Even the British, who placed him there, mock him behind his back."

Javed's exhale was heavy, his voice laced with bitterness. "Bengal was once ruled by men who built empires, who governed with strength and purpose. Now, we are ruled by a puppet, dancing to foreign tunes and mistaking indulgence for power." He watched the palanquin drift further into the winding streets, its opulence fading from view.

Mozammel's gaze hardened. "No usurper can sit easy on a stolen throne. The winds of change are coming. And when they do, even Mir Jafar will learn that no amount of luxury can silence the cries of the people."

• • •

Extract from a private letter by Robert Clive to his wife, Margaret Clive

Calcutta, February 1760

My dearest Margaret,

By the time you read this, I shall be at sea - returning not merely as a soldier, but as a man transformed by fortune. Bengal has been generous beyond all expectation. The Company's success has brought me a reward of **£210,000**[4] *- fitting recompense, I believe, for the burdens borne and victories secured.*

Let no one mistake this for mere conquest. It is enterprise. Discipline, resolve, and a willingness to act where others hesitated - that is what won us Plassey. That is what broke the back of native despotism and set this province on the proper course. The French have been swept aside, the Dutch cowed, and the Nawabs... tamed.

---

[4] Equivalent to £30 million in today's money

In London, I shall take my seat not as a supplicant, but as a statesman. Let the critics whisper of bribes and plunder. They do not understand the future we are building. Bengal is not simply a territory - it is a treasury, and we have learned how to make it sing.

You will see, my love, that history will vindicate the architects of dominion.

Yours always,

In victory and vision,

Robert

• • •

The winter sun hung low over the Bengal plains, its feeble warmth doing little to chase away the chill that clung to the damp air. Sergeant Thomas Hawke rode slowly along the rutted dirt path, his horse's hooves squelching in the mud. His crimson uniform coat, with its freshly sewn silver stripes denoting his recent promotion, sat heavily on his shoulders. The weight of the Company's expectations and his own conscience seemed no less tangible.

Thomas had fought valiantly at Plassey three years ago, rising from the ranks of a private to the coveted position of sergeant. He was proud of what he had achieved – proud of his service, of his country, and of the order that the Company promised to bring to Bengal. But the countryside he had been riding through told a different story.

The fields were barren, the irrigation channels choked with silt. Villages, once vibrant with the hum of life, were now eerily silent. Skeletal cattle stood tethered to posts, their dull eyes seeming to mirror the despair of their owners. Everywhere, the signs of economic ruin were stark. It was no secret that the Company had imposed crippling taxes and appropriated vast wealth, compounded by the ravages of the private traders under its indulgent eyes, but Thomas had never seen the true extent of the devastation until now.

He had passed three villages like this on his ride. But this one broke something in him.

He slowed his horse as he approached a small gathering of villagers. Their faces, sunken and hollow, bore the unmistakable marks of hunger. An elderly man, leaning on a crude wooden staff, stepped forward cautiously. His expression flickered between fear and curiosity.

"Sahib," the man greeted, bowing low, his voice tinged with a hint of fear. "What brings you to our humble village?"

Thomas dismounted, his boots sinking into the damp earth. "I am here to see the land," he replied, his voice measured. "And its people."

The villagers exchanged wary glances. After a moment's hesitation, a younger man stepped forward, his words brimming with suppressed anger. "See the land, sahib? Then look around. I hope the hunger, disease, and sorrow will not miss your eyes. The land that once fed us now serves only to fill the coffers of Calcutta's sahibs."

The words struck Thomas like a lash. He had grown up believing in the honour of the British – their justice, their fairness. But here, those ideals seemed grotesquely inverted. He looked around at the gaunt faces, the crumbling huts, and the barren fields, each detail gnawing at his conscience. His faith in the Company's righteousness wavered under the weight of their suffering.

"Is it true, sahib," an old woman asked tremulously, "that your people promised prosperity when they came? Where is it now? All we see is ruin."

Thomas struggled to reply. What could he say? That their sacrifice was for the greater good? That the Company was building something grander than they could understand? Even to himself, the words sounded hollow.

As the villagers fell silent, their eyes fixed on him, Thomas felt a surge of shame. He was a soldier, a servant of the Company, yet these people saw him as a symbol of their oppressors. He had fought for their subjugation, and now he stood amidst their suffering, powerless to undo it. The weight of his uniform felt heavier now, as if each silver stripe mocked his complicity.

Taking a deep breath, he turned to the village head. "Come with me," he said quietly, leading the man aside.

From his coat, he pulled a leather pouch. It contained his pay for the month, the reward for his service to the Company. Holding it out, he said, "Take this. Use it for whatever the village needs most."

As he watched the headman's trembling hands close around the pouch, an image of Gulabi flashed in his mind - her fingertips stained with turmeric as she cooked chattering with him, the way she casually brushed a stray lock behind her ear while stirring the pot, and above all her boisterous laughter during their private moments. This land was not foreign to him anymore. Its pain was no longer distant.

The headman stared at the pouch in disbelief. "Sahib," he whispered, his voice trembling, "this... this is too much. You are too kind."

"It is not kindness," Thomas replied, his voice tight. "It is justice."

The headman dropped to his knees, clasping Thomas's hands in gratitude. "You have given us hope, sahib. May the gods bless you."

Thomas mounted his horse, feeling a strange mix of warmth and unease. As he rode away, the villagers' words echoed in his mind, mingling with his own doubts. His pride in British honour and the ideals he cherished had been deeply shaken. But even as he questioned the Company's motives, he could not escape the feeling that his small act of generosity would change nothing in the long run. The suffering of these people was too great, too entrenched. What was one man's donation compared to the vast machinery of exploitation that kept them bound?

Ahead, the sun was sinking into the horizon, its light fading into shadows. And in the growing darkness, Thomas found himself unable to reconcile his duty with his conscience.

• • •

The late monsoon mist clung low over Calcutta, the Hooghly's waters swollen and sluggish. Atop the Company's riverside headquarters, beneath the crumbling arches of a shaded veranda, two men stood in quiet frustration. One of them was Henry Vansittart, the newly appointed Governor of Bengal - on whose shoulders the weight of Bengal's affairs had squarely settled after Robert Clive had departed for England. His wig, meticulously powdered that morning, now wilted under the humid air, and a line of sweat trailed down his temple unnoticed. Fresh from London, Vansittart had arrived bearing the expectation that British authority in India had matured into a smooth apparatus - that he would inherit a clock wound tightly by Clive's victories. What he found instead was something altogether different: a kingdom run into the ground by a man they had once called an ally.

Standing beside him was Warren Hastings. Younger, leaner, and far less adorned in title or ceremony, Hastings - calm, composed, observant - lacked the Governor's rank but bore an air of sharper intellect. He spoke sparingly, yet when he did, the weight of his words often lingered long after.

They stood together, surveying the city that festered beneath their ambitions.

Mir Jafar. That name had once brought gleaming smiles to the boardrooms in London and Calcutta alike. He had been their prize - hoisted into power by the barrel of British muskets and the veiled hand of subterfuge. In return, he had promised rivers of tribute, limitless concessions, and a kingdom rendered docile to the Company's ambitions.

And at first, he delivered. The wealth of Bengal flowed freely into the Company's coffers, drawn from the lifeblood of its people. Yet even the richest province cannot survive relentless extraction. What had once seemed inexhaustible proved frighteningly finite. The initial torrent slowed to a trickle. Years of forced tribute and unchecked corruption had drained the land. And now, as the Company's appetite only grew, Mir Jafar's ability to feed it fell far short. What little remained was squandered in court intrigues and private luxuries, while his ministers bickered and his soldiers went unpaid.

To Vansittart, Mir Jafar's collapse was a disappointment - a failure to uphold the promises of Plassey. To Hastings, it was something more dangerous: a threat to the Company's entire design in Bengal.

In truth, Mir Jafar had become an embarrassment - a hollow puppet whose strings had grown tangled in his own incompetence. Political dissent rippled through his court. Zamindars, once placated by promises of stability, now bristled under the weight of disorder. Even the sepoys spoke in barely concealed tones of revolt. It was clear to both men: the Nawab, once so useful, had outlived his purpose.

Hastings, ever the strategist, had already begun thinking beyond the disorder.

It was he who first named the alternative - Mir Qasim.

At first mention, Vansittart had dismissed the idea with a wave. Qasim was too mild, too quiet, too untested. A man of noble Persian descent, yes, but without reputation, without rank, and without the assertiveness one might expect from a ruler. What could such a man possibly offer?

But Hastings had seen something more.

He had read the letters from Patna administrators, heard accounts from Company agents posted near Qasim's estates.

Though Mir Jafar's son-in-law, Mir Qasim was cut from a different cloth. Where Jafar dithered, Qasim calculated. Though he lacked a warrior's laurels, he possessed an administrator's mind - shrewd, disciplined, and educated in the classical Persian tradition. He had impressed both officers and civilians with his integrity and had the backing of provincial elites and zamindars who longed for order over chaos.

To Hastings, that was enough. The Company did not need a lion on the throne - only a steward who would govern competently, quietly, and without presuming to rule.

Vansittart, under the weight of mounting disorder, found himself persuaded. Hastings' arguments were cold, precise, and difficult to refute. It was not loyalty they needed, but capability. Not grandeur, but predictability.

And so, as the mists of Calcutta thickened and the sounds of the city echoed faintly below, a quiet agreement began to form between the two men. An old ally would be cast aside, and in his place, a new figurehead would be seated - a man whose ambition could be contained, and whose gratitude would remain chained to those who raised him. No voice from the streets below would rise to challenge their decision; Bengal's fate would be rewritten by two men and a muttered agreement.

• • •

Mir Qasim entered the Governor's residence with confident, deliberate strides. There was nothing showy about him - just a quiet resolve that filled the space as he crossed the arched threshold. He was not tall, nor imposing, but his bearing held the assurance of a man who had waited patiently for the world to notice him.

At the head of a polished mahogany table sat Henry Vansittart. Across from him, Warren Hastings sat poised, his eyes keenly observing the young man now standing before them. Mir Qasim, dressed in elegant but restrained attire, was fully aware that this meeting held the key to his ambitions.

Vansittart gestured for Mir Qasim to sit, his voice calm but firm. "Mir Qasim, you know why we've called you here. Bengal is in a precarious state, and the Company finds itself unable to sustain operations under the current regime. Your father-in-law, Mir Jafar, has failed to govern effectively."

"Indeed, Your Excellency," Mir Qasim replied, his tone steady.

"The Nawab's maladministration has plunged Bengal into chaos. The treasury is depleted, debts are mounting, and the zamindars are restless. His inability to maintain order has left both the province and the Company in dire straits."

Hastings leaned forward, his gaze narrowing. "You speak of these failures with clarity, Qasim. But tell us, if the reins of power were to pass to you, what would you do differently?"

Mir Qasim's response was deliberate and measured. "To address the immediate crisis, I propose ceding the territories of Burdwan, Midnapur, and Chittagong to the Company. These lands are fertile and rich in resources, sufficient to finance the armies of both the Nawab and the British. By managing these territories directly, the Company can ensure a steady flow of income, eliminating the financial strain caused by Murshidabad's debt."

Vansittart's eyebrows rose slightly, impressed by the audacity of the plan. "An intriguing solution," he remarked. "These territories are vital, and their revenue potential is undeniable. But such a transfer of power is bound to stir unrest among the zamindars. How do you propose managing their reactions?"

Mir Qasim nodded, prepared for the question. "Your Excellency, many of the zamindars are already alienated by Mir Jafar's negligence. They are not fools - they seek a ruler who can preserve their privileges while restoring order. I have corresponded discreetly with several among them. With clear assurances of stability, they will fall in line."

Vansittart leaned back in his chair, a small smile playing on his lips. "Your proposal is bold, Qasim, and it addresses both the Company's financial difficulties and Bengal's instability. But let us speak plainly - what assurances do you offer to secure our support?"

Mir Qasim had anticipated this question too - and came armed with more tangible, personal assurances. He met the Governor's gaze unflinchingly, his voice calm but with a sharpened edge beneath the courtesy. "I understand the realities of power, Your Excellency.... To cement this partnership, I am prepared to offer £50,000 to you personally and £150,000 to your council. These funds will demonstrate my commitment to the Company's interests."

He paused, then added, with quiet assurance. "The funds will be drawn from private sources already pledged to my cause - men of commerce and standing who understand that Bengal's future depends on competent leadership. They know their fortunes are tied to stability, and they are willing to stake it on me."

Vansittart inhaled slightly, the sum - £200,000 - pressing against his composure like a tide testing a seawall. Finally, he stood, his decision made. "Gentlemen," he declared, glancing between Hastings and Qasim, "it is clear that Bengal cannot endure further under Mir Jafar's rule. His incompetence has become a burden too great to bear. Qasim's vision offers a path forward - a second revolution, if you will, to restore order and prosperity."

Hastings nodded in agreement, his voice calm yet resolute. "It seems the time has come to act. The Company's future in Bengal depends on decisive leadership, and Qasim, you have shown the will and strategy necessary for the task."

As the meeting concluded, the first steps toward deposition were quietly agreed upon. Company agents would soon approach key officers in the Nawab's army, gauging loyalties under the guise of inquiry. A discreet message would be drafted for Major Caillaud to position troops near Murshidabad, under the pretence of restoring order.

Hastings followed Qasim's retreating figure with narrowed eyes.

"A pliable ruler," Vansittart murmured.

Hastings did not answer. In truth, he was not certain whether they had just hired a steward - or set the stage for something far more dangerous.

• • •

THE TRAITOR'S BARGAIN

In October 1760, as the monsoon wind carried a low, uneasy growl through the streets of Murshidabad, the air inside the palace was thick with incense - and fear. Servants scurried in near silence. Somewhere in the distance, a drumbeat throbbed, steady and insistent, not ceremonial but furious.

Mir Jafar stood alone in the corridor outside the Diwan-e-Khas, the palace's inner sanctum, shoulders slumped, one hand resting on the gilded balustrade. From beyond the palace gates came a rising din - soldiers chanting, shouting, slamming spearbutts against the ground with the menacing rhythm of a storm about to break.

He had delayed their pay again. There were too many mouths, too few coins. Promises made in better days had curdled into threats.

By late afternoon, the palace was surrounded. Guards on the parapets gripped their muskets, eyes fixed on the swelling crowd below. As the sun dipped toward the horizon, the first stone struck the outer wall. Moments later, chaos erupted. Soldiers scaled the ramparts with crude ladders and hoarse battle cries. Attendants and guards scrambled for cover as chunks of loosened stonework crashed down from above. Officers stationed near the main gate were dragged from their horses. Servants peered anxiously from within as the sounds of fighting rose just beyond the walls. Royal banners, once flying proudly from the ramparts, were torn down and trampled into the dust. The mutiny - long simmering - had finally found its flame.

It had been weeks since the Company had quietly chosen their next Nawab. Still, they had waited - for a spark, an unrest, any chaos that could serve as pretext. That spark came now, in the form of mutiny.

Mir Jafar paced the mirrored chamber of his upper quarters, the clamour from below echoing off glass and marble. "Where is the palace commander?" he barked. No one answered. The guards had melted away.

He moved to the latticed window. The uproar below, muffled but relentless, pressed against the glass like a rising tide. Then something shifted. In the street beyond the palace walls - *he saw it*. A body, limp and broken, dragged by the heels. Not just any body. Siraj. Caked in blood and dust, head lolling side to side. He staggered back from the window, bile rising.

A sharp scuffle of sandals broke through the din - urgent, approaching fast. Then, a thud. A muffled cry. Silence.

Moments later, Mir Qasim – his son-in-law - appeared in the doorway, a streak of dust on his robe, a smear of red trailing down his forearm.

"Nawab Sahib," he said, breath tight, "the outer court has fallen. I had to force my way through a side gate - barely made it. There's no time."

Jafar turned, eyes hollowed by disbelief. "You risked that madness to reach me?"

"You are my family," Qasim replied. "And the Nawab. Your safety is paramount - whatever happens to me."

He stepped aside with a hand gesture. "Come. I've arranged a boat at the eastern ghat."

As Jafar followed, shaken, he never noticed that every turn they took was clear of debris, every sentry along the way stood back without question - men loyal not to him, but to the man now guiding him into the dark. The mutiny was real. The rescue was theatre.

Outside, in the shadowed rear passage behind the stables, a small detachment waited. Major Caillaud, his face carefully blank, offered Qasim a silent nod. The Nawab, trembling now, was hurried into a covered palanquin. "To Calcutta," Qasim said, voice low. "The English will keep you safe."

As the palanquin lifted, Jafar's eyes drifted toward the direction of the main gates, just visible through the archway ahead. "Yes," he murmured. "They always have."

Down the riverbank, under the cover of darkness, a Company boat awaited - its oars quiet, its direction certain. The palanquin was lifted aboard.

As the oarsmen pulled away from the shore, Jafar sat silently, watching Murshidabad recede into mist. After a while, he spoke, almost to himself.

"My son-in-law… he has taken my place, hasn't he?"

Major Caillaud said nothing, his features unreadable.

"The English placed me on the masnad," Jafar said, voice rising. "Now they cast me aside like a dog turned from the gate. But I kept my engagements - every one! I demand to speak to Clive Bahadur. He gave me his word. He will not have forgotten!"

Still silence.

"Then send me to Mecca," he added bitterly. "I will not endure this shame."

The boat drifted on, his words trailing behind in the wake.

Back at the palace, Mir Qasim climbed the steps to the throne room. The old courtiers hovered in the galleries and corridors - watching, waiting, weighing his strength. He seated himself on the throne, calm as stone, and issued the first orders of his reign: suppress all palace gossip, secure the treasury, and prepare a proclamation.

By morning, notices were posted across the city. The Nawab, it said, had abdicated for the good of the realm. Order had been restored.

In Calcutta, Mir Jafar would be granted a modest house and a meagre pension.

No explanation. No pilgrimage. Just a slow, state-sponsored oblivion.

• • •

THE ASHES OF A NATION

Calcutta - October 1762

A lean flame guttered in the oil lamp, its glow falling uneven across the paper-strewn desk. The night air, thick with the scent of the Ganges, seeped through the cracks in the chamber's shutters. A solitary figure hunched over the desk, the quill in his hand hesitating over the parchment. Warren Hastings, young but already wearied by the tangled loyalties and ambitions that shaped Bengal, dipped his quill into the inkwell and began writing.

To my honoured father,

It is with a burdened heart that I write to you today, for the state of our affairs in Bengal is not as we had once envisioned. The man we so carefully placed upon the throne more than a year ago, Mir Qasim, has proven himself to be no mere instrument in our hands, but a ruler of his own mind and mettle. Where his predecessor, Mir Jafar, was pliant, indulgent, and easily led, Qasim is a man of discipline, determination, and, dare I say, dangerous ambition.

From the moment he ascended the throne, it was clear he would not bow to our expectations. I recall our initial meetings with him – polite, measured, but with a resolve in his eyes that should have given us greater pause. His first actions as Nawab were swift and decisive, paying off rebellious sepoys from his own coffers and rooting out the corruption that had festered under Jafar's feeble rule. The treasuries we once expected to remain open to us have now become closely guarded and cautiously administered.

We had believed his need for our support would ensure his compliance, yet the man has outmanoeuvred us at every turn. The city of Murshidabad, once the heart of Bengal's power, he has abandoned for Munger – a fortress near Patna beyond our easy reach. The symbolic seat of governance matters little when the true reins of control are now clenched within his fist.

Yet geography was only the beginning of his defiance. In matters of commerce, he has proven no less bold. Our merchants cry foul at his latest decree – abolishing all internal trade duties. What may appear a gesture of fairness to the native trading classes is, in truth, a direct challenge to our privileges. No longer do we alone enjoy the rights of duty-free commerce, and the flow of wealth we so carefully ensured is now threatened. His mind, ever calculating, seeks to level the field, but at what cost? Worse, he sharpens his tools not just for governance but for war.

Father, this is not the rule of a puppet, but the work of a sovereign who will not suffer interference lightly. Even now, he strengthens his military with European instructors, trains his men in modern warfare, and has begun establishing small foundries and stockpiles in and around Munger. The bloated armies of old are gone, replaced by a lean, disciplined force – one that could, in time, stand against us.

Yet, for all his ambition and capability, it is said that Qasim has turned Bengal into a province thick with suspicion and fear. His bid to tighten his grip on power has unleashed an unholy storm – an increasingly repressive regime where whispers suggest that informers abound, and trust has grown scarce. Rumours speak of the Nawab's growing unease, of a climate in which loyalty is demanded, and even a hint of collusion with the Company invites swift and brutal retribution. Those close to his court are said to live in fear of his unpredictable wrath.

We are at a precipice. Our presence here, once secured through careful manipulation and a compliant Nawab, now finds itself in question. Should diplomacy fail, should Qasim's defiance turn into outright hostility, the consequences will be grave. The Company's ambitions cannot suffer a ruler who places his land's interests above our own. And yet, I cannot deny *the reluctant admiration I feel for this man, for he governs not as a mere usurper but as one who believes in the sovereignty of his realm.*

The winds in Bengal are shifting, Father. I fear that before long, the calm will break into a storm.

Your dutiful son,

Warren Hastings

He folded the parchment, sealing it with wax as he leaned back in his chair. Outside, the night was still. But beyond the river, the restless hum of Calcutta stirred - merchants grumbling of lost privileges, Company men debating their next move, and the distant clang of ships unloading cargo. A city on edge, awaiting what the dawn might bring.

• • •

Mir Qasim paced in his chamber, his fists clenched tightly, the veins on his forearms taut with the searing indignation of a man wronged yet again. The English traders, he reminded himself again, were no longer merchants; they had transformed themselves into rulers - rapacious, predatory, and shamelessly so - in all but name.

The immediate cause of the Nawab's agitation was the audience that he had just concluded in this chamber with Rahmat Khan, a senior official in his administration overseeing revenue collection in Patna. Rahmat had stood trembling before him, his face bruised and his turban askew.

"Speak, Rahmat Khan," Mir Qasim urged, his voice calm but tinged with an undercurrent of concern. "Tell me what has happened."

Rahmat Khan bowed deeply, wincing as pain shot through his ribs. "Nawab Sahib, it is the English at their factory in Patna. Under the orders of Ellis, they... seized and dragged me out while I was inspecting the warehouses." He paused, his voice faltering.

Mir Qasim's eyes narrowed, his hands clenching the edge of the divan. "They dared do that to a senior official of mine?" he said, voice low with fury. "In our own jurisdiction?"

"They paraded me through the streets like a common criminal," Rahmat Khan continued, his voice breaking. "Their men… they beat me with sticks, tore my clothes, and spat on me. They called me a thief, a leech on their trade. All while the common folk stood watching by the roadside. It was a humiliation beyond words, Nawab Sahib."

The Nawab's jaw tightened as he rose to his feet, his slight frame taut with tension. The intensity in his gaze made Rahmat Khan lower his eyes in deference. "And Ellis? The Company's man in charge at Patna?" Mir Qasim demanded, his voice sharp and rising. "Did he partake in this atrocity?"

Rahmat Khan nodded hesitantly. "He did not lay a hand on me, but he watched it all, Nawab Sahib. He grinned widely as his men carried out his orders. He made it clear that they answer to no one but their Company."

Mir Qasim's eyes blazed with fury. "What else? Speak freely, Rahmat".

Rahmat Khan knelt, his head bowed low. "Nawab Sahib, they have no fear of us. They flaunt their power, their muskets and their arrogance. They even have the temerity to undermine the authority of the Nawab of Bengal at every turn. The people… they whisper that the English are the true rulers of Bengal."

Qasim stopped in his tracks, his expression darkening. "Enough," he said, his voice trembling with restrained anger. "Rahmat Khan, you have suffered a grave injustice. Rest now. You will be cared for. But know this - the insult they have dealt you is an insult to me, to Bengal itself. And it will not go unanswered."

Rahmat Khan bowed again, gratitude flickering in his weary eyes. "Thank you, Nawab Sahib. Your justice will bring hope to all who suffer under their oppression."

Mir Qasim continued pacing his chamber. Was this their idea of free trade - or open plunder masked as commerce? Across Bengal, the Company bled the land dry. These were no merchants; they were predators, emboldened by power without check. His own traders were forced to sell their goods for a quarter of their worth, silenced by threats and violence. And the farmers - worse still - robbed of their grain and paid in baubles, goods claimed to be worth one rupee, but worth five in truth. How were his people to keep from starving, let alone preserve any dignity?

His mind turned to the sepoys - *their* sepoys, he corrected himself bitterly - fanning out across the countryside with unchecked license. No longer guardians of order, but enforcers of fear. They raided storehouses in the name of Company dues, demanded free lodging from peasants, seized carts of grain meant for market. Villages emptied at their approach; markets fell silent, shutters drawn hastily. All this, and not one among them had to worry about reprimand.

And what of his officers - men like Rahmat Khan? Upright, entrusted with upholding the Nawab's realm, now stripped of all authority. Beaten, humiliated, reduced to pitiable emblems of British contempt. The Nawab's sovereignty, once inviolate, now stood as an abject mockery.

His reforms - moving the capital to Munger, a northern province of the Bengal Subah, rebuilding the army - felt like whispers lost in the roar of the Company's greed. Every effort eroded - his laws ignored, his people left to suffer.

And Ellis… he spat out the name like a poisonous venom. William Ellis, the Chief Factor at the Patna factory had brazenly chipped away at the Nawab's sovereignty, imprisoning his officers, plundering his subjects, treating Bengal as personal fiefdom.

He remembered his first inspection tour to Patna after taking the throne - how the British officers received him not with deference, but with stiff civility, thinly veiled smirks behind powdered faces. Ellis had not bowed; he had merely nodded, as if to a minor official. The message was clear: Bengal may have changed Nawabs, but the leash remained in the Company's hands.

But Mir Qasim was not the one to be fazed by petty discourtesies from the Company's officials. He had resolved to play the long game, and made it a point to receive the Company's senior men with measured grace - offering pleasantries, masking contempt with courtly ease. Let them think him pliable. Let them think he was grateful. Let them even think he was another Mir Jafar. But even then, behind the silk of his words, he had sworn to sever the strings they had fastened to Bengal's throat.

• • •

The early morning heat had begun to settle over Patna. At the Company's fortified trading house, a punkah flapped lazily above, moved by the invisible hand of a sweating servant outside. William Ellis sat alone at his broad desk, a heavy chair pulled back just enough to let his boots rest imperiously on a nearby stool. His scarlet waistcoat was half-unbuttoned, and a tumbler of watered brandy already waited at his side.

His immediate attention was a letter that had just been placed on his desk by one of the servants. His brow furrowed at the seal - the wax bore the impression of the House of Jagat Seth.

Ellis allowed himself a thin smile. *The* Jagat Seth - kingmakers once, now perhaps little more than trembling bookkeepers, hedging their bets in whichever court still found them useful. It was more their ledgers than Clive's musket that had brought Siraj down at Plassey, he reflected, and for a time, they had basked in the illusion of a partnership. But Mir Jafar had proven too brittle, and Mir Qasim too bold. The latter had abolished internal duties, stripping the Seths of lucrative tolls and levies, then carved trade routes out of their hands, displacing them as Bengal's traditional financiers and logistical powerbrokers.

Now he commanded every rupee himself, bypassing the old banking houses.

Now, Ellis mused, they were scrambling once more, scurrying back to the side with the heavier guns.

Ellis cracked the seal with a knife and unfolded the letter in one swift motion.

To Mr. William Ellis, Esq.
Chief Factor at Patna
For His Eyes Only

Sir,

I write to you not as a merchant to a magistrate, but as a man who has watched the current of Bengal bend unnaturally, and now seeks to right its course.

Nawab Mir Qasim, in his haste to centralise all authority and wealth, has upended the delicate balance that long enabled Bengal's prosperity. His abolishment of internal duties, his state-controlled trade ventures, and his steady marginalisation of independent financiers have sounded a quiet death knell for Bengal's mercantile freedoms.

But the Nawab cannot be reasoned with, nor restrained by negotiation. He has made it plain that Bengal will be ruled by his will alone, regardless of the cost. In such times, correction must come not through counsel, but through might. And in Bengal today, only English arms can deliver such might - if they are given the means.

To that end, I place at your disposal a credit line of fifteen lakh rupees, to be routed through trusted agents in Patna and Calcutta. Should arms need to be procured, allegiances secured, or incentives delivered to wavering sepoy commanders, such transactions can be made in utmost discretion. English leadership, tempered by mercantile reason, remains Bengal's best hope for stability - and mine.

Should you accept this proposition, the means are already in place. But I ask one thing in return: once this letter has been read, let it be consigned to flames. Lest it fall into untrustworthy hands.

In quiet confidence,

Mehtab Rai
For the House of Jagat Seth

Ellis exhaled slowly, lips curling into the beginnings of a smile. He leaned back in his chair, holding the letter aloft like a prize freshly won.

"Just as I thought," he murmured to the empty room, "even the mighty banker begins to sweat under Qasim's grip".

That settled it. If men like Mehtab Rai were ready to gamble their fortunes, then Ellis saw no reason to hold his own hand back. Calcutta might hesitate, might weigh letters and dispatches and wait for some imagined diplomatic pretext. But here in Patna, he had the men, the guns, and now the money. Waiting was what had let Qasim entrench himself in the first place.

And entrench himself he had. The Nawab's foundries clinked day and night with the forging of arms. His sepoys drilled with growing discipline. His coffers filled with coin stripped from men who had built fortunes under the Seths - and freighted wealth for the Company. If Bengal was to be saved from slipping into native despotism, it would not be by words. It would be by force.

Ellis rose, spine straight, eyes gleaming with imagined victory. He could already picture the streets of Patna cleared of Qasim's banners, the muskets of his sepoys surrendered, the Nawab humiliated and worse. And if the cost of that glory was paid in Seth's rupees, so much the better. Ellis would pay him back in saltpetre and obedience.

His gaze drifted back to the last line of the letter, where Mehtab Rai had asked for the paper to meet flame.

Ellis gave a slow, cold smile. "No, sir," he muttered. "This stays with me. A card to play - not to burn."

He walked to the cabinet behind his desk, opened a lower compartment, and pulled aside a ledger to reveal a false-backed drawer lined in oilskin. The letter slid in without a wrinkle. He locked the drawer with practiced ease, then stood for a moment, listening to the rising din of sepoy drills outside.

The letter was safe. What came next, he would set alight himself.

• • •

Fear had begun to settle over Bengal like dust - fine, invisible, and everywhere. In market lanes and palace halls alike, voices dropped and eyes shifted before words were spoken. Everyday conversations grew guarded; letters burned more quickly. Trust grew scarce, even within families. It was whispered that the Nawab had begun placing informers in the households of men who held sway - landlords, moneylenders, court clerks. Nothing official was declared, but people understood: the rules had changed, and not knowing them could tempt disappearance.

Amid this suffocating climate, Mozammel Khan had withdrawn to his zamindari not far from Munger. The once-prosperous estate, now fraying under the Nawab's relentless demands, housed his wife Hamida, four adult children, and six grandchildren. Yet within its worn walls and fading murals, the strain was unmistakable - voices spoke in low tones, meals were taken in silence, and even the youngest had learned not to ask questions.

One evening, as the last of the daylight bled through the latticework and the estate fell into a hush broken only by distant cattle bells and the soft rustle of leaves in the courtyard, Hamida stepped into their private chamber and quietly shut the door behind her. For a moment, she stood watching Mozammel, who reclined on a divan, his eyes fixed on some distant corner of the room. Then, with measured steps, she crossed the floor and sat across from him. Her gaze steady, her voice low, she broke the silence.

"Miyan, we must talk."

Mozammel looked up. "What is it, Hamida?"

She leaned forward, her hands clasped tightly in her lap. "The estate is crumbling under the weight of the Nawab's levies and inspections. The harvest was poor, and his men show no mercy. Every month, I see more despair in the faces of our tenants. How much longer can we keep this household afloat?"

Mozammel exhaled deeply, his fingers drumming lightly against the divan. "You're not wrong," he said after a moment. "The situation is dire. But these are dangerous times, Hamida. Even hinting at our hardship - or appealing for leniency - could draw attention we cannot afford."

Hamida's brow furrowed, and she leaned closer, her voice dropping to a whisper. "I know, Miyan. But what worries me more… is Inzamam."

Mozammel stiffened, the fingers on his knee freezing mid-tap. His voice, when it came, was tight. "What about him?"

Her voice trembled slightly. "I have seen him, Miyan. Sneaking out at night, slipping into the shadows like a boy playing at being a man. He thinks no one notices, but I do. I've caught fragments - talk of standing up, of not bending to the Nawab's yoke' He's been meeting with Birju, the potter's eldest - whose uncle was jailed in last year's raid. I don't know everything they speak of, but I know it's dangerous."

She paused. "Inzamam is young and reckless. He believes he's doing something righteous. But he does not see the risk - not just to himself, but to this entire household."

Mozammel's brows knit together. "Hamida, are you certain? These things can have serious repercussions."

She fixed him with an unwavering look. "I am his mother. I know what I have seen and heard. If Mir Qasim's spies catch wind of this… You know what they do to families accused of treason. We cannot let him bring that upon himself and the rest of us."

Mozammel nodded slowly, his expression unreadable. 'You're right. I'll will speak with him, but we must tread carefully, Even within these walls, words can find ears we cannot trust."

Hamida leaned back, her breath unsteady as she pulled her shawl tighter around her shoulders. "Do it soon, Miyan," she murmured, her voice barely rising above the faint stirring of wind outside. "Before his fire consumes everything we've built."

Hamida rose and made her way toward the door. As she opened it, she nearly collided with Shaikh Umar - the newest servant in the household, a broomstick in hand and the vacant look of someone thought to be a little slow-witted. His gaze stayed fixed on the floor, posture meek as always. She waved him off without a second glance, and he shuffled away in silence.

As Hamida took her leave, Mozammel remained seated in silence, the lamplight casting slow, unsteady shadows across his face. Outside, the night deepened. Once the hush of slumber had settled over the mansion, he moved cautiously through the labyrinthine corridors of his mansion.

He slipped out of the mansion, thanking the night for being moonless. The silence of the night was broken only by the distant hoot of an owl, as he trod carefully along a narrow dirt path leading to the edge of a dense bamboo grove. His heart pounded. He paused briefly, glancing over his shoulder to ensure he had not been followed.

Some distance behind, half-hidden in the undergrowth, Shaikh Umar shrank back into the dark - just in time. He had followed Mozammel all the way from the courtyard, careful never to let his footsteps carry.

At the grove's edge, an Englishman stood waiting, his face obscured by the shadow of his tricorn hat. The faint glow of a covered lantern lit a small patch of earth, the surrounding bamboo swaying gently in the night breeze.

THE TRAITOR'S BARGAIN

Mozammel knew the risk he courted, but desperation had left him little choice. The Company was no friend to men like him, but the Nawab's reforms had turned landlords into targets - watched, squeezed, and discarded when no longer useful. He had reached out not for gain, but for survival. And now, there would be no turning back.

"You are late," the Englishman muttered, his tone clipped.

"Time is not an ally tonight," Mozammel replied, his voice low, the edges tight with urgency. "I had to ensure no one saw me leave the estate."

The Englishman huffed impatiently. "Have you brought what we discussed?"

Mozammel reached into the folds of his robe and produced a sealed letter. He extended it toward the official, his hand trembling ever so slightly. "This contains the details of my plea. Just... keep your promise. We can't survive this."

The Englishman took the letter, breaking the seal to glance briefly at its contents. "You seek protection against the Nawab's men? Arms and men to guard your lands?"

"Yes," Mozammel confirmed, his voice tinged with desperation. "The revenue demands have become unbearable. If this continues, my people will starve, and my estate will crumble."

The Englishman folded the letter and tucked it into his coat. "Very well. You will have what you require - arms, men, and perhaps and perhaps even a few men of experience to steady your position. But remember, this assistance comes at a cost."

Mozammel's eyes narrowed slightly, but he nodded. "I understand. As long as my lands and my people are safe, I am prepared to pay the price."

The Englishman turned to leave, his boots crunching softly against the dry leaves. "We will contact you when the arrangements are made. Do not attempt to reach out to us unless it is absolutely necessary."

Mozammel inclined his head. "Understood Sahib. Goodbye."

As the Englishman disappeared into the shadows, Mozammel remained frozen, a creeping dread coiling tightly around his chest.

Hidden in a nearby thicket, Shaikh Umar had caught just enough to understand. As Mozammel remained still, alone beneath the rustling bamboo, Umar slipped away into the dark without a sound.

Although the following day passed without incident, a little after the stroke of midnight, a thunder of feet broke the stillness of the night. Torches flared in the courtyard as the Nawab's soldiers surged through the gates, shouting orders as they fanned out across the estate. Inside, the inhabitants stirred from sleep, blinking into the darkness, their minds slow to catch up with the noise. Few yet grasped what was happening.

Mozammel bolted upright at the crash of his doors. His trembling hands struggled with his shawl, his mind racing for an escape, but it was too late. Soldiers poured into the room, their torches painting jagged shadows across his walls. Standing in his spacious chamber, he faced the soldiers with a sorry attempt at indignation.

"Mozammel Khan," the captain of the guard proclaimed, "you stand accused of treason against the Nawab of Bengal."

They dragged him from the room without ceremony.

By the time he was hauled into the courtyard, the household had awakened. Mozammel stood with his head bowed, his wrists bound in iron shackles. His knees quaked as his darting eyes sought solace, but found only despair. Hamida clutched their youngest grandchild, while his children stood frozen, their wide eyes betraying helpless terror. Inzamam made a sudden move forward, fists clenched - but his older brother caught his arm, holding him back with a whispered plea and a firm grip. Servants gathered in silence, their faces averted.

As Mozammel was led away, no one spoke. The children clung to their mother, an elderly servant wiped silent tears, and Inzamam stared at the ground, fists clenched at his sides.

Mozammel was hauled to Munger, where he was dragged through the fortified gates and into the labyrinth of dungeons that lay beneath the Nawab's stronghold.

The dungeon was where hope went to die. The air was thick with mildew; each breath felt like swallowing stone. Water dripped from unseen cracks, and the moans of other prisoners echoed faintly through the dark. Alone in his cell, Mozammel sat on the cold floor, drawing a shallow breath. He knew he would need every scrap of resolve to endure what lay ahead.

Like many of his kind, Mozammel Khan vanished into the tide of history - whether in the dungeons of Mir Qasim or the dusty alleys of Munger, no one knew.

• • •

The morning sunlight filtered through the shutters of the modest house near the garrison in Patna, casting warm patterns on the earthen floor. Thomas Hawke had continued his sterling rise within the ranks of the Company. He was now – in June 1763 – an ensign stationed in Patna, a hardened soldier with a deep understanding of the chaos and politics of Bengal.

Today he was seated cross-legged on a woven mat, utterly absorbed in entertaining his infant son, Billy. The boy, perched on his broad lap, gurgled with delight as Thomas dangled a carved wooden horse in front of him, its polished surface gleaming in the light. Billy clutched at the toy with tiny fists, his laughter echoing through the room.

Gulabi, dressed in a simple but elegant cotton saree, stood by the hearth, grinding spices for the morning meal. Occasionally, she glanced at the sight of her husband and child, her smile tinged with a contemplative shadow. "Thomas," she said, her tone cutting through the tranquillity, "do you think Ellis's provocations will truly secure what he wants?"

Thomas stilled, his hand holding the toy faltering. "I don't know," he admitted, shifting uncomfortably. "He seems set on forcing the

Nawab's hand. But it's reckless, Gulabi. Seizing Patna could turn this province into a battlefield."

"It's already becoming one," she replied, setting down her work and moving closer. "You've told me how the Company men sneer at Mir Qasim, how they take what they want and dismiss his authority. Do they think the people of Bihar won't rise against them for this?"

Thomas sighed heavily, setting Billy on the mat where he played contentedly. "Ellis thinks he can crush Qasim by taking this city. But Qasim's no fool. He's been fortifying Munger, raising an army. He won't bow without a fight."

"And yet you're drawn into it," Gulabi said, her voice steady but laced with concern. "A fight that should not be yours, Thomas. Does Ellis not see what war will cost?"

"Ellis sees what he wants to see," Thomas said grimly. "Qasim's abolition of trade duties angered him. Stripped him and the others of their fortunes. Now he calls the Nawab a 'meddlesome pretender' and seems bent on a confrontation with him" He ran a hand over his face, etched with frustration. "I respect the chain of command, Gulabi, but this plan... it feels wrong. I can't shake the feeling it'll spiral out of control."

Gulabi resumed preparing for the morning meal, contemplating in silence their conversation. But the contentment of seeing her two favourite persons together yet again settled her unease, if momentarily. Turning to them with an indulgent smile, she teased Thomas - "He has your stubborn chin."

"That he does," Thomas said, his voice soft with affection. "And my mother's grey eyes." His expression turned wistful as he looked at the boy. "She'd dote on him, Gulabi. I can almost see her cradling him in her arms, humming those old tunes she used to sing when I was his age."

Gulabi moved closer, her hand resting lightly on his shoulder. "You miss her," she said gently.

"Aye," Thomas admitted, his voice thick with emotion. "It's been eight years, Gulabi. Eight long years since I last saw her face. She was hale then, but her letters... they speak of failing health. I owe her a visit, if only to let her see her grandson before it's too late."

Gulabi knelt beside him, her fingers brushing against Billy's soft curls. "Then why don't you go, Thomas? Surely they'll grant you leave."

Thomas sighed heavily, setting the toy horse aside. "With the unrest here in Patna, the damned volatility, they won't let me go, not now. The Company needs every man at his post, they say." He ran a hand through his hair, his voice tight with weariness. "But how much longer, Gulabi? How much longer before I'm free to step aboard a ship and sail back to England?"

She took his hand. "Soon, Thomas," she said with quiet conviction. "You'll find a way. Until then, she'll know through your letters that her son has a family who loves him."

Thomas nodded, drawing her into a brief embrace, their son nestled between them. For a moment, amidst the scent of spices and the warmth of their home, the worries of the world outside seemed distant.

But peace was fleeting. An urgent, staccato knock rattled the door. Thomas had been reclining, eyes on Billy's wobbly crawl - until the knock jolted him upright. Gulabi froze mid-motion at the hearth, her grinding stone still in her hand, her brows knitting in concern.

When Thomas opened the door, the messenger outside was barely able to contain his urgency. "Ensign Hawke," the man said breathlessly, saluting. "You've been summoned to the garrison immediately. The commander has ordered all officers to report without delay."

Thomas nodded sharply. "What's the matter?"

"I don't know, sir," the messenger replied, shifting uncomfortably. "But it seems serious."

Thomas muttered under his breath, then turned back into the house. His face was calm, but his hurried steps betrayed his tension. "I've been called to the garrison, Gulabi" he said simply, retrieving his red coat from the peg by the door. He began dressing with practiced efficiency, tightening his belt and adjusting his scabbard.

Gulabi watched him in silence, her arms wrapped protectively around Billy. Her usually steady demeanour faltered, a shadow of unease crossing her face. "Thomas," she said softly, almost hesitantly, "this feels… different."

He turned to her, his expression softening despite the tension in his jaw. "It's probably another of Ellis's schemes needing oversight," he said with a half-hearted smile. "Don't fret, Gulabi. I'll be back before the day's done."

But Gulabi was not reassured. She stepped closer, her free hand brushing against his arm. "No, Thomas," she whispered, her voice trembling, "something is wrong. I can feel it. Please… promise me you'll be careful."

Thomas hesitated, his hand lingering on the hilt of his sword. "I will," he said finally, his voice low. "I'll always come back to you and Billy."

Gulabi's eyes brimmed with tears as she nodded, and her grip on his arm tightened. "Just in case…" She swallowed hard, willing herself to be brave. "Know that you are loved, Thomas. Deeply."

He leaned down, kissed her forehead, and then kissed Billy's tiny head, his voice cracking as he murmured, "Take care of him, Gulabi."

With one last glance at his family, he stepped out of the door and into the golden morning light, the sound of his boots fading as he strode toward the garrison. Gulabi stood at the threshold, holding Billy tightly against her chest, her heart heavy with an unshakable dread.

The attack on Patna under William Ellis began with surprise but unravelled in chaos. Discipline among the Company sepoys collapsed amid the looting of the bazaar, giving Mir Qasim's reinforcements time to counterattack. Ellis's men fell back to the factory, but their defences crumbled under overwhelming pressure. Fleeing by river, they were ambushed and forced to surrender.

THE TRAITOR'S BARGAIN

Shackled and marched to Munger Fort, Hawke now sat in a dim prison cell, the weight of failure pressing down on him. What had never been more than Ellis's reckless gamble had spiralled into catastrophe, emboldening Mir Qasim and rallying his fractured allies. War was no longer a looming threat - it was a grim certainty. And in the silence of his confinement, Hawke knew the bloodshed had only just begun.

• • •

War had come. In the wake of Ellis's disastrous assault on Patna, the Company Council in Calcutta declared open hostilities against Mir Qasim. Major Kilpatrick - whose long-postponed return to England had again been delayed by shifting priorities - was placed in command of a campaign to crush Mir Qasim's regime and reassert unchallenged Company authority in Bengal.

The campaign unfolded in the thick of the monsoon. Kilpatrick led his men from Katwa to Rajmahal and finally Gheria, through rain-soaked fields and fever-ridden forests. The enemy fought hard - Qasim's troops were no strangers to the land - but discipline, grit, and superior logistics carried the day. Supplies ran low. Men died by the dozen. Yet Kilpatrick pressed on, each victory edged with exhaustion rather than triumph.

By the time the final redoubt at Gheria fell, the cost was undeniable - but so was the momentum. Mir Qasim had retreated to the hilltop fortress of Udhua Nullah. And Kilpatrick, ever the realist, knew the hardest battle was still to come.

Weeks later, that prediction had borne out. The siege of Udhua Nullah was now deep into its second month, and the frustration was visibly etched into Kilpatrick's weathered face. Standing before the smouldering remains of his camp's cooking fires, he gazed up at the fortress towering above them. It loomed like a stubborn mountain, its thick walls seeming to mock his heavy artillery. The terrain itself was a daunting adversary. Not only was the fortress formidably located atop the hill, but it was also surrounded by thick forests and treacherous marshlands; and a deep moat guarded its walls. The moat was fed by the icy waters of a lake stretching from the mountains to the Ganges snaking through the lowlands below.

Behind him, Captain Frazier approached cautiously, his voice edged with concern. "The guns still haven't made a dent, have they, sir?"

Kilpatrick turned, his jaw set. "No, Frazier. Not so much as a scratch on those damned walls."

For weeks, the British batteries had thundered across the valley, their cannonballs slamming into stone with little effect. Rain-soaked powder often misfired, and the elevation made accuracy near impossible. It was siege by sound more than damage - a constant roar meant to wear down resolve, not walls.

Kilpatrick exhaled sharply, watching another useless volley echo into the hills. "Mir Qasim's engineers were cleverer than we'd hoped," he muttered, his voice dropping to a grumble.

Frazier nodded. "The men say they've seen torchlight dances on the battlements, sir. Drunken shouts, music - every night."

Kilpatrick's lips curled into a thin smile. "Fools. The more secure they feel, the less they'll see us coming."

Inside the fortress, Mir Qasim's generals had indeed grown lax. Wine and music spilled from the halls each night, the jingling of anklets drowning out the distant booms of English cannon. On the ramparts, sentries leaned on their spears, more interested in watching the dancers than the valley below. The fortress still stood firm - but its defenders no longer did.

Yet not all within the fortress had succumbed to complacency.

Mirza Najaf, the highly regarded cavalry commander, remained alert and deeply uneasy.

He had earned his reputation years earlier during the Afghan campaigns, where he led a shattered rearguard to safety through mountain passes others had deemed impassable. His exploits had since passed into regimental folklore - retold around campfires and in the shaded corners of officers' pavilions, as the mark of a man who defied odds and lived to tell of it.

Najaf had seen too many campaigns lost to arrogance. As others drank, he walked the ramparts alone, his sharp gaze fixed on the enemy campfires below.

"The English are clever," he muttered to his lieutenant. "And desperate men don't sit idle forever. If we grow too comfortable, they'll find a way through."

The lieutenant shifted uneasily. "The terrain protects us, sir. The marshes are deathtraps at night."

Najaf Khan's eyes narrowed. "Then that's exactly what makes it the perfect route - they won't expect us to come through it."

The generals drank. No one spoke of the Nawab. Najaf Khan did not ask for permission - he did not need it. The defence of the fortress, and its honour, was reason enough.

In the dead of night, Najaf's small force slipped into the marshes. Guided by locals, they moved like shadows through the icy water, every splash muffled by thick reeds and layered mud. The air was dense with the scent of damp earth and gun oil. Overhead, owls cried and fell silent.

They hit the British camp just as the first hints of light cracked over the eastern sky.

What followed was utter chaos. A sentry's scream was cut short by a blade. Another fired a shot into the air - the muzzle flash briefly lit up the darkness, just long enough to see the onrushing attackers. Men burst from their tents half-dressed, some reaching for weapons, others scattering into the shadows in panic. Cannon teams were overrun, supplies scattered, horses bolted in panic.

Kilpatrick burst from his tent, sword ready in hand. "To arms!

Rally, damn you!" he shouted into the confusion. Sparks flew from collapsing canvas shelters as fire took hold. Somewhere, ammunition crackled and popped in a smouldering wagon.

At first, the defenders flailed - but then, under the officers' shouted commands and flashing blade, a line began to form. Muskets barked, bayonets drove forward. The Company troops, bloodied but steadying, pushed back.

Satisfied with the disruption they had wrought - fires set, supplies ruined, and dozens killed – Mirza Najaf's men withdrew in good order. The raid had lasted less than an hour, but the toll was severe. Smoke drifted low over the valley like a warning.

Kilpatrick surveyed the wreckage grimly. The British were used to marching forward - not being dragged from sleep by knives in the dark.

Then, through the thinning haze, Captain Frazier came sprinting up, mud-caked and breathless.

"We've taken a prisoner, sir - a local guide," he said, unable to hide his grin. "He confessed to leading them through a hidden marsh path - the very one they used to strike us."

Kilpatrick looked out toward the fortress, his eyes narrowing. "Then we strike back - through the same path, and without mercy."

He hoped for more than just retribution. If the Nawab was still inside - as some scouts believed - then this assault could end the war with a single stroke.

At nightfall, the British troops moved. Waist-deep in the frigid waters of the lake, they pressed forward in silence, the night air clinging damp and heavy around them. Each step was a struggle - boots sucking into the mud, breath short from the cold, muskets and powder held aloft to keep them dry. Somewhere in the dark, a man slipped with a splash and was yanked up before his cry could carry. Overhead, clouds rolled across a sliver of moon. No one spoke.

Kilpatrick led from the front, his hand clenched tight around the hilt of his sword. "Steady, men," he whispered, just loud enough for the officers nearby. "Not a sound until we're over the walls."

As they reached the base of the fortress, the ladders came up - black silhouettes against the looming stone. The climb was agonising. Wet hands grasped at slippery rungs, limbs trembling more from anticipation than effort. A shout from above might have ended it all, but none came. When they reached the top, the sight that greeted them was almost surreal - guards slumped by cold brazier fires, snoring through the drunken fog of last night's revelry. The jingle of anklets still echoed faintly from somewhere within, a final vestige of misplaced confidence.

Kilpatrick gave a sharp nod.

The muskets cracked in unison, thunder ripping through the stillness. Flames burst from the barrels, lighting up startled faces and scattering sleepers. The defenders scrambled to arms, but it was too late. Steel flashed in torchlight, and the Company's soldiers poured over the battlements like a flood.

"Forward!" Kilpatrick roared, voice rising above the screams and gunfire.

What followed was not battle - it was carnage. Some defenders fought bravely, but most fled in panic toward the rear gates. Many tried to escape across the swollen river, but the monsoon had turned it savage. The current took men whole, dragging them under, while others were cut down mid-stream by musket fire, their cries lost to the roar of water and gunfire.

By dawn, it was all over. Smoke curled up from shattered rooftops. The stench of blood, ash, and powder hung thick in the morning air. Kilpatrick stood in silence, boots planted amid the ruin - the twisted bodies, the reeking ground, the silent rows of captured cannon spread out before him. Thousands dead.

Captain Frazier approached, boots slick with mud, face drawn from the night's ordeal. "It's done, sir," he said, voice taut with fatigue and grim satisfaction. "The fortress is ours."

Kilpatrick turned slowly, eyes shadowed beneath his soot-streaked brow. "And what of Qasim?" he asked, his tone edged with anticipation.

"No sign of him, sir," Frazier replied, shaking his head. "Must have fled before the siege closed in."

Kilpatrick did not respond at once. He stepped toward the battlements, the stone beneath his boots still tacky with blood. Below, the river swelled and hissed, dragging corpses under in silence.

When he finally spoke, Kilpatrick's voice was low, firm, and cold. "Then let them remember Udhua Nullah," he said. "Let them remember what it cost to defy us."

His words rang with command, but there was no triumph in them - only exhaustion, and a trace of something harder to name. Not doubt, not remorse - but the first crack in conviction.

Somewhere behind him, the Company flag snapped sharply in the morning wind.

• • •

The study smelled of damp paper and fading lamp oil. Dewan Harinarayan Sanyal stood near the shuttered window, arms folded tight, his gaze flicking toward the road beyond, then back to his master. Javed Hussain sat at his desk, the loan papers open before him - his own seal staring back at him, cold and counterfeit.

It was the work of Robertson - the private English banker who dined with governors and left ruin in his wake. His firm had fabricated the bond, and the court had accepted it without question.

"They've rejected our denial," Harinarayan said, his voice low and controlled. "The magistrate issued the warrant this morning. Charges: fraud and forgery."

Javed didn't move. "So the lie becomes law."

"They've stitched it up cleanly." Harinarayan said. "Robertson's firm submitted loan documents showing you borrowed thirty-five thousand rupees, three months ago, to cover revenue arrears in your zamindari in East Bengal. According to this" - he gestured to the document - "you pledged the estate as collateral."

"And I never saw a word of it," Javed muttered.

"We all know that. They forged everything - your signature, your seal, the execution date. Then they filed it with the court, submitting that you had signed it in private and had it delivered by your own agent."

Harinarayan hesitated, then added, "We made the mistake of dealing with them. When we approached Robertson's firm for emergency credit last year - you remember - they insisted we send a signed inquiry and affix your seal for authentication. We declined their final terms, but the papers stayed with them. That's likely how they copied your hand."

Javed's jaw clenched. "And when I denied it -"

"That was the second blade," Harinarayan said. "Your denial gave them grounds to accuse you of criminal forgery. They now claim you fabricated the denial to erase a legitimate debt. That's why the charges are no longer just civil - they're criminal."

He tapped the document. "Default on the loan activates estate liquidation. But denying a signature that the court accepts as yours - that's cheating, forgery, and intent to defraud."

Javed exhaled slowly. "So I'm being prosecuted for not repaying a loan I never took. And punished further for saying so."

Harinarayan lowered his gaze. "Yes, Sarkar. They don't care for truth - only a story that fits on paper. That forged document is now law. The court has granted Robertson the right to seize the estate - and the arrest warrant stands."

Javed closed the papers slowly. "So this is what conquest looks like now - not by sword, but seal."

A knock came at the door. Harinarayan flinched.

The captain of the household guard, Gopal Das, stepped in and bowed low. His brow was tight with unease.

"Malik... an English policeman waits below. Sepoys with him. He asks that you come down."

Javed said nothing at first. Then he rose - slowly, like a man peeling away from the last thread of belonging - and walked past Harinarayan without a word.

The stairs creaked under his steps. The hush in the corridor behind him felt heavier than footsteps.

At the foot of the stairs stood a broad-shouldered English officer in Company livery. Two sepoys stood at attention behind him.

"Javed Hussain," he announced, his voice ringing with a pompous authority, "by warrant of the East India Company court, you are hereby arrested on charges of fraud and forgery."

From the shadows, Gopal Das stepped forward, fingers tightening around the lathi - the long bamboo staff he always carried. He leaned in, close enough that no one else could hear.

"We can fight, if you give the word."

Javed looked at him. For a heartbeat, he almost said yes. But then he remembered the Company's might - how it had swept through Bengal, the fortresses taken with almost effortless ease.

He gave a slow shake of his head. "No."

The guard stepped back, jaw clenched, and said nothing more.

"You will walk with us, Hussain," the officer said, as iron cuffs snapped shut around his wrists.

They stepped into the street. The sun had dipped behind the rooftops of Murshidabad, but the lane still buzzed with evening life - vendors closing stalls, boys rolling dice on the stones, neighbours drawing water.

Now they stopped to stare.

"Clear the way!" the officer barked. "The accused is charged with forgery and theft of honour!"

Murmurs rippled through the crowd.

"That's Javed Hussain?"

"A forger?"

"No, he's a zamindar…"

Javed walked with quiet resolve, head held high. His robe - clean, faded - stirred in the breeze. He did not meet their eyes, but he felt their judgment pressing in: doubt, suspicion… and something colder still - pity he did not want.

"He gave to the mosque," an old man murmured.

"He paid my son's fees," said another.

But pity turned quickly. In the safety of the crowd, restraint gave way to resentment.

"Thief!"

"Forger!"

"Getting fat on ill-begotten money while we starve".

Harinarayan followed at a distance as they reached the waiting carriage - a plain Company transport with barred windows.

• • •

The prison cell was silent but for the slow dripping of water somewhere out of sight. A single oil lamp guttered in the hallway beyond the bars, casting long, broken shadows across the damp stone floor. The air was heavy with mildew, the stench of rusted iron and old sweat.

Javed stirred on the hard mat of woven jute. He had not truly slept - only drifted in and out of restless fog. The ache in his joints told him it was still deep night.

His body needed release. He rose, slowly, careful not to rattle the chains around his ankles, and shuffled to the corner where a dented brass bucket sat beside a cracked clay pot of water. The gesture was mechanical now, as stripped of dignity as the man who performed it.

He knelt, poured a little water to rinse his hands - and paused.

The rippling surface stilled for just a moment, and there, framed by grime and shadow, was his reflection.

At first, it was what he expected: gaunt cheeks, grizzled beard, eyes ringed with sleepless regret.

But then the water shifted - or perhaps his mind did. The face began to change.

The grime faded. The beard darkened. The robe straightened itself. The turban reassembled with impossible precision. The man in the water was no longer a prisoner.

He was the Javed of old - the courtier, the landholder, the man who once walked the halls of Murshidabad with quiet authority and the deference of others. But the face in the water did not carry pride. Only sorrow.

Javed stared, heart stilled.

The reflection looked up. And spoke.

"You remember me."

The voice was soft - his own, yet untouched by weariness. It held no anger. Only sorrow.

Javed's breath caught. He did not answer.

The reflection continued. "I was the man who believed honour could endure. Who thought dignity might still be found in loyalty, even to a flawed ruler. I held the line - until you let go."

Javed lowered his gaze, but the water pulled him back. "I thought I was saving us. And you… you saw what I didn't."

"Yes," the reflection said. "And in that moment, I held our last clarity. You silenced me. In a mirror, with wine and fear. You let the other voice speak."

"I had no choice," Javed whispered. "You saw what Siraj had become. I did what I thought was necessary - for my son. For Bengal."

A faint ripple stirred the water, yet the face held.

"And now?" the reflection asked gently. "Your son fights in the jungle. Your estate is in ashes. The Company you abetted calls you a forger and thief. Was this what necessity looked like?"

Javed's shoulders sagged. He wanted to look away, but couldn't. The water held him as firmly as the iron at his ankles.

"I thought we could control it," he said. "Steer the outcome. I thought if we gave them what they initially wanted, they'd let us keep the rest."

The reflection's eyes darkened with grief. "But they wanted it all."

Silence fell again. The drip of water resumed - slow, indifferent.

Javed looked into the face he once wore, now floating like a memory in a bucket of filth.

"What am I now?" he asked.

The reflection did not answer. It only gazed at him, with the quiet ache of something lost.

Then, slowly, the image began to dissolve - not in anger, but in mourning. A ripple blurred the eyes. Another swallowed the turban. The face wavered, then scattered.

Javed reached out, trembling - not to touch, but as if to ask forgiveness.

The water shivered. The face was gone.

He sat there long after, knees stiff against the stone, staring into the ripples, as if they might bring his old self back.

But there was no return.

Only a man in the dark. And the weight of what he had become.

• • •

The heavy scent of burning tallow candles filled the dimly lit chamber within Fort William. The warm, humid air barely stirred as Governor Henry Vansittart leaned forward, pressing his hands on the oak table before him. Across from him, Warren Hastings sat reclined, his fingers idly tracing the rim of his wine goblet, his expression unreadable - a man whose counsel Vansittart found himself relying on more with each passing day.

Vansittart exhaled sharply. "Ever since Udhua Nullah, Qasim's gone mad. His defeat should have broken him, yet it has only turned him into something far worse - he is a man consumed by vengeance."

Hastings did not respond immediately. He swirled the deep red liquid in his glass, watching the candlelight glint off its surface. "Mad? Or simply a man unravelling, as the grip on power slips through his fingers??" His voice was measured, contemplative.

Vansittart frowned. "That defeat should have ended his fight, yet it has only made him more dangerous. He is tearing his own kingdom apart - slaughtering merchants, purging his own allies, burning the very land he rules. His paranoia has turned his court into a dungeon - ministers disappear, allies are branded traitors, and a mere whisper of disloyalty ends in chains or worse."

He pushed back from the table, fingers drumming once on the wood as if weighing the madness aloud. "Last week, he had his own revenue collector in Bhagalpur executed - claimed the man was leaking grain prices to the British. No trial, no defence. Just a headless body thrown in the square. He sees it as treason - believes we're using price signals to track supply lines, undermine his tax reforms, maybe even distort the market to erode his base. Paranoia, yes - but not without a certain logic. What sense does that make?"

Hastings finally looked up, his gaze keen. "Sense? No. Nor strategy. You are right Governor, he has turned his intelligence network into an inquisition, hunting shadows. Even those who once stood beside him now live in fear of a stray accusation. The Jagat Seths miscalculated when they thought they could control him - he has turned on them too." He leaned forward slightly. "He is a drowning man. And what does a drowning man do, Governor?"

Vansittart rubbed his temple, irritation creeping into his voice. "Flails about wildly, dragging others down with him."

A slow smile ghosted across Hastings' lips. "Precisely. He knows he cannot win conventionally. So, he turns the ground into ashes, makes sure there is nothing left for us to inherit." He set the glass down with a quiet clink. "That is, unless we make sure his war serves our interests."

Vansittart narrowed his eyes. "Our interests? The man is turning Bihar into a wasteland. That doesn't serve us."

Hastings tilted his head. "Not directly, no. But think, sir. The zamindars, the merchants, the financiers - these are the lifeblood of Bengal's economy. Qasim is gutting them, one by one. And do you know what that means?"

Vansittart leaned back, thinking. "It weakens the province further."

"More than that," Hastings said smoothly. "It makes them dependent on us. When Qasim is finished with his vengeance, what few survive his wrath will not see him as a ruler, but as a scourge. What alternative will they have but to come crawling to us for protection? He is driving them into our arms."

Vansittart grunted. "If he doesn't kill them all first."

Hastings allowed a small chuckle. "Not all. Fear is a fine instrument, but it only works if there's someone left to be afraid. The men who survive this purge will not only seek shelter under our banner - they will owe us their very survival." He paused, then added, almost as an afterthought, "And when the time comes, we shall not merely be protectors of trade - but the arbiters of Bengal's future." He let the words hang in the thick air, watching as Vansittart absorbed the thought.

After a moment, Vansittart exhaled. "So we let Qasim do our work for us."

"We let him destroy his own support," Hastings corrected. "And when the dust settles, we shall be the only stable force left standing."

Vansittart drummed his fingers on the table. "And what of Qasim himself? He's like a cornered beast. Unpredictable."

Hastings shrugged. "For now. But beasts tire, Governor. And he is bleeding - badly. When the moment is right, we will strike the final blow."

A silence stretched between them, broken only by the distant creak of the fort's wooden beams. Then, Vansittart exhaled, nodding slowly. "Let him burn himself out, then." He hesitated, then added, "Though

I wonder how this will read in London a year or two hence - when the province lies in ruin and we've said nothing. Silence may serve us now, but history has a longer memory, and Parliament a shorter temper than we like to think." He gave Hastings a wary glance. "You are a dangerous man, Hastings."

Hastings merely smiled, reaching for his glass. "I don't make the storm, Governor. I only chart where it breaks." He paused, then added with quiet respect, "But it is for you to decide how best to sail through it."

• • •

The sea wind tore at Major Kilpatrick's coat as he stood on the deck of the westbound vessel, watching Bengal dissolve into mist on the horizon. He was finally going home – to England. He would not return. Not to the Company, not to the land that had soaked up so much blood - and so much of himself.

Somewhere behind that vanishing shore lay the officers' club in Calcutta - and a conversation he could not silence.

It had been his last night in India. The lamps had burned low, the wine had flowed freely. Harrington, an old companion from their junior days, lounged opposite him with his usual grin.

"To Plassey," Kilpatrick had said, lifting his glass.

"The turning point of all our fortunes," Harrington agreed. "Where else does one company earn £2.2 million in a single day? And Clive - two hundred and ten thousand richer. A merchant turned monarch."

Kilpatrick had nodded, but his voice had dropped. "Fortune, yes. But also ruin. I still see them - boys from Yorkshire, boys from Bengal. All gone, so a few men in London could count dividends by candlelight."

Harrington had shrugged. "Necessary sacrifices. The Nawabs wore the crowns, but we wrote the script. Bengal doesn't just fund the Company now - it bankrolls Britain."

He chuckled. "And let's not pretend we loot. We tax."

Kilpatrick remembered the bitter taste of claret in his mouth. "We've made an art of it, haven't we? Shaking the pagoda tree. But the roots are rotting. We've bled the land thin."

Harrington's eyes had glinted in the lamplight. "Then we squeeze something else. So long as we hold the forts and the treasury, India bends."

Now, on the wind-raked deck, Kilpatrick exhaled. That night, he had managed a smile. But it hadn't reached his eyes. It did not now either.

The sky ahead was pale with cold light. Somewhere behind him, the weavers, farmers, and merchants he had once watched with guarded admiration were still toiling under new taxes, stripped names, and dead sons. And yet the ship moved on, as if nothing were broken.

He reached into his coat and pulled out a folded scrap of fabric - Bengali cotton, finely spun, stained faintly with red.

He stared at it for a long time.

Then let it fall.

The wind caught it and carried it seaward, away from the ship, toward the mist.

• • •

The air in the prison was heavy with despair, the silence broken only by the occasional clink of chains. Jagat Seth Mehtab Rai sat in the corner of his cell, his face drawn, his once-proud demeanour now weathered by the weight of betrayal and impending doom. In an adjacent cell, his cousin and deputy, Swaroop Chand, fidgeted restlessly.

"They found the letter, didn't they?" Swaroop Chand's voice trembled, cutting through the stillness.

Mehtab sighed deeply, shifting in place. "Yes," he replied, his voice calm but heavy with resignation. "We thought ourselves invincible,

Swaroop. Our words to Ellis were meant to shape the future, not destroy us. But now, those same words may well seal our fate."

Swaroop's frustration spilled out. "If Ellis hadn't been arrested, if those papers hadn't been seized -"

"It doesn't matter now," Mehtab interrupted, his tone resigned. "We played the game, and we lost. All we can do is hope that four crores is enough to buy our lives."

Swaroop suddenly snapped, his voice sharp. "No. *You* played the game, Mehtab bhai. You dragged me into it. I warned you Ellis was reckless. I said we should wait."

Mehtab turned to him, but said nothing. The silence stung.

Swaroop's voice rose, trembling with rage and fear. "You thought you could pull their strings, just like you did with Mir Jafar. You thought your name alone could bend the Company. But you were wrong - and now we all hang for it."

"I thought..." he began, then faltered. His face twisted, not in anger, but in sorrow. "No. You're right. I was wrong."

Swaroop looked away, the heat of anger fading into something colder. He let out a bitter laugh. "The Jagat Seths, the great kingmakers of Bengal, outwitted at last. For decades, we shaped rulers like potters with clay. And yet, when it mattered most, we placed our wager on the wrong man."

Mehtab lowered his gaze, the weight of his misjudgement settling on him like lead.

"Mir Jafar - we thought him pliable, predictable. But we failed to see the true danger lurking in the shadows."

Swaroop's expression darkened. "The foreign merchants. We saw them as traders who needed us. We never imagined they would weave a net we couldn't escape."

Mehtab's voice hardened. "We thought we held the reins, but they were guiding the horse all along."

Swaroop's voice dropped to a whisper. "In our desperation to protect our wealth, we handed it Bengal to the English on a silver platter." His hands trembled as he looked at the cold, damp walls. "And here we are," he muttered. "Kingmakers no more. Just pawns, discarded when the game was won."

Meanwhile in the Nawab's court, Mir Qasim stood behind a table, his face a storm of anger and contempt. The officer before him, clutching a bundle of papers, struggled to keep his composure.

"This is their plea," the officer said, placing the Seths' letter and their offer of four crores of rupees on the table. "They beg for their lives in exchange for this sum."

Mir Qasim's eyes narrowed as he picked up the incriminating letter, the words glaring back at him. "Urging Ellis to attack me," he muttered, his voice low but brimming with venom. "And they dared to commit a fortune to fund it."

He looked up sharply, turning to his minister. "Do you see the audacity of these coin-counting jackals?? The same Seths who fancied themselves kingmakers, who thought they could pull my strings as they did with Siraj and Mir Jafar. Now, they think I can be bought."

The minister hesitated. "Four crores is no small sum, Nawab Sahib. Perhaps we could -"

"Enough!" Mir Qasim's voice thundered through the hall. "If my commanders hear of this, they'll march to the prison and release them themselves, dragging me with them as their price! No, their game ends here. Let them sweat a little longer. Send someone to deliver the verdict - not the bullet. Yet."

In the dim confines of the prison, the iron door groaned open. A burly man stepped inside, his shadow looming large against the stone walls. The faint flicker of torchlight caught the polished steel of his pistol. Mehtab Rai looked up, his heart sinking as the weight of inevitability settled on him.

But the man didn't raise his weapon. Not yet. He simply stood there, staring. The silence stretched.

"Orders," he said gruffly, "are to wait."

Swaroop let out a gasp - half relief, half confusion. "Then we live?"

The man did not answer. He turned and stepped back into the hall, leaving the door ajar.

Minutes passed. Each one stretched thinner than the last.

Then - footsteps. Heavier. Slower. Purposeful. The door swung fully open. He returned, the pistol still in his hands. Without a word, he stepped inside and shut the door behind him.

Mehtab looked toward the adjoining cell, where Swaroop's frantic pleas echoed loudly.

For a brief moment, Mehtab's eyes drifted upward - not to the cell walls, but to memory. He saw himself in silken robes, seated in the marble hall of Murshidabad, flanked by nobles and clerks, whispering in Mir Jafar's ear as the newly installed Nawab nodded. The treasury had been opened that day at his word. The court had listened - not to the throne, but to him. The Company men had merely stood watchful in the shadows.

"We make kings," he had told Swaroop that night, wine in hand. "And we unmake them."

The memory flickered, then died.

The assassin said nothing, stepping forward with a mechanical purpose. Mehtab closed his eyes, muttering a prayer under his breath. A moment later, the crack of gunfire shattered the silence. His body slumped to the ground, lifeless, as blood pooled beneath him.

Swaroop's voice had broken off mid-rant, leaving behind a charged stillness. Amidst this silence, the irony lingered like a curse. The Jagat Seths had crowned kings, shaped kingdoms - and in the end, mistook influence for invincibility. Mehtab had played the game too long, believing the rules still bent for him. Now, the wealth was ash, the titles hollow. And the ultimate cost - his life - offered no space left for regret.

· · ·

THE TRAITOR'S BARGAIN

The air in the haveli on the outskirts of Patna was thick with the warm, smoky aroma of the prisoners' midday meal. A long table stretched across the sunlit courtyard, where the sharp daylight carved shallow shadows beneath the arches and along the cracked flagstones. Around the table sat the British prisoners captured during William Ellis's ill-fated assault on Patna - men who had been confined in the haveli for four months. The edge of apprehension had dulled over time, worn down by routine and the absence of violence. They talked quietly, their voices punctuated by occasional laughter.

Outside, as the sun climbed toward its zenith, another rhythm stirred in the quiet street. Sumru, the grim-faced commander of Mir Qasim's forces, arrived with a platoon of armed sepoys. The soft slap of sandals and the jingle of harness buckles were the only sounds as they approached the gates of the haveli. Inside, the prisoners remained oblivious, their voices a faint murmur beyond the walls.

Sumru paused, glancing back once at the quiet street, then toward the heavy gates of the haveli. His jaw clenched.

"The Nawab wants vengeance," he muttered under his breath, as if reminding himself. "This is the reckoning" His voice was flat, but behind his eyes flickered something harder to read - duty, perhaps, or the last embers of fury. He nodded to his men. "Unbolt the gates."

"Bring me Ellis and Lushington," Sumru barked to his men once they were inside the compound. Lushington was Ellis' second-in-command among the prisoners

Moments later, Ellis and Lushington, still in their coats, were led out into the courtyard where Sumru stood waiting.

"What is this about?" Ellis asked, his voice low and wary, the stiffness in his shoulders betraying rising alarm. Lushington's eyes flicked from the drawn weapons to Sumru's face - and froze. "This isn't a parley..." he whispered, dread blooming in his tone.

Sumru stared at them a moment. "It's a sentence," he said. Then he stepped forward and drew his sword in one smooth motion. The blade flashed in the hard morning light as it arced across Ellis's chest. Ellis gasped, staggered, and fell without a word. Lushington lurched toward Ellis instinctively - but before he could reach him, a second slash opened his throat, cutting the cry from his lips. Both bodies crumpled to the cobblestones, their blood spreading across the dust-veiled stone.

Inside the haveli, the clamour of footsteps and the cries of their fellow prisoners echoed ominously. The remaining diners at the table froze, their laughter dying mid-sentence. With Ellis and Lushington being summoned away, it was Captain Watson who rose instinctively. Pushed back his chair, voice tight, he asked, to no one in particular. "What in God's name is going on out there?"

He never got an answer.

The crack of gunfire split the midday heat. From the terraces above the courtyard, the Nawab's soldiers opened fire, musket barrels jutting over the balustrades. Smoke rolled downward as the first volley tore through flesh and splintered bone. Plates and glasses exploded, screams rising as bodies collapsed. A few prisoners dove for cover; others sat frozen in disbelief, motionless in their seats, crimson pooling beneath their chairs.

"Fight back!" Watson shouted, grabbing a wine bottle and flinging it toward the terrace. Around him, a handful of others scrambled for anything at hand - stones, broken crockery, shattered furniture. But the unarmed and outnumbered prisoners never stood a chance.

One by one, they fell - some with defiant cries, others in stunned silence - as musket balls tore through the courtyard.

Sumru descended into the melee, sword drawn, his men close behind with fixed bayonets. A few survivors struck out wildly with makeshift weapons; others cowered or pleaded - both in vain. The soldiers moved through the courtyard with grim efficiency, silencing the last of the resistance.

By the time the massacre ended, the courtyard was eerily silent, save for the moans of the dying. The soldiers began dragging the bodies toward the well in the corner of the courtyard. Sumru watched impassively as the first of the corpses were thrown into its depths. The harsh afternoon sun cast stark shadows across the bloodstained cobblestones, a grim testament to the day's horrors.

Among the fallen lay Ensign Thomas Hawke, struck down by a shot to the abdomen. As he bled onto the stone, his fading gaze turned inward - to the tender image of his bibi Gulabi, cradling their son Billy. And then further back, to his mother, her frail hands waving him goodbye seven long years ago, and the rolling green fields of Devon - before the world around him dissolved into eternal darkness.

• • •

The dim light filtering through the narrow slit in the prison wall cast long, feeble shadows on the damp stone floor. Javed Hussain sat hunched in a corner, his frail body wrapped in a tattered shawl that barely kept the chill at bay. The once dignified aristocrat was now a shadow of his former self, his health rapidly deteriorating in the squalid confines of the Murshidabad prison. His breath came in shallow rasps, his chest heaving with the effort of simply existing.

The creak of the iron door broke the stillness. Javed looked up slowly, his sunken eyes meeting the hesitant gaze of the young man who entered. It was Rafiq, one of his former servants.

"Rafiq," Javed rasped, his voice weak but tinged with a fleeting glimmer of recognition. "What brings you here? There must be something important"

Rafiq hesitated, clutching a bundle of cloth in his hands. His lips parted, then closed again, as if the words refused to come. The silence stretched. He looked down, eyes flicking to the floor, then back to Javed - haunted, afraid. His lips trembled as he knelt before Javed, unable to meet his master's eyes. "Huzoor," he began, his voice low and trembling. "I came to see you... to bring you some food. But there is... there is something else."

"I did not want to be the one to say it," Rafiq whispered after a moment's pause, as though confessing a sin. "But no one else would come. They're afraid. But you deserve to know."

Javed's brow furrowed. He could already feel the blow forming in the pause, heavy and inevitable. "Speak," he commanded, his voice a hollow echo of the authority it once wielded. "Do not keep me waiting."

Rafiq placed the bundle on the ground and took a deep breath. "Huzoor, I... I bring news of Sarfaraz Malik," he said, his words faltering. "The young master."

At the mention of Sarfaraz, Javed straightened, ignoring the stabbing pain in his chest. A sudden urgency gripped him, brittle and raw. "Sarfaraz?" he repeated, his voice strained. "What of him? Has he come to Murshidabad? Has he... has he written?"

Rafiq shook his head, tears brimming in his eyes. "No, Huzoor," he said, his voice breaking. "Sarfaraz Malik... He is gone."

Javed's body stiffened as the words sank in. "Gone?" he whispered, his tone laced with disbelief. "What do you mean, gone?"

Rafiq's tears spilled over as he explained. "He... he was leading a rebellion of peasants against the Sahibs. They ambushed his group near the Company's granary. There was a fight... a bloody fight. They say he stood atop a rise, waving a bamboo spear, shouting for the others to fall back. He held the line alone until a musket ball struck him through the chest. Sarfaraz Malik fought bravely, but... but he fell."

Javed's breath hitched, and he clutched his chest as if the words themselves had struck him like a dagger.

"No," he breathed. "Not like this. He was just a boy with questions. I was the one who made the bargains... the one who -"

His voice cracked, and he pressed trembling fingers to his eyes.

"Not Sarfaraz. Not my boy. Not the only part of me that was still clean."

He leaned back against the cold wall, his hands covering his face. Memories of Sarfaraz flooded his mind - his boyhood laughter, his eager questions about the zamindari, the look of pride in his eyes whenever he spoke of justice and honour. Sarfaraz had been his hope, his redemption.

Javed spoke again, barely audible. "I betrayed my honour for this... for a future I thought I could build for him. I bore the shame of chains, the scorn of my people, thinking it would all be worth it. And now... he is gone."

Rafiq reached out to steady him, but Javed pushed him away weakly. "Leave me," he said, barely above a whisper. "Let me grieve alone. What is left of me... of my name... if Sarfaraz is no longer here to carry it?"

The young servant hesitated, reluctant to leave his master in such a broken state, but Javed's hollow eyes brooked no argument. Slowly, he rose and left the cell, his heart heavy with sorrow.

Alone in the silence of his prison, Javed Hussain wept. The man who had once walked marble halls with pride now curled against cold stone, hollowed by grief. His tears fell freely, mingling with the filth on the floor, as he kept whispering his son's name into the darkness.

• • •

The monsoon hung low over Murshidabad, thick and swollen with heat. A pall of silence had settled over the Nawabi palace, broken only by the lazy creak of punkahs and the faint gurgle of water in hookah pipes. A strange calm, too quiet for a kingdom at war.

After the Company had declared open war on Mir Qasim, they had turned to an old puppet gathering dust. Mir Jafar was hauled once again to the masnad - thin, tremulous, and wrapped in velvet he no longer filled. The throne had lost its shine. So had its master.

He now reclined on a divan in his private chamber, his fingers trembling around a half-burnt opium pipe. The room smelled of smoke, musk, and slow decay. Curtains sagged from rods, and the fanboys swayed as if unsure of their rhythm. His eyes, bloodshot and heavy-lidded, stared into nothing.

The door creaked, and Ataullah Khan entered, stooping slightly as if the weight of years had caught him too. He still wore the high plume of a nobleman, though it sat like a relic of another time. Once one of Jafar's most trusted lieutenants - present at every campaign since the Maratha raids, and the very man who had whispered treason into his ear - Ataullah had aged into something colder, sharper.

"Come," Mir Jafar said, waving a languid hand, "Sit, Ataullah. It's been long since we spoke without others listening."

Ataullah obliged, easing himself onto a cushion, his posture respectful. "You called, Nawab Sahib?"

Jafar inhaled deeply, then exhaled a trail of opium smoke that curled toward the crumbling ceiling. "Do you remember, old friend... the night we sat in my study, after Siraj handed Calcutta to that ink-smudged clerk, Manikchand?"

Ataullah's expression flickered.

"You said then that I had been humiliated. That a man who had held the Marathas at the gates should not be made to watch a courtier command the English. You said it was time for the ground to shift beneath Siraj."

"I remember," Ataullah said quietly.

Mir Jafar laughed, dry and bitter. "You were wrong. We both were. There are no old ways left. Only ledgers and contracts and muskets."

He set the pipe down, fingers twitching. "I thought I was choosing power. I ended up choosing servitude. And when I tried to hold my ground... they broke me like a servant's cup and tossed me in the shadows."

Ataullah said nothing. He looked at the floor, his silence carefully measured.

"And Miran..." Jafar's voice faltered. "My son. Burned to ash by lightning in an open field. They say it was chance - a storm, a flash. But

I've wondered since… if the heavens were settling a debt. Not his. Mine."

He wiped his mouth with the edge of his sleeve, unaware that his tears had already soaked it.

"I betrayed Siraj, yes. But I betrayed something older too… the marrow of what held this land together. I don't know its name now. Only that it died with us."

Ataullah placed a hand gently on Mir Jafar's shoulder. "You did what was needed to survive. All rulers do. You bore the burden for us all."

Mir Jafar shook his head, slow and dazed. "No. I carried it for myself. And even that was a lie."

They sat in silence a while longer, smoke curling around them like the ghosts of a dead durbar. Finally, Ataullah stood. "Rest, Nawab Sahib. You've carried enough."

He bowed and took his leave, the silk of his robes trailing behind him like a shadow.

Mir Jafar remained slumped on the divan, barely conscious, but still alert enough to hear. The chamber walls were thick, but the breeze from the half-open corridor carried voices faint and sharp.

"A goat in robes," Ataullah's voice snickered. "He weeps like a peasant girl and calls it wisdom. I thought he'd choke on his own self-pity."

A second voice, British and nasal, replied with a chuckle. "Still thinks he's a king, does he?"

"Thinks he's a prophet," Ataullah muttered. "Speaks of lightning and justice now. As if the heavens waste their thunder on weaklings."

Mir Jafar did not stir. He did not call out. He simply stared at the dying coal in his pipe, his features slack with wear, the sting of mockery deeper than any exile.

Outside, laughter faded into footsteps. Inside, the room fell back into silence.

And in that silence, the opium-sweet air grew heavier.

• • •

THE ASHES OF A NATION

The first light of dawn broke over Patna, casting long shadows over the straggling columns of Mir Qasim's retreating forces. The city behind him lay in ruins, its walls breached, its streets swarming with red-coated soldiers. Mir Qasim rode on, his weary eyes scanning the dust-streaked plains as the Karmanasa River came into view, shimmering in the early morning light - a silent witness to his final flight.

The night before, the distant echoes of marching drums and the tense reports of scouts had signalled the British approach. Mir Qasim wasted no time in abandoning the city, ordering his men to begin their retreat with what remained of his army. His soldiers moved in silence, their faces hollow with exhaustion and dejection. Once, they had marched with pride, carrying the banners of a ruler determined to cast off foreign dominance. Now, they trudged behind him, thirty thousand men strong in number but not in spirit, their loyalty fraying with each passing mile.

Over the last few months, the British advance had been relentless. Their forces had marched steadily across Bengal, and the towns and fortresses had fallen like ninepins before their might. Mir Qasim had watched in grim resignation as the pattern unfolded - one garrison after another lost, his officers defecting, his allies retreating into silence. Now in October 1763, defeat was no longer a mere possibility – it was an inevitability. But he refused to let the throne of Bengal slip away without a final act of defiance. The massacre of the British prisoners had been his last act of vengeance, his final statement before the world closed in on him. Now, he rode towards an uncertain refuge.

At the heart of the sprawling caravan, three hundred elephants lumbered forward, their massive frames burdened with more than just supplies. Some carried silk-veiled carriages said to shield noblewomen; others hauled crates swaddled in tarpaulin.

A young officer had ridden close earlier that morning, frowning at the tightly clustered column. "Why are so many elephants packed into the centre?" he had asked, his voice low but not low enough.

THE TRAITOR'S BARGAIN

Mohammad Rizwan, Mir Qasim's aide and keeper of the Nawab's logistical secrets, turned sharply. He said nothing. His stare alone, steady and unreadable, was enough to end the conversation.

Those carriages and crates, beneath their coverings, held what was left of the Nawab's treasury - gold coins, uncut diamonds, priceless ornaments. The deception was vital. Spies lurked in every shadow, and Mir Qasim had no intention of giving the British a prize beyond his throne.

Rizwan remembered Mir Qasim's instructions when they were about to begin their retreat. "The treasury moves at the centre. Surround it with our most trusted men. Let no word of it escape. If the British learn what we carry, they will hunt us with twice the fury."

As the march progressed, Rizwan rode up to Mir Qasim. In a voice only loud enough for his ears, he spoke. "The men, Nawab Sahib. They march, but their spirit is gone. The fall of Patna has broken them."

Mir Qasim's jaw tightened. He had seen it too - the ill-concealed doubts, the furtive glances toward the road behind them. Their fight was no longer for him, nor for any cause - it was simply to escape annihilation.

"We must give them a reason to stand firm," he said, though even to his own ears, the words carried little conviction.

The road stretched ahead, leading them toward the wealthy principality of Awadh which lay across the Karmanasa River. There, the last threads of hope remained. Before his fall, Mir Qasim had sent word to Shuja-ud-Daula, the Nawab of Awadh, and to his guest Shah Alam, the dispossessed Mughal Emperor. His message had been clear - *we are losing Bengal, but we do not have to lose Hindustan.*

As the first wave of soldiers waded through the river, a messenger appeared on horseback from the direction of Awadh. The man dismounted swiftly, bowing low to Mir Qasim before offering a bundle wrapped in white cloth. "From Badshah Shah Alam, huzoor," he said.

Mir Qasim unwrapped the parcel to find a Quran, its blank pages inked with the emperor's words. A promise of safe passage, sealed with the authority of the Mughal throne. He ran his fingers over the script, his lips pressing into a thin line. Shah Alam was a mere shadow of his forebears, a ruler without a kingdom, but his signature still carried the weight of centuries. Perhaps, with Awadh's forces and what remained of Bengal's will, they could yet strike back.

Mir Qasim closed the Quran and looked ahead. His throne was gone, his reins of power reduced to a desperate flight. He rode forward, past the river, past the ruined dreams of his rule. Beyond the horizon, destiny waited.

Far behind him, in the smouldering wreck of Patna, a barefoot woman crouched beside a blackened wall, her sari singed and streaked with ash. In her arms lay a half-English child wrapped in faded muslin, too thin for the cold. She rocked him slowly, her lips cracked, her voice a whisper. "Hush now, Billy," she murmured. No one spoke to her. No one asked her name.

• • •

The sun hung low over the village, casting long shadows across the dusty path that led to the crumbling remnants of Javed Hussain's once-grand estate.

From beneath a gnarled banyan tree, Harinarayan Sanyal, the aging dewan, watched in silence. His frail frame, wrapped in a threadbare shawl, trembled more from sorrow than from the evening chill.

The estate had been seized by Robertson's firm just weeks earlier. Now it was being auctioned off with ruthless efficiency, its treasures reduced to lots and ledgers.

Two days ago, the devastating news had reached him - Javed Hussain, his master and protector for decades, had succumbed to ill health in the squalor of his prison cell. The dewan's heart, already battered by the toll of recent years, felt like it had crumbled entirely at the news. The man for whom he had poured his life's loyalty was gone, leaving behind only memories.

And now, even his own life lay in ruins.

Once he managed accounts in a stately residence; now he lived in a crumbling hut at the village's edge, its roof leaking, hunger a daily companion. Yet he could not look away from the final, merciless desecration of his master's house.

The auction concluded in the fading light, claimed by a merchant from a nearby town. Harinarayan watched in silence as servants loaded the estate's belongings into a cart - chests, scrolls, and ornaments once handled with reverence, now tossed like refuse. The merchant barked orders, while a guard stomped past, kicking up dust.

A portrait tumbled from a cart - the stern face of Alivardi Khan, a figure Javed Hussain had revered. The guard glanced at it, then walked on, the heel of his boot catching the edge of the frame with a dull crunch. Harinarayan winced as if struck. The cracked portrait was left behind as the cart rolled away, its wooden wheels creaking under the weight of treasure.

He stood motionless a long moment, his heart twisting in his chest. Then, glancing around furtively, he shuffled forward. Kneeling stiffly, he gathered the broken frame in his arms. A shard of glass nicked his skin, but he barely noticed.

He clutched the cracked portrait to his chest and turned toward the village - toward his leaking hut, his hunger, his forgotten name - carrying with him the last fragment of a vanished world.

His steps were slow. The dust rose behind him.

And in the gathering dusk, one broken man carried the memory of Bengal's honour home.

EPILOGUE

A year after Mir Qasim's flight, In October 1764, on the windswept plains near the town of Buxar, the East India Company secured not just Bengal, but the future of British dominion in India. Arrayed against them was a formidable alliance: Mir Qasim, the exiled Nawab of Bengal; Shuja-ud-Daula, the Nawab of Awadh; and Shah Alam II, the Mughal emperor. United in a desperate bid to reverse the tide of foreign conquest, they fought - and failed. The battle was brief but decisive. The Company's disciplined army, led by Hector Munro, shattered the allied forces. It was a military triumph, but also a civilisational rupture.

In its aftermath, the Mughal emperor - holder of a throne under which much of India had once truly bowed - was forced to grant the Company the diwani rights: the authority to collect revenue from Bengal, Bihar, and Orissa. This gave the British not only the right to trade, but to tax. The Treaty of Allahabad (1765) formalised this arrangement, making the Company the official revenue collector of India's richest provinces, while placing Awadh under de facto British control and reducing Shah Alam II to a pensioner of a foreign corporation, ruling from Delhi in name alone.

THE TRAITOR'S BARGAIN

Mir Qasim, who had secured his throne through British favour and ruled with determined independence, now found no allies left. Hunted and reviled, he died in obscurity - broken, exiled, and unmourned. Mir Jafar, briefly reinstated as Nawab after Qasim's fall, spent his final days watching his throne become a hollow pretence. He died in 1765, his name becoming a byword for treachery in the chronicles of India.

Amid this reordering, Robert Clive returned to Bengal in 1765 as Governor and Commander-in-Chief of the East India Company's forces in Bengal - the supreme authority in the richest corner of India. He formalised the dual system: a puppet Nawab would reign in appearance, while the Company controlled revenue and power behind the scenes. It was efficient, profitable - and ruinous. Administration collapsed, the countryside starved, and famine loomed. Clive sailed back to England in early 1767, laden with riches but conscious of the fragility of British dominion. "We have made the most delicate and the most difficult conquest that ever was made in India," he would later write.

But Clive's empire of shadows would not endure. In 1772, Warren Hastings - a man of discipline and order - assumed control. He dismantled the dual system and became the Company's first Governor-General. A lover of Persian poetry and a student of Indian culture, Hastings spoke of balance and reform. But he ruled with a firmer hand than any Mughal had wielded in decades. Under his guidance, the East India Company became what Clive had only hinted at: not a merchant empire, but a government - complete with courts, tax codes, and armies.

Thus ended the first act of British India. What had begun with a trading charter and a coastal warehouse now stretched across the Ganges plain. The old aristocrats were gone. The jagirdars, the zamindars, even the kingmakers - all reduced to silence, ruin, or memory.

Those who tried to broker deals with the Company thought their standing would spare them. But the tide of conquest left no one untouched.

Author's Historical Note

This novel adheres closely to the historical record of Bengal's fall and the rise of the East India Company. Only one key liberty has been taken for narrative continuity: the campaign against Mir Qasim - historically led by Hector Munro - is here attributed to Major Kilpatrick to maintain internal character arcs. This adjustment does not alter the essential course of events but serves to heighten dramatic coherence.

In striving for historical fidelity, I consulted a range of secondary sources by leading historians. Among the most influential were William Dalrymple's *The Anarchy*, Nick Robins' *The Corporation That Changed the World*, Tirthankar Roy's *The East India Company: The World's Most Powerful Corporation*, John Keay's *The Honourable Company*, and John Wilson's *India Conquered*.

These works - rich in archival insight and analysis - helped frame the backdrop against which this fictional narrative unfolds. Any errors, deviations, or interpretations are, of course, my own.

About the Author

Rajat Roy is a historical fiction author and business consultant based in Sydney, Australia. An alumnus of the Indian Institute of Management Kozhikode, he blends analytical precision with a deep interest in the untold stories of colonial India. His debut novel, *The Traitor's Bargain*, explores the fall of Bengal and the rise of the East India Company through the eyes of rulers, conspirators, rebels, merchants, and men of war. It is the first in a planned trilogy tracing the arc of British conquest and resistance across the subcontinent.

When not writing, Rajat shares reflections on colonial history with a growing community of readers and researchers interested in the legacies of empire.

Printed in Dunstable, United Kingdom